THE
WOLFE
WIDOW

Center Point
Large Print

Also by Victoria Abbott and available from
Center Point Large Print:

The Book Collector Mysteries
The Christie Curse
The Sayers Swindle

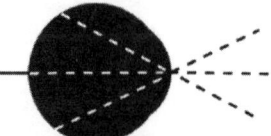

**This Large Print Book carries the
Seal of Approval of N.A.V.H.**

THE
WOLFE
WIDOW

VICTORIA ABBOTT

CENTER POINT LARGE PRINT
THORNDIKE, MAINE

This Center Point Large Print edition is published in the year 2015 by arrangement with The Berkley Publishing Group, an imprint of Penguin Publishing Group, a division of Penguin Random House LLC.

The text of this Large Print edition is unabridged. In other aspects, this book may vary from the original edition. Printed in the United States of America on permanent paper. Set in 16-point Times New Roman type.

ISBN: 978-1-62899-524-4

Library of Congress Cataloging-in-Publication Data

Abbott, Victoria.
  The Wolfe widow : a book collector mystery / Victoria Abbott. — Center Point Large Print edition.
    pages cm
  Summary: "Shortly after Muriel Delgado makes an uninvited appearance at Vera Van Alst's home, Jordan Bingham is fired as Vera's assistant. When Jordan discovers a deadly connection between Muriel and the Van Alst family, it's up to her to put the house in order and stop a killer"—Provided by publisher.
  ISBN 978-1-62899-524-4 (library binding : alk. paper)
  1. Book collectors—Fiction. 2. Murder—Investigation—Fiction.
    3. Large type books. I. Title.
PS3601.B394W65 2015
813'.6—dc23
                                                    2014049684

ACKNOWLEDGMENTS

We are both grateful to Rex Stout for bringing to life the inimitable Nero Wolfe and the dishy Archie Goodwin, two of the great characters of modern detective fiction. No wonder poor Vera was besotted with those books.

Readers make the mystery world go round and we have loved hearing from you as we work our way through the book collector mysteries. Fans, librarians, reviewers and bloggers: Your reactions to *The Christie Curse* and *The Sayers Swindle* really gave us a boost. Walter appreciates your affection and we all enjoy the suggestions for the Kelly kitchen. Special thanks to Mare Fairchild for Cheez-Its. The Siamese are most appreciative.

Meanwhile back in the real world, Giulio Maffini offered endless support and made many excellent meals. At drop-dead deadlines, he got stuck with dishes too. Speaking of meals, the legacy of Irma Maffini and Lina Arno inspired the magnificent meals that the signora produces at the drop of a hat.

A shout-out to the rest of the family who keep our spirits high: G-Bird, Barry, Devan, Zlatka, Jesse, Julian, Sam, Cassandra, Jason, and the squid-lets, thank you!

Special thanks for our wonderful friend, Linda Wiken aka Erika Chase, who once again took the time to read this manuscript with good humor and on short notice, and to John Merchant for his eagle eye, time and advice. The staff at Odgensburg Public Library offered us a warm welcome and solid information.

Victoria would like to thank Dave and Connie Martin for their support and friendship over the past three books, and also the funky and fantastic Kelly Connolly whose bright, adventurous personality is the inspiration for Tiffany. She sends a big hug to all those at the Farm, especially Pat, Shawn McRae and Haley Mallory, our little Lady Gaga–in-waiting. Special thanks to Luc Lavigne and Candy St. Aubin, two of Victoria's lifelong friends, for never letting her get bored or down on herself.

We are lucky to have the very patient and supportive Tom Colgan as our editor at Berkley and we really appreciate the rapid response to every question from Amanda Ng. We know that our agent, Kim Lionetti, always has our backs. Thanks for making time for us and taking our calls.

To our wonderful friends and colleagues at The Cozy Chicks, Killer Characters, The Ladies Killing Circle, and Mystery Lovers Kitchen, thank you for ideas, support and enthusiasm and for all you do to make this a more mysterious world.

CHAPTER ONE

THE DOORBELL RANG. Now, this would be no big deal in most places, but at Van Alst House ten days before Thanksgiving, it seemed to create a collective panic. It was just after eight on a night that had already brought us some serious wind, making the unseasonably early snow flurries seem like a blizzard fit for the arctic. My boss, Vera Van Alst, and I were grumbling about the cold white stuff arriving in mid-November as we waited to be served our main course in the historic ruin that is the grand dining room. My Uncle Kev, the world's oldest and largest child, was defending the fun factor of early snow.

When the bell rang, I thought I'd ignore it. It sounded again, a serious, rich and commanding ring, perfect for a massive historical home. It should tell you something that we all reacted with shock.

Everyone froze. Vera's cook, Signora Panetone, put down her vast platter with the mountain of gnocchi and crossed herself. The signora won't see eighty again, but usually that doesn't stop her from heaping food on your plate. This time her black eyes bugged out and her unlikely ebony hair seemed to plaster itself a little closer to her scalp.

The doorbell ringing was not a regular occurrence at Van Alst House. Nor was it a welcome one.

Vera hulked unmoving in her wheelchair, her face like an Easter Island moai. Apparently her majesty was not amused. Kev—usually ebullient where food was involved—vanished like an ice cube in a bowl of minestrone. Even the Siamese cats took refuge under the mile-long Sheraton table. I felt their tails swishing against my ankles. Would claws be next? Why hadn't I worn something higher than ankle boots? In the six and a half months I'd worked for Vera, lived at Van Alst House and taken my evening meals in this dining room, you'd think I would have learned, but sometimes fashion wins over feline, and then inevitably feline turns the tables and triumphs once more.

Another ring of the bell.

It was mildly eerie, because all the people brave enough to cross the threshold of this house were present and accounted for, except for Eddie, our recently retired postal carrier who was floating somewhere off Florida on a cruise with his ninety-year-old mother. Eddie wasn't expected back anytime soon. As Eddie had been nursing a crush on Vera for nearly fifty years, I wasn't sure how that would work out for him. But anyway, it wouldn't be Eddie at the front door. He always came in the back.

So who could it be? A wrong address? Some poor wretch who'd braved the long lonely driveway to the large and pretentious front entrance to our crumbling Victorian pile o' granite to ask for a donation to repair the church organ? A random serial killer about to have the worst night of his life? A stranded traveler?

I was prepared to wait it out. Vera broke the silence at last. "Miss Bingham."

I responded with my eye firmly fixed on the platter of gnocchi. "The doorbell, I think."

"Of course, it's the doorbell. Don't be ridiculous. Can you make whoever it is go away?"

I shouldn't have been playful. "What if it's missionaries? Will I give them something?"

"What part of 'away' is unclear to you, Miss Bingham?"

"Or they could be collecting to get gifts for the needy."

"Not from me they won't."

I knew my place. Researcher and minion. Answerer of bells. Opener of doors. I rose, gazed longingly at the platter of gnocchi and headed down the endless corridor to the front door. I grabbed my handbag as I went. Vera might be grinchy, but I wasn't. I could manage a donation if it came to that.

The doorbell pealed again as I reached the front

entrance. I pushed it open, ready to drop a dollar into the palm of some forlorn waif while whispering, "Run for your life."

I stared up at a tall woman dressed entirely in black, much of that a vast black cape, swirling like the snow behind her. I am five foot six, but I felt like a dwarf next to her. She was quite aware of that, I thought. She gazed down imperiously. "I want to speak to Vera Van Alst."

What to say? It was a pretty safe bet that Vera would not want to speak to her.

I raised my nose and stared in her general direction, trying not to gaze at her capacious chest. "Miss Van Alst is not available. Perhaps you could call tomorrow and make an appointment."

I could hardly wait to shut the door. The wind was whipping snow past our visitor and into the grand foyer. Even though the snow stung my eyes, I made a point not to blink first.

"I am here now. And I believe she *will* see me."

I might have said, "Want to make a bet, lady?" but my uncles raised me right and I couldn't quite utter those words. Instead I said, "I am sorry. As I mentioned she's not available tonight."

She took me by surprise and stepped into the foyer. Stunned, I lurched back and said, "Don't make me call security." Obviously, I'd been watching too many movies. Security would be Uncle Kev. He was also maintenance, gardening and soon-to-be snow removal. There was a good chance that right now he was hiding out under the dining room table with the Siamese. For some annoying reason, they never scratched him.

"Why don't you tell her I'm here and let her decide if she's unavailable?"

I stuck to my story. "As she is unavailable, I will be unable to accommodate your request."

"Accommodate this, then: Tell her my name is Muriel Delgado and I have something she wants badly."

I can dig my heels in with the best of them, and so I simply said, "Excuse me, but no."

Behind me a voice said, "I'll check."

I whirled to find Uncle Kev. His wicked smile complemented his ginger curls and the matching expressive Kelly eyebrows. His Hooters T-shirt mocked me as he strutted off. How did he get away with that at the Van Alst table? I once wore flip-flops to lunch and was subjected to a lengthy talk about hygiene from Vera. But that's our Kev, always where and when you don't want or need him, charmingly inappropriate and apparently deaf.

"It's all right, Kev. Under control."

"I'll check with Vera. Don't worry about a thing, Jordie."

That left me and Muriel Delgado—if that was really her name—facing off in the grand foyer. She gazed around, sending the message that she didn't have time for the lower orders. I retaliated

11

by not offering her a seat. To top it off, a Siamese appeared and rubbed itself up against her still-swirling black garments. Aiming for the ankles, I figured. I didn't bother to warn her.

Half a lifetime later, Kev reappeared, flushed and triumphant and smelling of Axe.

"Miss Van Alst will see you now. In the study."

What? I almost fell off my gray suede stiletto ankle boots, not for the first time, but my balance wasn't the issue here. Vera was going to see someone? And in the study? During the dinner hour? Not even in the dining room where my delicious plate of gnocchi sat unattended?

Vera might not care about her food, but I was starving and now this woman was infringing on Vera's privacy and my dinner. I had no choice but to follow them down the hallway. Kev's notorious charm seemed to bounce right off the intruder. So that was good. At least she was immune to him. Things have a habit of getting out of control when Kev's in high-charm mode.

The study is down a second endless corridor, parallel to the one that leads to the dining room. To reach it, you must pass the sitting room, the ballroom and the sort-of-gallery housing the portrait collection. I always try not to let my gaze rest on any of the formal images of Vera's various ancestors. They all appeared to be suffering from serious constipation and major dental problems. Vera might have been born to wealth and influence, but life hadn't done her any favors when she was fished out of that particular gene pool.

As I trailed Muriel Delgado down that corridor, my vertebrae stiffened to near the snapping point. This woman radiated negativity. She was all about power and not the good kind. I felt it. I could practically hear and taste it.

Kevin scurried back and forth, attempting to curry favor, I suppose. He can sense power. He always wanted to be on the right side of anyone who possessed it. That usually didn't last long. I smoothed my cream tunic and adjusted my posture to center myself. I needed to pay close attention to this conversation.

A short time after, Vera propelled her wheel-chair down the corridor from the opposite direction. Behind her, the signora fluttered, a panicky black bird. "Vera must eat! Come back. Gnocchi tonight! Eat now! No no no yes!"

I opened the door to the study. I've always liked that room. After all, this was where Vera first agreed to hire me. Vera rolled on through the open door, without so much as a glance at Muriel Delgado's striking appearance and flowing black garb. She pivoted in the wheelchair. "That will be all, Miss Bingham. Mr. Kelly. Fiammetta, I will not be eating. Stop babbling. Please leave us."

We stood there, frozen, although our bodies still indicated our intention to enter.

So, I wouldn't be joining Vera and this strange black widow persona to soak up the atmosphere of the ten-foot walls, the tall Georgian windows with the timeworn silk draperies and the formerly red velvet sofa now faded to amethyst, not to mention the gorgeous Edwardian desk. My gut told me that I would be absorbing more than beautiful antique design if I had gotten my foot through the door. And now, I wouldn't be there to cushion my boss from whatever negative intentions this strange woman had for her. My job was to make sure that bad things did not happen to Vera's collection of rare first editions and to her investment in them. By extension, I felt that included making sure that bad things did not happen to Vera herself.

I hesitated.

Vera's eyes narrowed. "Go find something to do, Miss Bingham. I don't require your presence."

My mouth was still hanging open when the door shut behind the black-clad pile of drama that was our visitor. On the other hand, I wouldn't have to avert my eyes from another batch of Vera's ancestors staring down from the walls of the study in disapproval. Even so, I didn't feel good about not being there.

Kev scratched his head. The signora let out an enormous sigh.

Kev was the first one to regain composure. "No reason to let our food get cold."

He had a point.

The signora almost brightened, although she stared at the closed door with trepidation.

I didn't like it, but then I didn't have to like it. I wasn't paid to like things. I was paid to do whatever Vera Van Alst wanted whenever she wanted it. And she wanted to be alone with this visitor who had arrived without an appointment and without an explanation.

"A bit of history there apparently," I said.

The signora crossed herself.

Kev said, "No kidding."

I wondered if there was a way that I could hear what was going on by pressing my ear to the door. Or the wall of the next room. That didn't work. Whatever its other drawbacks, Van Alst House is well insulated with solid mahogany doors.

"Let's go," I said, after my failed attempt. "Gnocchi waits for no man. Or woman."

"*Dio!*" the signora said. "No no no cold gnocchi! No! Come. Eat!

"Eat, drink and be merry." Kev giggled.

For tomorrow we die. I shivered. I told myself not to be silly.

We ate. We drank. We were not merry and we wondered.

"What was that about?" Kev said, as he accepted a second helping of *Pan di Spagna*, an Italian sponge cake he had developed a weakness for. He layered on some whipped cream and a small lake of the signora's homemade blueberry syrup.

"Nothing good," I muttered.

Vera doesn't suffer fools gladly. Her home is her castle and she needs us to achieve her goals, so she does suffer us, but not gladly in the least, come to think of it. Yet she'd gone into a room with a seeming stranger, closed the door and sent off her palace guard without a blink.

My intuition told me that something was up. Something bad. What was going on? We weren't to find out that night. Vera never reappeared. Kev spotted La Delgado's Grand Prix leaving in a swirl of snow around eleven. I heard the elevator creaking up to Vera's second-floor quarters around the same time. But I learned nothing. It didn't sit well, and heartburn flared on top of the uneasiness.

Trouble for sure.

IT WOULD HAVE been helpful to discuss this odd occurrence with someone. It's never easy to talk to the signora, and Kev is a lost cause when it comes to sensible, or any other, advice. But I had options. My best friend, Tiff, was now living in Harrison Falls. I've been bouncing my problems off her since we were roommates in our first year at college. We'd bonded on so many things. I'd done my best to help her cope with her mother's death from leukemia during our second year of studies. My mother died when I was a child, so I understood something of loss and devastation and

16

survival. In turn, Tiff had been a shoulder to cry on when my cheating ex-boyfriend dumped me, after maxing out my credit card and draining my bank account.

We could always rely on each other. But Tiff didn't pick up. I figured she'd have a good reason. Now that she was back from her stint in Africa and working in our neighboring town of Grandville as an ICU nurse at Grandville General Hospital, she pulled a lot of extra shifts. She hadn't mentioned it, but perhaps she'd been called in to work. I sent her a text.

Strangely, my buddy Lance—arguably the world's sexiest librarian—wasn't answering his phone or texts either. Lost in a good book, perhaps.

Ordinarily, I would have called the would-be man in my life, Officer Tyler "Smiley" Dekker. He was an excellent listener, but I knew he was out of town on police training and not due back until the morning. He'd been mysterious about the "training assignment," but apparently outside communication with cell phones or other devices was discouraged.

My uncle Mick was tied up with a "project" that involved being out late every night. He'd also been busy acquiring a few new properties near the shop including the building across the street, through a discreet third party, I understood. I couldn't imagine what he'd do with a vacant dress shop and the apartment overhead. Better that way.

As I am the first person in my family to go straight, the less I knew about any of Mick's activities the better. My uncle Lucky was still lost in the newlywed world with his bride, my good friend, Karen Smith. Their current activities were probably legal. The newlyweds were off on yet another little mini-moon, as Karen called their frequent trips. Still, after a month, you'd think they'd let their four feet touch the ground, I thought sulkily.

Speaking of four feet, I did have two sets of those. Walter, Karen's pug, was spending the weekend with me, as was Cobain, Tyler Dekker's large, shaggy dog of no known breed. I was in charge of him until Smiley's return whenever from wherever. I loved the dogs and that was fine. Not that I was complaining. Not in the least; I was merely thinking that someone in my life might have answered their phone or texts.

As conversationalists went, the dogs were light on dialogue—if you didn't count snorting and snuffling and passing gas—but on the other hand, they didn't hog the conversation and weren't prone to melodrama. They were curled up on my bed with the flowered comforter in the attic accommodations that I adored. Next to the books, my little garret was the best part of my job with Vera. It was relaxing to cuddle up with the dogs and stroke their fur, but it wasn't enough to take my mind off the sense of doom that Muriel Delgado had brought with her. I felt a little shiver thinking about it. I had a feeling this visit was about money, as most things are. I spent a lot of time worrying about Vera's money, her champagne tastes and what I knew was a beer budget. The Van Alst fortune isn't what it once was. These days, there was hardly enough money to cover the basics around this vast estate, let alone take a hit from some con man—or woman, in this case.

At two in the morning, I was still awake worrying about Vera's visitor and listening to the wind howl. The midnight walk in the snow with the two dogs hadn't helped me get to sleep. All around me were signs that the Van Alst fortune was in decline. In the harsh floodlights and frosty air, every crack was clearly visible. The lifting tiles on the vast roof resembled an old reptile, lying down for the last time. I itemized the immense expenses Vera and her estate must have. The house needed a combination cook and housekeeper. It required someone to keep the extensive grounds and maintain the building. The signora was devoted to Vera. I wasn't even sure if Vera paid her. The signora had her quarters and her food. What else would she want except to have Vera finish a meal for once? Kev was about the same. Mostly he needed a place to lie low where nobody would think to search for him, as a consequence of a small disagreement about a large amount of money with some impatient "colleagues" down in Albany. Kev had a "suite" of rooms above the garage. This suited him. The three monster-sized meals (minimum) a day suited him even more.

I had my dream attic, the run of the house, a job I loved and food to die for. Vera paid me a reasonable rate, but as I had no real expenses, that allowed me to save to get back to graduate school. In turn, while I did research, I also managed to find good books at good prices and sell many of these finds, which gave Vera a good return.

Although I believed she was getting some perks from having me on staff—such as keeping her and her collection from harm's way—for the most part. In fact, I figured I was a bargain.

Vera's growing collection was a big money drain. The estate was hemorrhaging cash. Her better artwork had been disappearing and there was a lot less sterling silver than when I'd first come on the scene. No one in their right mind would buy any of these portraits of the Van Alst ancestors, no matter who painted them. I thought I'd better try finding out about this Muriel Delgado woman in case we were about to say adios to our Francis I forks. Or worse, maybe she was making an offer on the book collection. I sat upright, sweating. Maybe Delgado was a real estate agent and Vera was thinking of liquidating

20

the contents and selling the house. What would happen to us then?

How to dig up some dirt?

By now it was past two, so maybe Uncle Mick was back. I gave it a try.

I picked up the phone and called.

"What is it? Bail money?" he said.

I could imagine him sitting there, big Irish grin, ginger eyebrows and matching chest hair, an older, saner version of Uncle Kev, without a bounty on his head.

"Very funny. Just need a bit of information."

"Anything for you, my girl. You know that. And while we're talking, how's our Kevin getting on?"

"As well as can be expected."

"Always have a backup plan, Jordan."

My family are masters of the backup plan, which is why they live free and happy days instead of breaking rocks somewhere without antiques and Kraft Macaroni and Cheese.

"I do, but I hope I don't need it. Do you know anyone called Muriel Delgado?"

"It might ring a bell but I can't say right off."

"Any chance you can ask around? See what you can dig up?"

"For my favorite niece, the sky's the limit."

"Your only niece."

"Even more so. I'll inquire. But I should mention that your uncle Lucky's kind of mopey since you don't live here anymore. Don't suppose you could drop in more often?"

"Uncle Lucky's in Manhattan with Karen."

"Still."

I grinned. "I'll come by tomorrow. I miss you too."

"I SEE YOU have another Archie Goodwin book on the go, Vera," I said cheerfully as I arrived in the conservatory the next morning. We breakfasted at eight every day. We were not late if we knew what was good for us. Vera had a passion for Nero Wolfe, because her father had introduced her to the Rex Stout books when she was a child. It seemed to have been the only interest they'd shared. Now as a collector, she had a thing for a lot of classic mysteries, but Wolfe held a special place in her icy heart. Today the book was *Black Orchids*. She wouldn't read it, of course. It was for fondling only, being a deliciously fine first edition. Her father's well-thumbed paperbacks were stashed between her bedroom and her office, where I'd found her reading and rereading them. The fact that she had this edition of *Black Orchids* with her in the conservatory, away from its normal, safe habitat in the temperature-controlled library, told me she was in her Wolfe-ish mode. Not that it mattered to me. Archie Goodwin was my man. The only one who counted.

Mind you, I'd had quite a literary crush on Lord

Peter Wimsey not that long ago. It seemed that the minute I got my bearings again I had fallen hard for the suave, smooth, wise-cracking and well-dressed right-hand man to the eccentric Nero Wolfe. I was trying to keep up with Vera and while she was rereading Rex Stout's works for the umpteenth time, I was just discovering these treasures. I'd now been luxuriating in the world and characters he'd created long enough to know that if I couldn't have Archie Goodwin, I wanted to be him. I'd even considered a fedora. Maybe two-toned shoes.

I took a glance out the splendid windows of the conservatory at the snow-dusted Van Alst property. Picture perfect.

"Nero Wolfe book, you mean," Vera sputtered. "Archie Goodwin is merely an adjunct, a side-kick, an also-ran."

I raised an eyebrow provocatively and took my place at the table.

"The hired help," she added with a hint of a sneer.

I grinned, the same way that Archie used to when he teased Wolfe. "Where would Wolfe be without Archie? Who would keep the cops from the door, drive the Cadillac or escort the suspects, strong-arm difficult clients and pull a gun on the villain? The great detective wouldn't be able to function without him. All Wolfe does really is obsess over those flowers."

Vera scowled. "Orchids. Hardly just flowers."

Vera reminded me a lot of Nero Wolfe, without the charm. I did have the brains not to mention this. People can admire and even venerate the man, but did any of them want to be him? Of course, with Vera you never knew.

I said, "Right. Thousands of orchids. But without Archie that detective business would go down the tubes. Archie is absolutely necessary."

"He's absolutely replaceable," she snapped. "Men like him were a dime a dozen in New York in the thirties and forties."

"Unlike me," I said with a straight face.

You could feel the temperature drop a good ten degrees. The signora's eyes widened. Uncle Kev's fork paused in midair. I smiled and accepted a Dutch baby pancake from the signora. It was puffy and delicious and loaded with pancetta, mozzarella and Parmesan cheese.

"Even you, Miss Bingham, can be replaced."

"Uh-huh," I said, as if I didn't believe a word of it. To tell the truth, I don't know what had gotten into me. Maybe I was channeling Archie, picking up his glib speech patterns and cocky attitude. Come to think of it, I did have trouble leaving the garret without a fedora that morning. Whatever it was, poking this particular Nero Wolfe in a wheelchair was a death sport and I needed my job.

"Yes. You, whether you have enough wit to

realize it or not," she said, waving the signora and the Dutch baby away.

"I suppose," I said, digging in. Again, I put my reaction down to the Archie factor. He probably needed his job too. Come to think of it, Archie also had his comfortable live-in digs and at least three of Fritz's fabulous meals a day in the brownstone as part of his compensation. But he didn't let Wolfe bully him. He stood his ground. He made his points. He wasn't afraid to argue. Sometimes he had a little hissy fit, but in a manly way. Archie was definitely a good influence on me. And Wolfe was definitely a bad influence on Vera. Not that she needed any bad influences. She was already too much like the eccentric detective: wealthy, irascible, difficult, demanding, obsessive. I could go on, but I believe the point has been made.

In fairness, she wasn't much like Nero Wolfe in appearance; she was bony and angular, as opposed to Wolfe's bulky person. Of course, she used a wheelchair and he was mobile. But there the difference ended. Neither one of them ever left the house if they could help it. The homes they lived in were large and imposing, although Vera's was in a small town in upstate New York. They both had cooks, although a bird feeder would probably have done for Vera. Wolfe had fine clothing. I grinned thinking about those vast yellow silk pajamas that Archie described in almost every book. Conversely, no one knew where Vera got her drab moth-eaten sweaters. Today's was the color of old vomit, with fraying cuffs and a missing button.

Despite their having intelligence, self-focus, conceit and snobbery in common, I think even Wolfe would have trouble communicating with Vera. Wolfe had his ten (or was it twenty?) thousand orchids, Vera had her thousands of fine first editions, but she wasn't so good with living things. Nero Wolfe might give Vera pointers on being more of a people person.

I wasn't sure what Wolfe's voice was like. Vera's sounded like the crunch of gravel.

The gravel crunched. "Archie Goodwin. An errand boy, nothing more."

"Agree to disagree," I shot back merrily.

Signora Panetone swooped down with a refill of the Dutch baby. I wouldn't say no to that.

Really, I should have been more sensitive to Uncle Kev. He actually needed his job even more than I needed mine. After all, no one with mob connections was actively hunting for me to my knowledge. Kev had landed on his feet here at Van Alst House. Even though he could turn practically any everyday situation into chaos or disaster, here everyone thought the sun shone out of his tight knockoff Levi's.

"More snow coming," Kev said. I think that was what he said. He had a pretty big mouthful of breakfast.

Vera didn't like snow but she didn't need to care if it snowed. She never went anywhere except to the bank and her quarterly meetings of the hospital board, driven by Kev in her ancient Cadillac. The signora didn't care either. Between her two freezers and her pantry she had enough food stocked up to feed Harrison Falls through the coming winter. Kev was probably thrilled. He'd get to ride the tractor plow along the driveway and back once the serious snow arrived. And he'd be able to play with the snowblower in all the smaller, hard-to-reach areas. Toys for boys. Kev was in heaven. I could imagine him carving figure eights in the snow.

I said, "I sure hope the mail can get through."

That got her. The mail and courier pickups were her lifeline. How else could she keep up her collection?

I went back to my breakfast. Life was good.

I knew darn well Vera would put me in my place one way or another before too long, but I wanted to savor the moment. It was just over a month to Christmas. The snow made me think of it. I pondered the idea of yellow silk pajamas for Vera. Despite her persnickety nature, I had actually become fond of her. So, that morning I was anticipating my first Thanksgiving at Van Alst House and then Christmas. Yes. Yellow silk pajamas for sure. I could manage that.

What for the signora? Thirty pounds of cheese?

Bail money for Kev. Bound to come in handy sooner or later.

I shot a playful glance at Vera. "With luck *Fer-de-Lance* will make it safely through the blizzard conditions and past the coyotes."

Vera quivered. She'd been waiting for this one: a first edition of Rex Stout's initial Nero Wolfe mystery, published in nineteen thirty-four. It was what they called a near fine first, and an upgrade to her previous copy. This *Fer-de-Lance* would roll in at twenty-four hundred dollars, plus shipping. It was in lovely, but not perfect condition. I had tracked it down. Mind you, the copy she really wanted was going for twenty-three thousand dollars, but we'd have to wait for that. In the meantime, we'd settled for near fine. Both editions had the same pink orchid against a black background on the cover. The previous copy had netted us seven hundred in a private sale that pleased me and the buyer that snagged it. That had been one of my early finds for Vera and I felt proud that we'd turned a nice profit on it. I'm pretty sure that Vera had wanted to keep that copy too. But at the rate antiques were disappearing from Van Alst House, she would have to make some compromises. I'd felt lucky that I'd persuaded her not to sell the Georgian silver candlesticks that graced the table. In fact, I'd barely talked her out of it, citing family history.

Kev said, "Weather doesn't bother me."

Vera's haggard face relaxed as she gazed at Kev. That was the closest she ever came to a fond smile. The signora beamed and headed straight for him with refills.

I glanced out at the snow dusting the lawn, as the signora filled my coffee cup with fragrant Italian roast. The day ahead consisted of hunting online for missing copies of Rex Stout books that Vera didn't already own or better copies of the ones she did.

While I was on the hunt, I'd be flogging my own latest finds, a cute little collection of three Trixie Belden adventures that I'd found for a quarter each at a garage sale. It paid to be the one who got there at six in the morning. The family selling off the grandmother's belongings were glad to get rid of those drab and faded children's books from the forties and fifties. I barely stopped myself from shrieking with glee as I took them off their hands. Vera does not do children's books. I am pretty sure she had never been a child. I expected to get about five hundred dollars for them. This close to Christmas, I was glad of a bit extra. Who knew how much those yellow silk pajamas would set me back?

"As I said, Miss Bingham, everyone is replaceable."

I shook my head. "Not Archie."

"Let me be clear. Not Archie Goodwin—

although he most emphatically could be replaced—but I am speaking of you."

I stared.

"This discussion is quite timely. Our association must come to an end."

I felt a buzzing around my ears. Perhaps that was why I had trouble making sense of her words. "What do you mean?"

"I mean that you are fired."

CHAPTER TWO

A JOKE, OF course, I told myself. But Vera doesn't joke. Not at her best moments. And this hadn't been one of her best moments.

"What's that, my girl?" Uncle Mick said when I reached him. Sounded like he'd just woken up.

"Let Uncle Lucky know he can stop moping in Manhattan. I'm coming home."

"You quit? Well, how many times have we told you that those Van Alsts are too big for their britches?" There was only the one Van Alst and she didn't wear britches, but Mick was still seething at some of the long-dead ones. He wasn't alone in that view in these parts.

"Fired," I said, clearly.

The line was silent. Finally Uncle Mick's voice came back. "Thought you said 'fired,' my girl; nobody fires us—"

"I'll need a van for my stuff. Kev will help me load it."

Uncle Mick's lovely tenor voice quavered. "Kev? Has Kev been fired too?"

"No need to panic. He's still king of the castle here. Nope. It's me and, as I said, I'm moving back."

I was glad I hadn't sniffled or wobbled when I was speaking to Mick. My knees were still weak as I packed my belongings in my beloved attic. "Replaceable. Fired." Vera's words ricocheted around my head. "No longer welcome at Van Alst House."

The signora kept fluttering up the two flights of stairs and into my room, bearing cakes, toast, tea, coffee, cookies and what might have been veal cutlets.

"Eat! Yes! Yes! No, Vera will change mind."

Nothing could stop the signora and I had given up, even before the cutlets. I had such a knot in my stomach that I thought I'd never eat again. Of course, aside from my bad feelings, it had only been an hour since breakfast. I emptied my wardrobe and the little walnut dresser. I had brought my own midcentury modern Lucite coffee table to Van Alst House, as well as my books and my collection of vintage clothing. Lately, I'd been collecting inexpensive vintage reprints of the Nero Wolfe (meaning Archie Goodwin) books. Now I'd have more time to read some more of them.

The two dogs lay on the flowered comforter, faces in paws, and watched me with concern. I tried not to sniffle and feel sorry for myself. There was no time to waste on that. I had until noon to be off the premises.

The most humiliating part was having to hand over my key to Vera. I noticed she didn't meet my eyes.

• • •

UNCLE KEV WRESTLED all my gear down the steep stairs from the third floor to the back door.

"Don't worry," he whispered to me, "I'll get to the bottom of it."

"What?"

"I'll find out what's going on."

Oh boy. If Kev started getting involved anything could go wrong, and things were plenty messed up already.

"Please, Kev," I said, firmly. "Don't try to find out what's going on."

He wore his hurt feelings on his face. That usually worked for him, although not so well in our immediate family.

"I'm serious," I added.

"But I'm in a position to find out—"

"Come on. You have a great job here and a good life. Don't do anything to jeopardize that. Please."

"Vera really likes me."

"You know what? She likes me too in her own curmudgeonly way. But see what just happened?"

"I think that was because of this Muriel Delgado. Vera turned on you right after she barged in here."

You mean, after you got her invited in, Kev. Luckily, I managed to keep that thought to myself. No point in rubbing it in. "Yes, I was just wondering about that myself. I'm pretty sure Vera was really happy with my services. I know my

33

firing has something to do with whatever was said in the study. I wish I were as good at barging into rooms as Ms. Delgado."

Kev opened his mouth.

"Don't. This is Vera we're talking about. She's unpredictable and she can be vicious. My point is that she could turn on you too. Leave it alone."

"She wouldn't fire me." Kev batted his ginger eyelashes.

"She could. And she would. Then you'd lose the best job you ever had." It might have been the only job Kev had ever had. I couldn't actually remember another one, unless a parole officer had been involved. Or unless there had been some awkwardness involving a getaway car, which wouldn't be a real job.

"I really like it here. The food is amazing."

"And there's the lawn tractor and the snow-blower and the plow," I reminded him.

"It's a great old place and the property is really special."

"Yes, well, don't question Vera or argue for my reinstatement or anything like that if you want to stay on. Promise?"

Kev moved his head in a way that could have meant anything from "Yes" to "No" to "I'm choking on a fishbone."

I pressed on. "Keep in mind, Vera will be stuck here and whatever hold this Muriel Delgado has over her will get worse. I'm counting on you, Kev.

Keep your eyes and ears open and your mouth closed."

He nodded.

I said, "We'll keep in touch with each other and you can make sure I'm always in the loop."

Kev brightened. "I won't miss a trick. I'll be your man on the inside. Don't worry about a thing."

I wished he hadn't said that because, after all, he was Kev.

AT 11:58, UNCLE Mick showed up with a van that was big enough for my belongings, spraying gravel and scattering the flock of wild turkeys that had been hanging around in recent weeks.

As we loaded my possessions into the back and the dogs into the front, he grumbled.

"What are all these coolers?"

"Um. Food from Signora Panetone. Lots of stuff."

"Why does she need to send food? We've got lots of good food. You never went hungry growing up with us, my girl. Good American food. You sure you want to take this?"

"We can freeze it for emergencies," I said tactfully. An emergency would be any time Uncle Mick was out of the house. I knew for a fact he was planning Alphagetti for lunch, with Pillsbury rolls as a special treat. And chocolate marshmallow cookies for dessert. Of course, they'd be good.

"Humph."

He stared around truculently, watching out for Vera, but she didn't show her face. Uncle Mick would have had a few choice words for her. Besmirching the honor of the Kellys and all that; even though I was technically a Bingham, I was definitely part of the Kelly clan.

"Bite your tongue, if you do see her," I said. "Remember that Kev still has his job and we both agree that we don't want him coming home."

Uncle Mick's cheerful pink face paled and he was uncharacteristically quiet for the drive home. I was glad. I needed the time to brood.

MY OLD BEDROOM in my uncles' home was pink and white, the girliest place ever. Think of it as an oasis of frills in a houseful of Kelly green knickknacks and ginger chest hair. I sat on the bed and glanced around. Nothing had changed. This was my second time in eighteen months finding myself in my childhood digs. A herd of My Little Ponies gazed at me with pity. My uncles would always take me in. They'd raised me and they loved me, but ending up back where I started felt like failure to me. The first time was after my ex-boyfriend left me too broke and broken to continue grad school. At least I understood what had happened that time. Now here I was again. What was this about? I thought Moon Dancer shook her head a little in shame.

So I'd been fired. Big deal. People get fired all the time. Not in my family, of course, since all my uncles are what we like to call "independent businessmen." Sometimes they call themselves "entrepreneurs" or operators of "creative start-ups." But people who do get fired must get fired for a reason. I'd always supposed that as a rule, they'd done something wrong. I couldn't think of anything that I'd done, except maybe tease Vera about Archie Goodwin.

Hardly a hanging offense.

I jumped when my iPhone sounded. Smiley!

"Hello, Officer Dekker," I said trying to work a casual tone into my voice without much success. It would have been nice to cry on his shoulder, but we don't really have a crying-on-shoulders kind of relationship. Anyway, he wasn't there, was he?

His voice was low. "Sorry, I can't talk long because we're not supposed to be on the phone. I won't be back for another week. Didn't want you to worry."

Didn't want me to worry?

"I've been fired!" I wailed. It's not like me to wail, but, in my defense, let me plead lack of sleep and extreme stress.

"What?"

"Fired. I've been fired."

After a brief silence, he said, "The line is pretty bad. I thought you said you'd been fired."

"I did say that. I have been fired. That's what I'm trying to tell you." This was like being stuck in a Three Stooges film in which I got to play Curly, Moe and Larry.

"There's a lot of noise here," he said. "But who would fire you?"

I didn't mean to snap at him. "Vera. Who else? She's the person I work for, make that worked for."

"But you do everything for her. You put your life on the line. You—"

"Thank you for the vote of confidence, but she did fire me and I had only a couple of hours to get my stuff out of Van Alst House."

"Really? That's incredible."

"Yes and that's because I was fired, and the apartment was part of my compensation for working there. Therefore, no working, no apartment."

"But—"

"And no signora's food."

"What are you going to do?"

"I don't know. Right now I'm back in my old bedroom at Uncle Mick's. I don't know what people do when they get fired. I don't even know anyone who ever got fired."

Smiley said, "I was fired once."

"What? You never were!"

"For sure. From the ice cream shop the summer I was fifteen. Something about supplies running low whenever I was on duty."

I laughed despite myself. "I don't know what reason Vera had. Supplies weren't running low, for sure."

He said, "In the adult non-ice-cream world, people get fired because their jobs aren't necessary anymore and they disappear, the jobs I mean."

"My job didn't disappear. In my position, I had lots to do."

"Well, it's not corporate downsizing, but she could be cutting costs. You said she sold some things lately, didn't you?"

I thought about that reason. I knew well that the Van Alst pockets were not as deep as they once had been and Vera had been liquidating assets to keep her book addiction going. I said, "But even if that were true, I would have worked for less or worked less for room and board. I brought in money and I could have helped her bring in more. We could have arranged something that would have suited us."

"Well, we can rule out any competency issues. You are one top-notch book hunter, Jordan."

"Thanks." He was right. I knew my stuff. I was valuable to Vera and I was getting better every day.

I said, "I suppose people get fired because they're light-fingered. Vera would have had me tied to a chair and interrogated if that had been the case." I take pride in my law-abiding life, so there was no chance that I had pilfered anything or otherwise crossed any legal or ethical lines.

He said, "Vera knows you're not a thief."

"I would have thought so too, but here we are." I sighed. "How about down at the cop shop? What does it take to get handed a pink slip?"

"It's pretty hard to get rid of us unless we start shooting innocent bystanders or sleeping with the chief's wife. Even then—"

"Funny. So you're immune?"

"Nope. Just hard to fire. But there's lots of politics in policing, and people's careers can take a beating because of departmental politics."

"Like what?"

"Like someone hates them and starts a rumor. Someone is jealous and turns other people against them. Someone wants their job and undermines their credibility or messes with their mind or their cases. Politics. It's everywhere."

"I don't think I was in any political danger from the signora or from Uncle Kev. Vera can barely find someone to deliver her paper, she is so despised in this town, as Uncle Mick enjoys telling me. Let's face it, no one wants my job."

I sat on my little pink bed surrounded by the trappings of my childhood and an empty case of beer, a holdover from the brief period when Uncle Kev had been living in my room before he hit the jackpot and moved into Van Alst House. I scratched my head. Smiley was giving it his best shot, but I needed to know the real reason behind my sudden dismissal.

"Nothing explains it," I said.

He wasn't giving up. "Sometimes people get fired because someone more powerful influences their employer to dismiss them."

Twenty-four hours ago, it wouldn't have made a bit of sense, but that was before Muriel arrived and changed the rules of the game. Kev was right. And now Smiley had put his finger on it.

"You know what? Last night a woman came to the house and Vera made us let her in and shooed us all away while she met with her in private. We didn't see Vera again until the morning, and at breakfast she fired me with no warning."

"But who is this woman?"

Right. I hadn't explained that yet. "Muriel Delgado. She walked into Van Alst House with more confidence than anyone has ever faced Vera with, like she had a handle on something that the rest of us didn't."

"What do you know about her?"

"Not a thing. I've been checking the Internet and coming up empty." Of course, Smiley was an agent of the law, and who better to find out about Muriel than my own personal police officer? "And that reminds me, I really need you to—"

I thought I heard bellowing in the background.

He lowered his voice. "Gotta go. I've been spotted talking on the phone. Sorry."

I said, "But—"

Naturally, the phone was dead.

Fine.

I didn't have the slightest idea why Muriel would want to get rid of me. None. But in the deepest fiber of my body I was now sure she was behind it. The question was, why? And not only why, but how? Even coaxing a smile out of Vera was impossible, but actually swaying her behavior? Vera was a mountain, never to be moved.

Was Muriel after the money that Vera paid me? It seemed a small amount for such a big presence. I couldn't imagine her dancing to Vera's tune or happily lounging in the attic room with the curling cabbage rose wallpaper while making deals for old mystery books. No. There was something bigger going on. And why would Vera even listen to her? Vera Van Alst was the least likely person in the world to tolerate a large imposing woman giving her orders and changing the comfortable facts of her existence. Perhaps Vera owed a debt to this woman and was too ashamed to share that with anyone.

From under the Care Bear lamp, I grabbed a Hello Kitty notepad with renewed purpose. I had to find out three things: Who was Muriel Delgado? What did Muriel Delgado want from Vera and Van Alst House? And why did she want me out of the way?

I felt Uncle Mick's presence as he loomed in the door.

"You don't mind so much being back here?" he said.

I got up and gave him a hug. "Never." His flannel shirt smelled like Old Spice and Irish whiskey.

"You deserved better treatment. There's reasons everyone hates that woman," he said, darkly.

"I do deserve better treatment. But I don't hate Vera. I think this woman who came to the house last night is the reason I was fired."

"Sounds like it. But why would she want the Van Alst female to fire you?"

I shrugged. "I really have no idea. But I guarantee you, there's something there. And I'll make it my business to find out."

It was taking Mick a while to get Vera out of his system. "I thought I'd come to like her or at least respect her over the past year and a bit, but this, this makes me think my original opinion of her was right."

"I don't want to judge her, Uncle Mick. I'd like to find out what's going on before I make up my mind about it all."

"Anything I can do to help?"

"Thanks. In fact, there is something—"

"Anything in the world. But it'll have to be later, my girl. I'm on my way out. Pressing business elsewhere, as they say. A bit of business is bubbling up. Your lunch is on the table. Keep your strength up for the battle."

With Uncle Mick gone, I let Walter and Cobain feast on the Alphagetti. They licked tomato sauce off each other's whiskers after cleaning their plates. I guess this was my team of associates now. I reheated the signora's cutlets and pasta alfredo. I did hang on to the marshmallow cookies. I'm sentimental about them. But for some reason, everything I ate tasted like sawdust.

There's nothing like a good walk to clear your head if you've been fired and evicted on the same day. And there were two dogs to encourage me in this kind of thinking. I bundled up in my nineteen-sixties red wool, hooded cape, a vintage find that made me feel like a streetwise Red Riding Hood. I headed downtown to stomp out my frustrations on the sidewalks of Harrison Falls. It didn't help that signs of Thanksgiving were everywhere. If it wasn't a pumpkin, it was a sheaf of dried corn. If it wasn't a Pilgrim hat, it was a cornucopia. If it wasn't a turkey, it was a . . . well, there were lots of turkeys, none of them real, thank heavens. Never mind that Harrison Falls was done up à la Norman Rockwell, I wasn't feeling thankful in the least. I did realize that it could have been worse. I could have been arrested or dead or . . . but it wasn't a situation suitable for celebrating.

I needed to find a way to make a living again and quickly. For sure, the uncles wouldn't toss me out, but I would need a place of my own before long if I wanted to retain my sanity. I had to keep saving too. That part might prove to be tricky. What could I do to make a bit of money?

On Main Street I stepped into Betty's Boutique, a vintage clothing shop, to check it out. The fifties and sixties fashions in the window showed well against the backdrop: a framed poster of Norman Rockwell's famous *Freedom from Want*, the archetypal Thanksgiving image. I decided not to think about my own Thanksgiving, which was probably going to consist of beans and franks, with Uncle Mick's signature Heinz ketchup.

I had to find the bright side. I probably had plenty of vintage I could sell on consignment to Betty's. The shop tended to be pricey and catered to out-of-town and online customers. Normally, I wouldn't think of getting rid of any of my clothing, but this was no normal time. Betty, the owner, didn't mind dogs and they were pleased to be allowed to sniff around in this new space with so many scents.

I always liked seeing Betty with her nineteen-fifties pageboy and her cinched-waist outfits, jet-black drawn-on eyebrows, bloodred lipstick and fingernails, plus cigarette holder. Back in the day, I bet that Archie would have been drawn to her. There were many great rumors about Betty's background. According to wagging local tongues she'd been romantically linked to two of the Beatles, a Scottish lord, and several U.S. senators. Whatever her life had been, for sure it had been interesting. The cigarette remained unlit, of course. I chatted with Betty a bit and then snooped around, enjoying the many racks of sixties and seventies outfits. Fun stuff. Too bad I found lots that I wanted to buy and buying wasn't in the cards.

Never mind, I made an appointment with Betty for the following week to show her some of my favorite dresses with a "mod" pedigree from the sixties. It might hurt a bit to sell them, but I knew I had to be tough. And in a week, I'd have a better idea of what I really needed to do to get my life back on track.

Betty waved her cigarette holder languidly as I headed out. I grinned back at her. The visit had cheered me up a bit and shown me that I could find ways of making money without Vera and her books.

Next we trooped into Second Time Around to see if there were any pickings. I managed to seem bored after twenty minutes of pretending to browse through other things when I selected three Bobbsey Twins books in great shape from a mess of worthless bestsellers, with their curled, yellowed pages and bent covers. I could sell these without a problem on eBay for at least twelve dollars each and turn a nice profit from a three-dollar investment. It would be more than worth the trouble of listing them.

I tried not to smile as I paid for them. The dogs

seemed to be sensing my suppressed excitement. I thought Cobain's tail would clear the nearest shelf of mismatched glasses and shaky table lamps. I don't have many vices, but the thrill of a good find keeps me creeping around in dank corners of dusty shops.

Harrison Falls has been improving somewhat of late, and small businesses have been making their way to the downtown area. Some have failed quickly and spectacularly, and others have held on. The Sweet Spot and the Poocherie seemed to have weathered their first couple of years. We gave the candy store a miss, although I waved as I went by. I couldn't resist strolling through the pet shop, where both dogs got homemade crunchy treats. We missed the young manager, Jasmine, but we'd drop into the Poocherie more often now that I was living in the area.

I figured I'd better enjoy this walk, because it was only a matter of time until everyone in Harrison Falls found out that I'd been fired by Vera. I had to practice keeping my head held high, as befitted a Kelly or a Bingham. It was easier if I didn't run into everyone I knew all at once.

The walk did me good and as I passed the Hudson Café, I paused. I could see the new owner, Lainie Hetherington, inside. Lainie loved me, perhaps because I was such a good customer. I got a warm feeling every time I spoke to her. My best friends Tiff and Lance and I count it as our favorite place. I could get a job there in a flash. But did I want to go back to the job I had after my first year in college? The job where I'd worked with Tiff and Lance? It had been great that summer, but I hoped my life would continue to be in the book world. I wanted to go forward, not back.

Lainie spotted me and waved. She opened the door and enveloped me in a big hug. As I said, she loved me. I could smell wonderful aromas through the open door. Was that pumpkin pie? For sure there was a tantalizing hint of cinnamon and nutmeg and something baking. It was all part of that Thanksgiving mood on Main Street. I decided to be thankful for the delicious smells in the restaurant.

"How are you?" Lainie said, sympathetically. "You seem a bit down."

"Nope," I fibbed. "Not down at all. Couldn't be better. How are you?"

She shrugged. "The same. Soldiering on."

"It's really good to have you here in Harrison Falls. You've kept our beloved café afloat." Lainie had moved to town the past summer after retiring from her therapy practice in New York City. She'd bought the venerable Hudson Café with great ideas to update and expand it, only to discover that her restaurant was soon struggling in the bad economy.

"A person likes to hear that," she said with a

bright smile. "How about a bit of a late lunch?"

"Thanks, I can't." I chose not to mention that I wouldn't be lunching in upscale bistros or cafés until I got my job back or found a really good alternative.

"On the house," she added with a sparkle. "Cheer you up."

It was hard to say no to her. For a small person, Lainie's presence was larger than life. Her silver ponytail was sleekly gathered in the back and her slightly pear-shaped figure was hugged by snug jeans that might have been designed for her. The asymmetrical black cashmere sweater and the large silver hoop earrings and dramatic silver ring gave her a casual glamour that most women would kill for. Classic red lipstick was invented for a woman like her. She was probably almost ten years older than Vera but seemed much younger and more vital. When I'm midsixties I want to look as good as she does, but I knew better than to mention that.

"What are you grinning at?" she said.

"Sorry, I've already eaten, but I'm starting to realize how many inspiring women are running successful businesses in this town. It gives a girl hope for the future."

"Does it now?" She laughed her throaty laugh. "Well, it ain't all roses."

I knew that. Lainie hadn't realized that the café had been in trouble when she'd sunk her life savings into it. The reality of running a restaurant in tough times had been a shock to her.

Still, she had managed to keep the Hudson Café humming along even through the ups and downs.

I said, "It's your perseverance I admire most. Please tell me it's worth it in the end?"

"I guess so. I've sure learned a lot, like making sure I'm on the premises and not paying other people to manage my investment. You have to take charge of your life and be tough, Jordan. You need to seize the moment."

I nodded. A good bit of advice.

I fought the urge to gush about her place as a role model in my life; I didn't want her to feel put on the spot.

She frowned and two little lines creased her forehead. "What's wrong, Jordan? You can tell me."

I opened my mouth to give her my litany of troubles when Uncle Mick's words echoed in my brain. *Never be needy. It makes you vulnerable. If you really require help, turn to your family.* This was kind of a Kelly code that Uncle Mick had instilled into my head when I first moved in as a small child. It had stood me in good stead in the schoolyard, where I'd learned to stand up for myself early and often.

I squeezed her hand and said good-bye. "Don't worry about me. I have a lot of errands to do and these two dogs waiting. I'm a bit distracted. I hope to be back for a wonderful lunch soon."

A few stores down, I noticed that an abandoned diner had been set up as a food depot for needy families by Phyllis Zelman, Harrison Falls's most energetic volunteer.

Where Lainie had welcomed me, Phyllis pounced.

"Look at you!" Phyllis said.

I stared. Walter cocked his head and snuffled. Cobain reserved judgment. Maybe it was the close-cropped salt-and-pepper hair or the over-sized round black-framed glasses. Or it could have been the track suit with the Nordic sweater over it or the clumpy white running shoes. The thick knitted socks were a possibility too. It was really nippy in the space, though, so I figured all those clothes were a good idea.

"I bet you've got lots to be thankful about this season," she said. At least she hadn't heard about my unceremonious firing. One good thing.

"Actually . . ."

She raised a hand. "We all have some troubles, but do you have a roof over your head?"

I paused. Not the roof I wanted, but a roof. "Yes."

"Enough to eat?"

I thought of the cupboard full of mac and cheese. "Yes."

"So then please don't complain because you don't have the latest cell phone or a trip to the Caribbean or new and fashionable clothes."

I stared at her. "These are vintage," I said. "I choose to wear them."

She snorted. "I'm not speaking of your actual wardrobe. I'm talking about your advantages. Lots of people have almost nothing, including not enough to eat. So give some thought to helping us with our Thanksgiving dinner for people who really need help."

"Sure," I said. "I'd be glad to help." All she'd had to do was ask. I would have said yes without the guilt trip.

She wasn't done, though. "Makes you put your own problems in perspective, doesn't it?"

It did. But I still had them. They were big enough to me and they weren't going to disappear without me doing something about them. But never mind; whatever happened with Muriel and Vera, it was a good idea to help with this project, even if Phyllis was a bit of a pain.

She said, "What would you like to do? Collect food? Cook? Serve?"

"I'll serve. I'd like that." It seemed a lot more straightforward than figuring out how to collect food or, worse, how to cook it. I couldn't see that ending well for anyone.

Luckily, I'd already reminded myself not to be needy. So I didn't really require Phyllis's approval. And that was probably a good thing. I had to stand on my own two feet. And that wouldn't prevent me from giving a helping hand to someone else.

I gave Phyllis my cell number so she could leave me a message about where and when to show up. "And," she said, "there might be a few extra errands required. You never know."

MURIEL DELGADO KEPT a low profile on the Internet. I had plenty to do and the first order of business was to try harder to find some information about her. Back in my room alone, I continued searching and I found people with that name in Canada, Europe and South America. Harrison Falls? Zip. Upstate New York? The same. In fact, Muriel Delgado didn't appear to live in the USA.

Whoever she was, she wasn't active in the book world as far as I could tell. I tried a few more search engines, knowing that can make a difference, and also tried the image applications. I found nobody even faintly like the tall imposing person with the swirling black clothing who had appeared at our door last night. I shook my head. Was it only last night? Less than twenty-four hours and my life had been turned upside down, sideways and inside out. How could that be? I willed myself to focus on my search. Where there's a will, they say. But this time, there seemed to be no way.

It wasn't the sort of quest you could quit. I stared around at my My Little Pony gang and the bookcase with my Goosebumps collection,

'N Sync CDs and well-worn *Newsies* video-cassette. I really needed to get out of that room.

I WALKED THE dogs through the lingering snow on the sidewalks of downtown Harrison Falls and headed out to the library. I figured Lance was out of town as he still hadn't answered any of my texts, but I was a big girl with a serious degree and I knew how to use a library.

In my family, we make sure we are always pulled together when we head out. It makes a difference in our mood and in how people react to us. Even those of us who are engaged in legal activities (that would be me) believe this.

I might have been fired, but no way was that going to be apparent to anyone who saw me. I'd ditched the red cape and was wearing wide brown slacks, with dangerously pointy brown boots and a raw angora cable-knit sweater, topped with my green suede fur-trimmed jacket. Earlier in November, I'd spied it in our Harrison Falls Saturday Flea Market with a ratty fur fringe and was lucky enough to find a replacement. It was my late-fall-with-a-bit-of-snow *Charlie's Angels* ensemble.

MY JAW DROPPED as I headed over to the reference desk. Lance glanced up and blinked. I blinked back. I forced a smile onto my face and said. "You're working today." A little pang of hurt feelings settled across my chest. Why hadn't he returned my text?

He nodded.

On my back, I felt the beady eyes of the brigade of elderly women who spend hours in Lance's presence. Since he'd joined the staff at Harrison Falls Public Library after getting his master's, interest in local history had exploded. Everyone seemed to have a small, unique research project. I wasn't fooled.

"Great. I need some help and you are the best."

"Excuse me," a quavery voice said at my elbow. "I require some assistance here."

It would not be an exaggeration to say that Lance leapt to his feet to help one of his posse. Any more enthusiasm and he would have vaulted over the desk.

I did my best to pick my jaw up off the well-worn carpet. Where was my usual over-the-top greeting? The hug? The "beautiful lady" or "mademoiselle"? Some remark about getting lost in my eyes? What was wrong with my Lance?

I felt shaken to my core. What if it was really something wrong with me? Clearly something about me was . . . well, the word "repellent" came to mind. Lance and I had been friends since the summer after our first year in college, when we worked together in the Hudson Café along with Tiff. We were close. We flirted. We were the best of friends. We loved each other. There had never been any coolness between us, let alone the cold shoulder like this. I gingerly pointed my nose to my armpit region, testing for offensive odors.

Literally, I smelled like roses.

Every time I made visual contact with him, he shrugged apologetically and at the same time let his eyes slide away. If I didn't know better, I'd swear he was feeling guilty. But what could Lance have to feel guilty about?

Never mind.

That was a setback, but of course, he wasn't the only librarian in the world. Still, Lance knew his way through the myriad vertical file materials and historical files and other library magic. If there was a sentence about Muriel Delgado on some yellowed sheet of paper in the Harrison Falls Public Library, Lance DeWitt would be able to track it down.

Unwilling to admit defeat, I made my way to the shelves of city directories. The service had been discontinued, but volumes were still available up to the seventies. There was only one Delgado. I found a C. Delgado living at 10B Willows Road in the early sixties. After that, a C. Delgado around nineteen sixty-five at 22 Lilac Lane. I found no M. Delgado in any year. Finally in the midseventies, a C. Delgado showed up at 153 Maple Street.

I made a note of each address. At least I had somewhere to start.

I left the library without having made eye

contact with Lance again. He didn't rush after me to make things right. Whatever was going on with him today, I couldn't deal with it. I put his strange and hurtful behavior behind me and headed off to find answers to my other problems.

But mostly I lay on my bed for the rest of the evening sulking and sniffing. Occasionally I paused to stuff my face with chocolate marshmallow cookies.

The dogs understood that part.

WHEN I WASN'T walking, feeding and patting the pooches, I spent the next morning polishing up my all-purpose résumé on the off chance that a part-time opportunity might present itself. I found a few lackluster opportunities online and decided to apply anyway. I could not help but notice the complete lack of attention from the man in my life and my two best friends. I had, after all, been unceremoniously dumped from my wonderful job. Surely that was worth a pat on the back. And speaking of pats on the back, Uncle Mick was not around either. I was alone in the world.

A trip to the post office to mail off some résumés to totally unappealing possible employers did nothing to help my mood. Even if I love that historic building. Usually.

I WAS ALTERNATING between hurt feelings and anger as I eased my beloved vintage Saab in front of Michael Kelly's Fine Antiques and parked. I felt I needed to give Lance and Tiff the benefit of the doubt, as they'd been good and loyal friends for such a long time. Tyler Dekker had his career to think about. And Uncle Mick was probably busy with . . . it was better I didn't know with what. As I stepped out of the car, an elderly black Cadillac Seville shot in front of me and braked abruptly. Uncle Kev jumped out and left the motor running. This was Vera's car, of course, and Uncle Kev wouldn't be paying for that gas. Most likely he wouldn't be paying for any fuel ever.

To my astonishment, the signora got out of the passenger door. Both of them ran toward the Saab. I closed my mouth and stepped out to meet them.

"*O Dio!*" The signora clutched my hand, her round little body shaking. "*Il demonio.*"

Demons were new to conversations with the signora. Speed demon, maybe?

"How fast were you going, Kev?"

Kev interrupted to translate. "It's not my driving. She's really upset. About you-know-what."

"Thanks, Kev. I can see that by the way she's hopping around. But I don't know why. If not your driving, what demon is she talking about?"

"Demon?"

"*Demonio.* That's what she's saying."

"Obviously, it must be the demon that's moving in," he said.

I felt a little throb in my temple. Kev can bring that on. "Try to talk sense," I said as kindly as I could.

"I mean Muriel."

"What about her? Wait. Are you saying—? You don't mean she's—"

"Yup."

"No!"

"I wish it weren't true, but Muriel Delgado has moved into Van Alst House. Lock, stock and barrel. Today."

The signora crossed herself.

CHAPTER THREE

MOVED IN?" I said stupidly. "Today?"
"Yup."

"Really?"

The signora did a little dance of desperation, wailing.

"To Van Alst House? Am I understanding correctly? How is that possible?"

"Truck pulled up. Two guys brought in her trunks and suitcases and boxes."

"Trunks?"

"What can I tell you. That's what we saw."

I swallowed. "Is she in my . . . the attic rooms?" I actually felt violated.

"Ho ho," Kev boomed. "No way, little peasant niece of mine. She gets the guest suite on the second floor."

"The guest suite? The one Vera's grandfather had designed for visiting dignitaries? Governors? Wandering British aristocrats?"

"That's the one. The only guest suite that I know of."

The signora continued to dance around in distress, muttering things I couldn't hear and probably wouldn't have understood.

I was just short of screeching. "I can't stand it! The guest suite! The Art Nouveau guest suite with the gilded rococo mirror and the Roman tub?"

Vera could have put royalty in that and no one would have felt shortchanged. It had a sitting room, bedroom, magnificent marble bathroom with the aforementioned Roman tub, dressing room and a writing alcove with a burled walnut and ivory table that fit perfectly under the faceted window and on the Aubusson carpets. I could go on and on and on. It was roomier than Vera's own suite and a hundred times grander than my former digs in the attic or than Kev's spartan accommodation over the garage or than the signora's modest rooms on the first floor. Still I felt a surge of relief that the *demonio* hadn't taken over my beloved spot.

"A visit?" I said, getting my voice under control.

Kev shook his head. "Permanent. Moved in. Period."

"*Povera Vera!*" the signora wailed.

Poor Vera indeed. But how had this happened? Vera was tough as nails and not one to be pushed around, so if Muriel had moved in, then Vera must have okayed it. "I can't believe that Vera gave her approval."

Kev said, "I wouldn't say she exactly approved it, judging by the expression on her face when the truck showed up with those trunks. But

61

Muriel said she was moving in and Vera seemed to accept it. She didn't put up any kind of a fight."

"It's hard to believe any of this. I mean, who is this woman?"

"It's all true," Kev said, placing his hand over his heart. "I couldn't make that up. I think she's got some sort of hypnotic powers."

"This is so strange and sudden. And I think we all know how Vera feels about change. Wait, does she know you're here?"

"No!"

"You don't have to shout. I just asked."

"We're under strict orders not to contact you."

"Vera told you not to contact me? How did she think that would work? I mean, you are still my uncle."

"She said we weren't to call you or visit you or—"

"I suppose that instruction included not having Signora Panetone squeeze my hands hard enough to cut off circulation." I pried my fingers free of the signora's grasp. "Call me crazy, but you are here."

"Well, you don't think we could follow those orders. What's the matter with you, Jordie? Do you think we would let you slip away?"

Everyone else seems to have, I thought. Only the two least likely to solve my problem were there in my corner. But I was glad of them.

"Thank you," I said, my heart filling with gratitude.

"For what?" Kev said, puzzled. "We really need your help. Something bad is going on. Vera needs you even though she doesn't know it."

So, even their support had been too good to be true. Kev was still talking. "Vera thinks I'm taking the signora to get supplies. Do you know that Muriel Delgado won't even eat Italian food?"

"*Dio mio!*" The signora was now practically spinning. She managed to grab my hand again midspin.

Kev said, "You're going to be our secret weapon. We'll feed you information and you can overturn . . . let's see . . . whatever is going on. You've got to figure out what this broad has on Vera. It's no good, Jordie, I'm telling you."

"Listen, Kev. Vera fired me. I don't feel much like helping and I am in no position to overturn anything. It's okay, Signora, please let go of my hand." Any more squeezing and bones would start to break.

Kev said, "Show a little spine, Jordie."

"Show a little spine? Are you insane, Kev?" My outrage came out as a series of squeaks.

Didn't help my case much.

"Nope. Just telling you straight. Vera was good to you. She gave you the perfect job. You loved everything about it. You gotta admit that. It was like it was made in heaven for you."

"Uh, yes, and then she took it away with no explanation, no severance, no talk of references. Nothing but a firing. Out by noon. No contact with you or the signora. That was a humiliating end after what I've tried to do for her. Not exactly a golden parachute, Kev."

"But you do have contact with us." Kev was never all that hung up on logic.

"*Povera Vera*," the signora wailed.

I said, "Stop wailing, Signora, and stop making excuses for Vera, Kev. Don't you realize that if she did it to me, she can do it to you?"

Kev blinked. "But I do everything she wants."

"Yeah, well. How did that work for me?"

"You were teasing her at breakfast. Maybe she—"

I snapped, "Hardly a firing offence."

Kev must have finally sensed my anger and frustration. He said, "None of this was Vera's idea. I don't think she wanted to fire you. That Muriel Delgado made her do it."

Even though I was sure all along that Muriel was behind my firing, I found myself arguing against Vera as the innocent pawn in Muriel's game.

"Have you ever seen anyone make Vera do anything?" I countered.

"This is different. It's like—"

"*Il demonio!*"

"You have to find out about this woman," Kev said. "Where did she come from? What kind of a hold does she have over Vera?"

"It's not that easy. She doesn't seem to leave any tracks. I've been trying to find her online."

Kev brightened. "You have been trying? So you do want to help. That's the spirit, Jordie."

"I'd like to know what's going on, that's all. I'm digging for information about this Muriel. There's nothing out there. And I don't have a lot of time for it. I'm going to have to get on with my life, get another job and figure out how to make a living."

"Come on. It's not like you found yourself on the street. Mick would never throw you out."

"Of course, he won't. It's not a matter of being thrown out."

"You can stay with him forever. He'll be thrilled."

"But I won't be thrilled. I need to be independent." Was that a whine creeping into my voice? Something else to be mad about. Archie Goodwin wouldn't whine and I wasn't going to either.

"Whatever. But you'll find out about this Muriel."

"I didn't say that. I said I already tried and it wasn't easy." Of course, I hadn't tried hard. And I did want to know.

"Try again. We are all depending on you. Vera will be too, although she might not know it. I don't care what kind of cable channels we get now."

"Cable channels?" Whoa, hold the phone. Vera

had always ranted against the evil "boob tube," which she overenunciated and called a "boob tee-yube."

"Yeah, cable channels."

"But we, I mean you, don't have cable. Vera would never allow it. All books all the time is her motto, except for the little black-and-white number in the kitchen."

"Used to be. But as soon as the moving truck left, they called the cable guy."

"They? Who's they?"

"Vera and Muriel."

"Vera actually called—"

"Muriel's totally addicted to cable channels. So Vera actually picked up the phone and spoke to them, Jordie. They were there pretty fast. The cable company, I mean. She was practically going through withdrawal symptoms."

"Well, I can't think of much that's more surprising than Vera agreeing to it."

"I can." Kev's eyes widened and he drew in close, as though he were about to share his magical knowledge of a hidden treasure. "Cherie," he said, mouth open in awe.

"What?"

"Cherie."

"I repeat: What?"

"The cable guy, much more surprising."

"Um, the cable guy's name is Cherie? And why do you have that besotted expression on your face?" I wasn't being judgmental. I only wanted it to make sense.

Kev's blue eyes danced. "Yeah, she's awesome. She turned in off the road, driving that cable truck like it was on rails." He made eye contact with me, as though I would have full appreciation for whatever that meant. "I've never seen a woman drive like that."

I let it go. Kev had his own standards for women and they were unique. I said, "So Vera ordered cable, for Muriel?" I glanced toward the signora, who was turned away slightly, her lips unusually pursed. I was sure she would have preferred to be watching her *telenovelas* on cable, instead of the snowy local programming that her digital antenna picked up through the stone walls for her ancient black-and-white television in the kitchen. But somehow, it seemed that her feelings were hurt. I assumed that it was by Muriel's influence, but maybe it was this Cherie.

"Yeah, she did. Right away. I could hear Vera on the phone yelling at the cable company from down the hall. Then, like an hour later," his eyes glazed over again, "Cherie shows up."

The signora said, *"Si, si, bella, bella!"*

Kev glowed. "You can say that again. And she was good too. She didn't cut any corners or freak out about the spiderwebs in the crawl space or anything." He was nodding, but clearly he'd drifted off to an imaginary place where he and

Cherie could drive like lunatics and celebrate their lack of arachnophobia.

While I'd been living at Van Alst House, I had made a bid or two for cable. The nights got kind of long sometimes. Vera had gone as far as to say that she would consider legal action against anyone who brought, and I quote, "that kind of filth and drivel" into her home.

Something was really bothering me about this news. That anyone could waltz in and be watching *Duck Dynasty* all day on A&E within twenty-four hours was astounding. This Muriel woman must have had dark powers.

I hesitated. I did want to know what had happened to me and why. And I didn't want the same thing to happen to the signora and Kev. Surely the signora was safe. She'd been with the Van Alst family since Vera was a child. Kev would land his feet somewhere, hopefully not in jail, and create chaos in someone else's life. But if this woman was trying to separate Vera from the people who cared about her, I had to do some-thing.

And first I needed to find out more about her.

"The truck," I said. "What company was it?"

"What truck? Cherie's truck?"

"Not the cable company truck," I said patiently. "I mean the truck that delivered Muriel's trunks and boxes and suitcases."

Kev frowned. Details were never his best thing.

Actually, he doesn't have a best thing, if you don't count being fairly irresistible to older women who should know better.

"Dunno," he said.

"You want me to act, you'd better give me something."

"Um, green."

"That's a start. So I assume that Muriel doesn't own this truck. Did it have a company name on it?"

Kev looked wounded. He specialized in that. "Why do you need to know?"

"Because if I can find out where she came from, I can dig around and learn a lot more about her."

I didn't mention that I had a couple of addresses from the city directories. C. Delgado. And how many Delgados could there be in Harrison Falls? I didn't want Kev showing up at either address and attracting the type of disastrous attention that he had such a knack for.

"Work on remembering. I'll see what I can do in the meantime."

Kev nodded. "You'll let us know what you find out?"

"Sure. But you're also supposed to be finding out something. We need information about the green truck. If you remember anything or if you see it again or if it comes back, get some details. License number. Company name on the side. Anything."

"There was a company name on it."

"That's great, Kev. What was it?"

"I don't remember, but there was one. And Jordie, if you find out anything, don't call me about it. I told you that we're not supposed to speak to you. Or make any contact. Including seeing you. Which we're doing right now. Against orders, if I make myself clear."

"You do. I'll text you."

Kev's voice went up a notch. "What if she sees your name on my phone?"

"It won't be my name, you goofball. Uncle Mick will have a burner phone that I can use. We'll use that to stay in touch. Let's use some code name for Vera and another one for Muriel."

"Good idea. How about Little Red Riding Hood and the wolf?"

"Let's use real names that won't sound like obvious code if Vera or Muriel snoops on your phone."

"They might do that. They're really serious about keeping you out of whatever's going on. That reminds me. Don't try to sneak back in for any reason. They changed the locks. And they changed the alarm code."

Huh. "What did they change the code to, Kev?"

"Well, my password is 'HANDYMAN.' "

That was all I needed. Locks are nothing.

After some haggling we settled on Cruella for Muriel and Wheels for Vera, and for no reason at all, Kevin insisted that he now be referred to as the Eagle. I was Bo, as in Peep.

As I watched Kev and the signora pile back into the Caddy and rocket down the street, I wondered what we had all gotten ourselves into.

On a bright note, I found myself with a couple of additional large containers of the signora's food. Every cloud and all that.

IT WASN'T LIKE I had anything else to do. I headed back to the rooms behind Michael Kelly's Fine Antiques and checked the usual spots for a spare burner phone. A childhood favorite, an industrial storage unit with fifty drawers, loomed behind one of the glass-topped counters. From the bottom left, I counted five drawers in and five up, but that hiding spot was bare. Things had changed more than a little around here. But I guess a few sprays of bullets into your business and home-stead can inspire reorganizing. Had Vera forgotten about that whole incident? I'd put my life on the line for her. As I lamented my shabby treatment by Vera, my eye settled on a copy of *Moby-Dick* on top of the storage unit. Bingo. I chuckled and opened the hollow book and removed the burner phone and left a note for Uncle Mick promising to replace it, although I knew he'd tell me not to worry about it.

Then I headed back to my bedroom to check out my wardrobe. If I was going to be hunting for a trail to Muriel Delgado, I needed to do it as someone other than Jordan Bingham. Okay, I don't need much urging to don a disguise; wigs are fun, and I thoroughly recommend them. I still had the kicky red shoulder-length wig I'd used during our Sayers adventure. The hair takes all the attention and no one even notices my face. Even if they did, the red picks up my blue eyes and seems to brighten and intensify them. It changes my appearance completely. I look nothing like the real me with my dark hair and blue eyes "put in with a sooty finger," as they say. Black Irish, they call that coloring. The wig gives me a "Pippi Longstocking gone wild" vibe. I picked a pair of jeggings with my knee-high leather boots, the tunic again and a shrunken jean jacket. I looped my vintage Pucci scarf around my neck and headed out, red hair blowing in the breeze. I left my deep-orange purse at home, as it would be too distinctive. I used a serviceable but boring black bag that might suit the person I would be pretending to be.

By now, the snow had almost melted away and the day was pleasant enough for late November. Of course, my powder-blue Saab would be a dead giveaway, so I borrowed one of the spare cars that Uncle Mick keeps for occasions such as this. This one was a black-cherry Honda Accord, old and unremarkable but reliable. Not as much fun as the Saab, but never mind. I left a note, of course. I also left the Saab sitting conspicuously in front of the shop. I was here at home and as far as anyone needed to know, I was intending to stay there, sulking to the death. I left a light on in my bedroom and the radio playing loudly.

You can never be too careful.

I STARTED WITH Maple Street, as it was the last street in Harrison Falls showing C. Delgado living there. Maple Street was a plain but cheerful street of sixties brick bungalows, some a bit dowdy, others on the upswing with freshly painted shutters and new interlock pathways. Even the dowdy houses seemed to be well groomed, the lawns raked again now that the snow had melted. Everyone seemed to have their Thanksgiving decorations out and their leaves bagged for pickup by the side of the road. Most people had the biodegradable paper bags, but a few used burlap bags.

I love fall, but sometimes it does seem like it's a lot of work. I imagined the more industrious neighbors hauling their biodegradable leaf bags into the safety of their garages when the snow came and then back out again for curbside pickup once it melted.

Number 153 was one of the lucky updated houses on the street; it had a new red door, wire window boxes with coconut fiber, interlock pathways and shiny white shutters. A large, expensive double stroller was parked out front. Twins? A baby and a toddler? I figured either would explain why it was the only house with the leaves still thick on the lawn.

I rang the doorbell and waited. A young woman with a perky blond ponytail answered with a smile. She was balancing a baby on her hip. Behind her, a curly-haired toddler clung to her yoga pants. Both children had wide, green eyes, the same as their mother's. A lovely legacy for sure. Everyone's cheeks were pink, a sign that they'd been out for a walk in the pleasant weather.

I smiled back at the three of them. The toddler hid her face shyly behind her mother's back.

"What beautiful children," I said. "Those eyes."

"We like them." She grinned. "Although you have to push them for miles before they will go to S-L-E-E-P."

I got down to business before we went down the life-with-babies conversational path. "I am representing the legal firm of Lawson and Loblaw. We have information that could benefit a C. Delgado of this address."

She said, "Oh."

I kept smiling to encourage a bit more than the "oh."

"There's no one here by that name. We moved in last year. Our name is Bennacke."

I tried to avoid saying "oh" again. "We did have this address, so perhaps . . ." I paused to glance at the paper in my hand . . . "C. Delgado was the person you bought it from. We are following up on an inheritance."

"My! An inheritance," she said with interest. She seemed like she wanted to help. "We never met the owners, but I don't think the name was Delgado. It was a bit more ordinary."

"Is there a way you could find out?"

"My husband takes care of all the legal papers."

"Do you mind checking with him?"

"He's at work. He often works weekends. He'll be back this evening. I could ask him then."

"I have to do that myself quite often, like today," I said, keeping my disappointment to myself. I wrote down the number of my new cell phone, gave myself the name Clarissa Montaine, for no good reason except that I liked the sound of it, and made a note to myself to leave a greeting from Lawson and Loblaw on the burner.

No point in people knowing that Jordan Bingham was nosing around, in case someone was in touch with some lurking Delgado.

"Clarissa," she said, "that's such a beautiful name. I'm Audra. I'll let you know."

"What about the neighbors?" I said, smiling at her. "Have they been here awhile?"

"The ones on both sides bought after we did. We've been here a little over a year. Across the street they're new too. This is a great street for a bargain. Our own home was a fixer-upper," she said, with pride. "We did most of the work ourselves."

"Terrific," I said, gazing around admiringly. "You did really well on this."

She beamed. "We are planning to move on up, but I do love our little house. It will be really hard when the time comes."

Speaking of time, I needed to get back on task. "So no one around who might know about this C. Delgado?"

"Oh. Well, there's an older couple three doors down, in the house on the corner. Their name is Snow. They're retired and they're in and out all the time. I see them coming and going when we're out on our walks. I'm pretty sure they're the original owners. They might be able to help. And I'll ask my husband to call you."

"Thanks."

I headed to the corner, hoping that I would find the couple at home. But no one answered the door. There was no garage, and the carport stood empty. Timing is everything, as they say. If I hit a wall, I'd have to come back. I wrote down *175 Maple Street/Snow* and *Check with the Bennackes about previous owner*. Then I headed back to the neutral Honda I had used to travel there.

Next stop: 22 Lilac Lane, where C. Delgado had been in residence back in nineteen sixty-five. Lilac Lane was at the far end of Harrison Falls, but no end of Harrison Falls is far from any other end, so I tootled over. Number 22 had been something but was now nothing. Well, not exactly nothing, but a vacant lot with the remains of a crumbling old foundation and a sign that said, "FOR SALE—ZONED FOR MULTIPLE DWELLINGS."

Not so good for my purposes. Lilac Lane had seen better days and there was no sign of the upgrading I had found on Maple Street. There were other older homes on the street, but no sign of anyone around. Never give up. That's my motto. I tried the house on one side. A woman peered out the grimy window in the front door and refused to open up. She turned her back and walked away from the door. Maybe it was my red hair? Pretty eerie. Fine. I tried the house on the other side of the vacant lot.

No one answered. I considered that it might have been unoccupied, because the front window was boarded up and graffiti tags covered the worn paint of the clapboard siding. But I thought I detected movement on the side of the house. Stepping quickly, I zipped down the front steps and around the side. An elderly man was dozing on an ancient sofa parked by the side of the house. Over the top was a roof of sorts made from a sheet of yellowed corrugated vinyl. At the end of the enclosure stood the garbage can. The roof was good because it was now starting to drizzle. The rain pattered on the vinyl, but the man kept snoring softly in his little getaway.

"Excuse me," I said.

He awoke with a start and stared at me—well, at my hair, actually, which was what I was counting on. He kept on scratching and staring.

I said with my fake smile, "Hello, I am trying to find a C. Delgado who used to live at number 22."

"What? Speak up!"

I raised my voice and repeated it.

He cupped his ear and I tried a near shout.

"No need to yell. They're gone now," he said, still staring. "Been gone for years. The house has been torn down."

"I can see that. But do you know where they went?" He'd said "they." So more than one of them. That was good.

"Can't remember. Must be more than fifty years since they left."

"I'm from Lawson and Loblaw. The law firm," I said importantly. "I may have good news for that family. Especially"—and here I took a chance— "Muriel."

"Humph. Muriel? She was just a little kid then. She'd be all grown up now."

I felt goose bumps on my arms when he said Muriel's name. I tried not to show my reaction.

He said, "Funny girl. Not like other girls around here if you ask me. Bit strange."

I hadn't asked him about Muriel's personality, but I was glad he'd volunteered that information. She was still strange, but also forceful and, in my opinion, dangerous.

"Strange how?" I said.

"What kind of news?" he said, a bit more awake now. "That sounds like it means money."

"It might mean money. If it's the right Delgados and it sounds like it is. It would help if you could give me C. Delgado's first name.

"C. Delgado. I guess you mean Carmen."

Carmen is not my favorite name. Maybe because of those issues that Uncle Kev had with Big Carm Spitelli, a guy with way more throwing knives than anyone needs. Or maybe because of the unhappy resolution that Uncle Mick and Uncle Lucky had with Carmen "Dead Meat" Lobocoff on the jewelry experiment. Whatever. I guess I made a face.

I hadn't noticed her arrival, but we'd been joined by a woman. She could have been a twin to the old man, only without the white chin stubble. She was dressed in a faded and drooping (possibly blue at one time) housedress that made Vera look like a fashion model.

"Yes," I said, "Carmen. That's exactly right. I have some news that will be of great interest to him. Do you know where he's moved?"

The woman spoke. "I don't know what you're nosing around for, but you don't know crap about

Carmen Delgado. Get your butt off our property before I call the cops."

"What?"

"You heard me. Don't think that we're going to turn on our neighbors. Off with you."

"Neighbors" was pushing it, as the house the Delgados lived in was nothing more than a field now. "But it's not a matter of turning on them. I do have information for Carmen Delgado. Important information of benefit."

She sneered, "If you did, you wouldn't have said 'he.'"

Of course. All the Carmens I knew were men, most of them quite dangerous. But Carmen is a woman's name as well, and, although dramatic, it doesn't seem quite the same at all. I said, "Oh! I don't think they had that information at the office. They thought C. Delgado was a man. Well, the information would still be in her interest. Gender has nothing to do with it."

I tried again after noting his blank face and her hostile glare. "There's a small but nice legacy. Doesn't matter if C. Delgado is a man or a woman in terms of inheritance."

Why had I leapt to that conclusion? Because C. Delgado was listed first, indicating head of household. That was silly of me, with all the women heading households in the world.

He said to the angry woman, "Gotta be Carmie. She's the only one that could be a C. Delgado.

Could be money for her." He turned to me. "Too bad. I heard that Carmie died. Years ago."

"I'm sorry to hear that," I said. I meant it too. I had nothing against Carmen. Muriel was a different story.

He nodded, accepting my sentiment. "She was all right, Carmie. A real looker."

"I'm sure she was. But I need to know how to reach her or her family. The legacy may pass to another family member now. Let's see. Was she sister to Muriel?"

He shook his head. "Muriel? Muriel don't have no sisters."

"Well, then what was the relationship?"

"Carmie would be the mother. Muriel would be the daughter. But they've been long gone from here. Maybe fifty years. I told you that."

"That is too bad," I said.

"Well, nothing to me really. I liked Carmie well enough, but we weren't what you'd call close." He flicked a nervous glance toward the woman.

I pressed on. "Are there other relatives that you know of?"

She had been quiet for a while, standing with her thick legs in a wide stance, burly arms on her hips. Now she butted in pugnaciously. "Who did you say you were?"

"I'm from Lawson and Loblaw. We're a legal firm from Albany."

She raised a white eyebrow. "My fat fanny, you are. And I'm the First Lady."

"Really," I said, with what I hoped was outraged innocence. "I am here to ensure that Ms. Delgado gets what's coming to her." That was true enough in a different sense.

"I think you better get out of here and leave folks alone or you'll get what's coming to you. Don't come back neither. Or I will call the cops."

CHAPTER FOUR

B Y ALL MEANS, call them," I said, nose in the
air. "I'm not doing anything wrong."

"We'll see what the cops say about that."

I had what I wanted and I raised my hands in
mock surrender. I kept my spine straight as I
walked to the car. I could feel her eyes on my back.
As I got into the vehicle, I glanced around again at
the side yard. There she was, on the phone. Police?

Mental note to self: Maybe the bright red wig
didn't mesh with the law firm gofer persona.

Oh well, I was committed to this cover now.

I wasn't doing anything illegal, but I didn't want
to have to explain myself or my red wig to anyone
I knew on the local police force. I'd met a lot of
the officers since I started to see more of Tyler
Dekker. Of course, that whole idea made my
uncles feel faint, so I tended not to mention it. I
made tracks back to Uncle Mick's second garage,
keeping an eye in the rearview mirror for anyone
on my tail. I didn't think anyone would be
following me, but that was how I was raised.

BACK IN MY bedroom I pondered exactly what
I had learned. Carmen Delgado was Muriel's

mother. She was a widow or divorced, I supposed. She had been described as a "looker." Muriel hadn't gotten her features from her mother, in that case. Carmen had gradually moved her way up a bit to a better neighborhood, perhaps with Muriel's help? But Muriel would have been a child when they'd moved from Willows Road.

The elderly woman had been immediately suspicious of me and my inquiry. Why was that? I had fooled Audra Bennacke. In fact, my track record for fooling people was so solid it was a good thing I'd decided to go straight. I would make an excellent criminal, but you know how kids are: always rebelling against the family.

The woman on Lilac Lane had said they weren't going to turn on their neighbors. I'd been talking about a legacy. A small but nice inheritance, not a request to "turn on" their neighbors. She didn't seem to have bought that for a minute. Perhaps she knew enough about Carmen Delgado and her family to realize that the legacy idea couldn't be true. Some people have no relatives and that may have been the case. Even if Carmen had had relatives and this woman had known about their existence and financial state, that didn't rule out an inheritance. A former employer, a friend, a benefactor could easily have left her a bequest. So why the hostility to me? And who had she been phoning? Would she really have phoned the police? I doubted that. I had a strong feeling that on Lilac Lane, no one encouraged a visit from the authorities. They were probably used to knocks on the door from bail bondsmen, repo men and bounty hunters. In lean times, those guys always had work, and they often employed the same methods I'd used. At least I was polite enough not to kick in any doors or tow away cars or pry Christmas gifts from the fingers of crying children.

Never mind. I had some of what I wanted. I knew that Muriel Delgado had lived in Harrison Falls as a child and that she was the daughter of Carmen Delgado, Carmie to some people. I knew Carmie had died.

I wasn't sure where else this would get me, but it was a start. I'd set out to learn something about Muriel Delgado, and I had already found out quite a bit. Knowing where she'd grown up and some details about her family took her down a peg from the tower of swirling black garments, a malignant black widow. Let's face it, this woman who seemed to want to ruin my life and who also seemed to have the power to control Vera Van Alst was one scary lady. What was the rest of Muriel's story? What events had she lived through that created such a menacing personality? Whatever was in her background, I intended to ferret it out and use it to get back to my rightful place.

My cell phone vibrated. *Audra Bennacke,* it said. Uh-oh. What was my name again? Oh right.

"Lawson and Loblaw," I chirped as I answered it. "Clarissa Montaine speaking."

"Clarissa?" she said.

"Yes," I purred.

"You remember me? Audra? From Maple Street? You were asking about who we bought the house from?"

"Yes, of course. Thanks so much for getting back to me. Was it Carmen Delgado?"

"No. My husband remembered the second I asked him. The previous owner was Bob Smith. It was rented out."

"Really. Bob Smith?"

"Yes. Almost like a joke."

"But an answer, anyway. He may have been a second owner or a relative. I appreciate your call."

"Oh, and the other neighbors are back now. The Snows. I saw them pull in with their shopping a few minutes ago."

I wigged up, left through the back and climbed into the black-cherry Accord again.

On the way, I decided to check out the third and earliest address for C. Delgado.

Willows Road sounds more picturesque than it was. Prior to the closing of the shoe factory during Vera's father's time, Harrison Falls was a pleasant and prosperous town, but every town has its seedy side and Willows Road seemed to be part of that. It was the closest thing to a row of tenements we had. I couldn't imagine that there had ever been any willows. The "road" was narrow with no parking and shabby houses that came right up to the edge of the street. No gardens for this area. Not even a scrap of lawn. Every unit had peeling paint and most of the front steps had rotten boards I thought were ready to collapse. More than one window was boarded up. I saw no sign of life. Number 10B looked as though it would tumble to the ground if you blew on it. A half-starved feral cat scurried past.

I shivered.

Somewhere, someone had been cooking cabbage, and most people hadn't picked up their garbage. A feeling of hopelessness hung in the air, as palpable as the odor of bad food. Whatever else I knew about Carmen and Muriel Delgado, their life couldn't have been easy in the early days.

I knocked on every door, but although I could clearly hear television sets booming behind those doors, no one answered.

I tried not to be too discouraged. I figured I might find some answers on Maple Street. The wind picked up, pierced through the weave of my coat and reawakened that shiver, or maybe it was my Spidey Sense telling me to be wary. I scurried quickly to the Accord and drove back to see the Snows.

Here I got a bit lucky. The Snows, as Audra had mentioned, were indeed home. I parked midway between the two houses thinking I might like to say hello to Audra first and thank her for her call. I knocked on the door but got no answer. The stroller was gone so I figured she was off for a little ramble with the children. I headed for the house three doors down, getting into my legal assistant mode. Shortly after, Clarissa Montaine of Lawson and Loblaw walked up their immaculate front path and glanced with approval at the flags flapping in the breeze, the freshly painted yellow front door and shutters and the artfully displayed pumpkins with the cute wooden turkey (cuter than the real ones for sure) and the lovely sheaf of dried corn on the wall behind the display. I also admired the attractive wreath with fall leaves that decorated the yellow door. A tantalizing aroma was drifting from the slightly opened window to the left.

A row of burlap leaf bags sat in a precise row by the side of the road. The lawn was leaf-free. This did not come as a surprise.

When the door swung open, I held out my hand and introduced myself. Turned out their names were Tom and Mindy and please don't call them Mr. and Mrs. Snow, and don't blame this weather on them either. They were both round, white-haired and pink-cheeked. Behind their bifocals, their eyes twinkled. Hers were sharp and blue, his were warm brown. They had finished unpacking their groceries and were sitting down to a cup of hot tea and some cinnamon buns. The cinnamon buns must have been the source of the tantalizing aroma. Up close, I upgraded the scent of the fresh baking from tantalizing to intoxicating. I had already mentioned the law firm of Lawson and Loblaw, but I got the feeling that they would have been glad to see me no matter who I was.

"Mindy made these buns herself," the husband told me, ignoring the talk of law firms. "They can't be beat. Come in and have one with us. If we eat them all, we might put on some weight." He patted his belly, indicating that he'd consumed a few cinnamon buns in his time.

No one needed to ask me twice. I wasn't afraid to take sticky buns from strangers.

"Sure thing."

I joined them in the small, cozy kitchen and squeezed into the corner bench at the compact pine table. A border of candy-colored hearts topped the walls and ran above the yellow painted cupboards. I found myself grinning. These people were so cute. I never knew my grandparents on either the Kelly or the Bingham side, but "Call me Tom" and "Call me Mindy" were like the perfect fantasy grandparents. With my luck, though, maybe they'd turn out to be featured on *American Justice*: "when octogenarians attack." Never mind, I'd take my chances for another cinnamon bun.

Those cinnamon buns will live on in my memory forever. They were close to the most delicious thing I had ever tasted, from the fresh dough to the brown sugar, cinnamon and butter mingling inside the swirls, and the melting sugary glaze. Oh boy. Clarissa Montaine had pretty well died and gone to heaven.

As soon as one bun was finished, another one took its place on my plate.

"It's a practice batch," Mindy said, modestly. "I don't bake quite so much anymore, but with Thanksgiving almost here, I have to get back at it."

"Practice?" I laughed. "They're perfect."

After that we were friends for life. Still, remembering my reception from the couple on Lilac Lane, I finished my second cinnamon bun before I brought up the topic of Carmen and Muriel Delgado.

When I did, they both smiled. "Audra told us you were asking. A legacy for them? That's something, isn't it?"

I wondered what that meant.

"Yes. Assuming that I have the right person."

"I wonder who the legacy is from?"

I shrugged. "I'm afraid I don't know. I'm only a lowly assistant new to the firm. I've been sent out to try to find them. I don't mind, though. It beats being in the office and I've met some very nice people, especially you two and Audra." I beamed at my new fantasy grandparents.

Her sharp blue eyes grew slightly guarded. "You never know who you're going to meet in these circumstances."

"So you knew Carmen Delgado?"

They nodded together. "We did."

"And Muriel?"

"Yes."

"I've been told that Carmen has, um, passed away."

A shadow crossed Tom's face. "She did, poor girl. Never was that strong."

"Was Muriel the daughter? I didn't get a good reception in their previous neighborhood and I wasn't quite sure."

"Yes, the daughter. So I suppose she'd get the legacy, would she?" Tom asked, his brown eyes bright with interest.

"I think she may be the one to get it. Mr. Lawson will know all about that. I've been tasked to bring back the information. It hasn't been easy finding Carmen Delgado. I had to check the city directories here." There was something to be said for old-school sleuthing.

"So Muriel lived on this street with her mother?"

"Not for that long, really," Mindy said. "Does that matter?"

"And it was just the two of them?"

Tom said, "Muriel stayed on after she finished school. She was here until her mother died. We thought she'd leave when Carmie married. She was so hostile to Carmie's new husband."

I blinked. "Oh. She married again?"

They didn't quite stop themselves in time. I

caught the glances. So there was something there. Something about marrying again. But what?

"She married a nice man. He'd carried a torch for Carmie for a long time," Mindy said.

"He did. Carmie was a beautiful woman," Tom said. "Very beautiful."

"Was she?" This was the second mention of Carmen's attractiveness. I found it hard to picture her, especially after seeing Muriel. She was imposing. Grand. Mount Rushmore–like, yes. Beautiful, no.

"Oh yes," Mindy said. "She was lovely to *look* at." Ah, a bit of subtext there, I thought. Maybe not so lovely in other ways.

"And a good neighbor?" I said.

"Well . . ." Mindy said, turning away slightly.

"Poor thing was not a well woman, ever," Tom said, in the late Carmen's defense. "She had a lot of problems, you know, health. She wasn't strong. In any way."

I wasn't sure what the subtext was to "in any way." But there was something worth finding out.

"More of a taker than a giver," Mindy said, a bit waspishly. Tom glowered. I figured he'd liked "Carmie" a lot more than she had.

"Life didn't treat her that well," he said.

I had nothing better to do than nudge them for more.

"I guess she didn't have an easy life."

Had I imagined that Mindy snorted? The temperature in the room had certainly dropped a degree or two.

I blundered on. No way to find out without digging a bit harder. "Did her first husband die? And leave her with the child? That would have been so hard for her back then."

Tom shot Mindy another look. There was no missing the warning in it. This time Mindy stared up at the ceiling fan as if she'd noticed a long-lost treasure up there.

"Well," I said. "Not my business really. I didn't mean to pry into her personal history. I'm curious and sometimes these little inklings are what help wrap it all up."

"Well," Mindy said. "You young people look at these things differently, I suppose."

What things? I wondered.

Tom added, "Something to be said for that."

So what was it with the first Mr. Delgado? Did he desert them? Was he abusive? A criminal? There was something, and I knew that I wasn't going to get the answers here.

"Well, I'm glad things ended up better for her. Was the new marriage happy?"

"As happy as it could be, considering," Mindy said, shifting her eyes to the cuckoo clock.

Tom couldn't resist adding, "Muriel wasn't happy about it. I think that broke Carmie's heart. Wasn't the first time she'd had it broken."

I could have sworn that Mindy smothered a snort of laughter. What do the Germans call that again? Oh right, *Schadenfreude*, shameful joy. And it's not that difficult to elicit negative information from someone experiencing it, so I pressed on.

"And then?" I said.

"After Carmie died, Muriel moved away. That was it."

"Hm. I wonder where she went," I said, trying not to sound too desperate for an answer.

"Here and there. She was always restless."

"Oh, so you don't know where?"

"No idea," they said in unison.

"But for a while, Carmen and her new husband and Muriel stayed here?"

Tom said, "It's a sad story. Carmie got sick not long after they married."

This time, Mindy flashed *him* a warning glance.

So far, things weren't perfect with my fantasy grandparents. Tom had a bit of wishful thinking toward his former neighbor Carmen Delgado, and Mindy had been well aware of that. There was something else at work, though. I figured that Mindy was strong and practical. I didn't see anything vindictive in her. She hadn't approved of Carmen for more than one reason, if my Spidey Sense were to be believed. What were those reasons?

"Oh dear," I said. "I need to locate her heirs. Mr. Lawson will need to know that."

"Of course," they said in unison.

"Could be the daughter. Muriel." I gazed at them, waiting. "But I'll probably need to check with the husband."

Mindy said, "Rest his soul. He's dead now too."

"Oh, I'm sorry to hear that. I didn't even catch his name."

"Pete. Peter Delaney. He was a lovely man," Mindy said with yet another glance at Tom. "A saint, really. Too good to live."

This time, Tom shot *her* the warning glance.

So Pete Delaney. That didn't fit with Smith as the owner. Perhaps Pete had sold?

Tom nodded in agreement. "Pete loved Carmie, no matter what, and he took good care of her."

Hmm. No matter what. I wondered what that was.

"Did he die before she did?"

Tom said, "Yes. But not long before. She was having treatments in Grandville General when poor Pete was killed in a hit-and-run back in, let's see, must have been 1974. That right, Mindy?"

Mindy nodded and Tom continued. "It happened as he got out of his car near the hospital on his way to visit her. He died instantly, I believe. It was a great shock to all of us. We all liked Pete. Carmie was devastated. She only lived a few months after that."

I thought Mindy suppressed a sigh.

Tom seemed not to notice. He said, "So he wouldn't have inherited anything from her."

Mindy said with a bit of asperity, "She didn't have anything. She never had anything to leave. She would have inherited whatever Pete left to her. He was practical and sensible in most things." I took that to mean aside from his feelings for Carmie.

"But the house must have been hers. Did she own it or did he?"

Again with the glances. "We don't know anything about that," Mindy said.

"Nothing at all," Tom added quickly.

Okay.

"Fair enough. So the daughter, Muriel, would have been the heir, most likely. We'll have to follow up and see if there was a will. Mr. Lawson could do that. I hope she didn't die intestate. I suppose there's no way to know who their lawyer would have been."

Tom said, "Well, it must have been—"

Mindy cleared her throat.

She was tough, that Mindy, even if she did seem like the perfect fantasy grandmother.

This time Tom stood his ground. "What harm could it do? They need to find out what Carmie's wishes were. She probably had a will. Pete was good about things like that. She might have left things to Muriel. Muriel was her daughter. No matter what."

Mindy pondered that and nodded. She reached over and squeezed Tom's hand. "You're right. That's not a secret we need to keep."

I wondered what secret they did need to keep and exactly what "no matter what" referred to.

"Lovely," I said. "You have been so helpful. I hate to go back empty-handed. I try to do a good job, but sometimes circumstances make it difficult."

Mindy said sadly, "Yes. Sometimes circumstances do make it difficult."

"Dwight Jenkins was her lawyer. I know that because he was ours and we passed his name to Carmie and Pete when they got married. Pete wanted to make sure that Carmie was taken care of. I assumed that meant a will," Tom said.

Mindy muttered, "Well, you couldn't count on Carmie to get things done."

If Tom heard her, he chose to ignore the comments. "Dwight's in his seventies but he still has a law office in his home, right in downtown Harrison Falls."

Mindy said, "In fact, we updated our wills not long ago and the previous ones were still there on file. Dwight's taken care of us. Carmie's papers will still be there and anyway, doesn't a will have to be filed?"

"I can't thank you enough," I said, getting up to leave before there were any legal queries that "Clarissa" should know but I wouldn't. I felt sure that Mindy didn't want any secrets to leave with me. But maybe I'd be back.

Even if there were no secrets, Mindy made sure I left with a plate holding enough cinnamon buns to feed my private army, if I had one. "I'll think of you with every bite," I said, meaning my words on several levels. "I hope I'll see you both again sometime. I'll let you know how things turn out. I appreciate your help."

In fact, I looked forward to seeing if I could catch Tom on his own. I figured there would be answers there and he seemed keen to share. I needed answers about secrets and about Carmen Delgado. To make sure that happened, I let my silky Pucci scarf slip onto the floor underneath my chair. Naturally, I would have to come back for that.

"I'll leave you my telephone number," I said, writing down the number of my burner phone on a page from my notebook. "I wonder if you'd mind giving me yours."

Tom didn't mind. Mindy seemed less than sure. But at least I knew I'd get another chance to see them and maybe get something more out of them about the Delgados.

I waved as I reached the edge of their neat walkway. Tom waved quickly and disappeared out of view in the house. I headed for the Accord, which was parked halfway between the Snows' house and Audra's. I hauled out my iPhone and checked for an address for Dwight Jenkins in Harrison Falls. I was smiling as I walked around to the driver's side of the Accord. I turned back to gaze at the Snows' perfect little home. I didn't pay much attention to the roar of an engine.

I didn't feel a thing until the shock of the collision.

I never saw what hit me.

CHAPTER FIVE

I DID HEAR people screaming, sirens, ambulances screeching to a halt. I could still smell the baked treats, which gave me comfort and something to focus on. As the pain set in, all I remember thinking was, *Not the cinnamon buns!*

But once off the asphalt and without my magical cinnamon smelling salts, I lost consciousness before my arrival at Emergency at Grandville General Hospital. I guess I missed a lot of the exciting stuff.

Kev's face was the first thing I saw when I opened my eyes. I didn't mean to scream, but he can have that effect on people.

"What's going on?" I whispered.

"You're lucky! Talk about a horseshoe up your—"

Uncle Mick shouldered him out of the way. "What happened, Jordan?"

Kev bleated, "She was smacked by a truck and thrown ten feet. Right through the air."

Mick was pale as milk and his gingery freckles stood out in sharp relief against his skin. I stared at the freckles, fascinated. They must have given me something for pain or nausea, because the deep orange spots began arranging themselves into patterns and shapes.

He tried again, "Do you know what happened, my girl?"

I blinked. I really was hoping someone else would be able to tell *me* what happened. What Kev had said couldn't be right. I tried to shake my head "no" but that didn't work out all that well. Suddenly everyone had four heads.

"Where am I?"

"Emergency. Grandville General Hospital."

I blinked again and regretted it instantly. It hurt when I blinked. Everything hurt. I've read somewhere that swearing can reduce pain. I was ready to blurt out a doozy.

"Why?"

Kev's disembodied voice said, "Apparently you got hit by a truck."

"Hit by a—? Really?"

Kev stuck his head around Uncle Mick and said, "Yeah. You were doing something on Maple Street and someone slammed into you and took off."

Was he eating something? For the first time in ages, I was not tempted by the idea of eating.

"I don't remember anything. Except somebody screaming. Maybe that was me."

"Shock," said Uncle Mick, stepping in front of Kev and blocking him from my view. "It will take a while."

Now Kev's head appeared on the other side of

Uncle Mick. "The docs say you're going to be all right. You're pretty well drugged up now, so don't worry if you feel woozy."

I did feel woozy. I needed to start worrying soon.

"Lucky, though," Kev chirped.

Mick turned on him. "Stop saying that, Kevin. She's not lucky. She could have been killed."

Kev never knows when to shut up. I realized that even if he didn't.

"But she should have been killed when that truck whacked her and tossed her through the air like an old—"

Uncle Mick cleared his throat warningly.

Kev blundered on. "But hey. She's all in one piece. If that ain't lucky, I don't know what is."

Even in my drugged state, I could see that Uncle Mick was on the verge of a medical event himself.

Kev babbled on. "You can thank those leaf bags."

"What?"

"You can thank those leaf bags."

Uncle Mick stomped out of sight. Probably needed to get away so he didn't pop Kev in the jaw or something.

I had no idea what he meant. "Leaf bags," I said. "What leaf bags?"

"Just what I said. Leaf bags."

I would have stomped off to join Uncle Mick if I hadn't been flat on my back on a gurney with my head swimming. "I heard you, Kev, but I still don't know what that means. Why should I thank them?"

"You went flying through the air and landed on the leaf bags by the side of the road."

"And the driver?"

"Gone. Vanished. Vamoosed. Up in smoke. Disappeared." Kev was even wordier than usual.

Uncle Mick had returned, but it wouldn't take much to set him off again. The freckles on his forehead now formed the word "DANGER." He said, "We get the point. Will you settle down, Kevin?" Uncle Mick's cheeks were now Christmas red, but Kev never really notices details about people. He added, "The driver was nowhere to be seen."

Uncle Mick glared at him. "Could you ever keep quiet for one minute of your life?"

I felt like a spectator watching a play on a distant stage.

"Lucky me," I said with a smile.

"Double lucky," Kev said, "because this other woman was out walking her kids in the stroller. She came around the corner, saw you get hit and called 911."

"Right. That must have been Audra."

Kev said, "Yeah, yeah. That's her name. Nice-looking lady. She called me."

"She called you?" I was spinning again. I closed my eyes. I felt like I was being flushed down a toilet.

Mick glared at Kev. "Keep quiet. And Jordan, maybe it would be better if you didn't try to talk until later."

I said, "But what happened to all those cinnamon buns?"

With that, I drifted off to sleep, watching Mick's shape-shifting freckles turn into cinnamon swirls.

IT TOOK NEARLY an entire day before I was back at Uncle Mick's. There was quite a welcoming committee. Uncle Lucky and his new wife, Karen, were bustling around. Mick was busy whipping up a giant batch of macaroni and cheese dinner with a wiener upgrade. Walter and Cobain thought that kisses would make me get better, and they may have been right about that. They were curled up on the end of my bed while I recuperated. Uncle Danny and Uncle Billy were visiting as well but mostly telling tall tales in the kitchen. I knew most of those tales by heart, but it was soothing to hear snippets of them and the whoops of laughter drifting up the stairs. I thought I'd overheard Uncle Connie's, Uncle Tiny's and Uncle Paddy's voices, but why would they be there?

Kev was back too. I guess it was one step short of an Irish wake.

Every now and then, I heard them whispering. Wakes bring out the conspiracies in the Kellys.

I was starting to be more aware, glad to be alive

and conscious. The sight and sound of all those Kellys in wake mode told me I must have had a really close call. I wiggled my hands and my feet, fingers and toes. I lifted my arms, one after the other, and bent my elbows. I tried the same thing with the legs. Bent the knees. Lifted my feet, one after the other. I sat up and moved my head from side to side. Major aches and some pain, but everything appeared to be working. Well, maybe not the sitting-up part. I closed my eyes and let my head rest on the pillow again. Walter's curly tail thumped against the pink bedding. Cobain licked my hand.

Everyone was supposed to let me rest, but Kev couldn't resist sneaking upstairs. "So, do you remember anything?"

"No. I do remember the doctor saying that I may never remember what happened."

"Lucky for you that woman can describe the vehicle that hit you. The cops will want to talk to you about that."

"I can't tell them anything. I didn't see it. I didn't even know I'd been hit until I heard about it from you in the hospital."

"Why were you on Maple Street anyway?"

"Oh. I am starting to remember that. I was talking to Tom and Mindy Snow about the Delgados. They are Audra's neighbors. They were very helpful. Except they were holding back on something to do with Carmen Delgado. Not sure what it was, but I intend to go back and see them."

Kev blinked. "Who's Carmen Delgado?"

"Apparently, she was Muriel's mother. There's some kind of story there. Some bad things happened."

"That reminds me: This woman, Audra Something, was trying to see you at the hospital. She seems to be a bit mixed up about your name."

"Oh boy. I really liked her. I told her and the Snows that I was Clarissa Montaine and that I worked for Lawson and Loblaw down in Albany and was searching for a C. Delgado. I left my Pucci scarf at the Snows' so I'd have an excuse to go back again and try to get some more information on Carmen."

"This Audra saved your life."

"I am grateful." Even though I'd deceived her.

Kev said, "And then she called me. Otherwise, I don't know what would have happened."

I let that go. Didn't want to think about the other possible outcomes. "How would she know to call you?"

"That burner phone was thrown right out of your hand, I guess. She must have picked it up and I was the only contact except for herself and the geezers down the street."

"The Snows."

"Whatever. Anyway, she said you were being taken to Grandville General Hospital."

"And did she really say 'the geezers'?"

"Not exactly those words. She mentioned older neighbors. The geezers came out to help too, I guess. Put a blanket on you and kept you warm until the emergency vehicle arrived."

"One more time, Kev, the geezers are the Snows. Do they know who I am?"

He had the grace to look sheepish as he so often does. "You mean the gee—the Snows? I think so. The paramedics checked your wallet and you're listed as yourself here at the hospital. I didn't know enough to keep them in the dark. You should call me first when you're out pretending to be someone else. I love that kind of thing."

My head hurt. "Does Vera know I've been hit?"

Uncle Kev couldn't meet my eyes. "She does."

"How did she find out? Was it on the news?"

"I told her after I got the call. I thought she needed to hear it. The signora was hysterical. More hysterical than usual, anyway. As it wasn't you calling me or me calling you, I figured the no-contact rule wouldn't apply."

"And did it?"

Kev frowned. "She didn't say one way or the other."

"Well, what did she say? Was it 'Unless Jordan's at death's door, no one is to make contact under any circumstances'?"

He shrugged. "You know Vera. Stranger things have happened."

I tried not to roll my eyes, mainly because it hurt. "Back to the question, Kev. What exactly did Vera say?"

He shook his head, still not meeting my eyes. "She didn't say anything."

"Nice." I'd treated her cats' hairballs with more consideration than she'd given me.

"I don't get it," Kev said. "I think the news really bothered her, but she didn't let on to Muriel. She spent the rest of the day in her room, if it's any consolation."

It wasn't.

"You said that Audra saw the vehicle that hit me."

"That's what she told me when she called."

"Did she say what kind of truck it was?"

"She didn't tell me. She was pretty upset."

"Well, I bet she told the police. I don't suppose you spoke to them?"

Kev paled. He's not good with police and in fact is skilled at avoiding them. Probably all for the best.

I lay back against my stacks of pillows and closed my eyes. "It has to be Muriel. Nothing else makes sense. I was snooping into her past and talking to her former neighbors when someone did a good job of trying to kill me."

"And would have succeeded if those leaf bags weren't there."

"Thanks, Kev. But how would Muriel have known I was checking out her background?"

"What do you mean? Oh, maybe she followed you. No, she couldn't have done that. She was at home—" A guilty expression stole across his face. "I meant she was at Van Alst House all day."

"Even when I was hit?"

He nodded.

"It's all right, Kev. She may have been at Van Alst House, but I know she's still behind it. Even if I can't prove it, I'm not going to let her mess with my head. I'll concentrate on finding out about her and her hold over Vera. I don't want to be distracted by negative emotions."

Kev nodded. "Like wanting to kill her?"

It only hurt when I laughed.

"Why yes, Kev, like that. How would Muriel know that I would be in that neighborhood? She must have gotten spooked by one of her previous neighbors. A woman on Lilac Lane was making a phone call to someone after she saw me. Muriel could have arranged to have someone else follow me, but she wouldn't have known it was me. Jordan Bingham was nowhere to be seen. I was out and about as Clarissa Montaine. I didn't use my name. I didn't drive my car. I wore the red wig. I left the Saab parked in front of the shop."

Kev's ginger eyebrows furrowed in puzzlement. I'd lost him at "why yes."

I said, "And you of all people—as a Kelly—should be aware of how easy it is for people to appear to be somewhere and yet to be somewhere completely different."

"I wish she didn't have such a great alibi."

"Maybe it's not airtight."

"It is. She was in the house in full view. She's usually in her suite doing who knows what. But at the time you were hit, she was in the kitchen meddling with the signora's cooking, telling her what kind of menus she wanted. Did I mention she hates Italian food? I was there too. She got everyone into a real flap. Even Vera got called into it and she got really riled up and you know she couldn't care less about who eats what."

I found myself pouting a bit. It happens if you're around Kev for too long. I said, "Fine, so even if she had found out I was there on Maple Street and her previous addresses or even if she decided to stage an attack on anyone asking questions about her, she still couldn't have been the one to hit me."

"Yeah. It would have been great if she had."

"Oh thanks."

"You know what I mean."

"Yes, Kev."

He prattled on. "Well, if she'd tried to kill you and she was seen and then the police could tie her to the vehicle that hit you, she'd be arrested and we'd be rid of her."

"I can't believe I'm agreeing with you. Did she talk to anyone—?"

The door was flung open at that minute and Uncle Mick made sure that Kev was out of the room.

"For the last time, Jordan needs to rest. You know what they said at the hospital, Kev. Out. Now."

I wanted to protest that Kev's presence was less of a disaster than usual as we were in the middle of an important conversation, but instead I slipped off to dreamland instantly.

WHEN I AWOKE, I stared around at my room. I lay there trying to think clearly, although my thinker was kind of messed up. Still, I could feel a glimmer of intelligence trying to assert itself.

I was clinging to a thought that had finally bubbled up from my subconscious. I fumbled for a scrap of paper and a googly-eyed troll-haired pencil and scribbled it down. I was afraid that it might vanish forever otherwise. I knew it was important. My subconscious had made a break-through. I wasn't the first person linked to Muriel to suffer a hit-and-run collision. So I wasn't going to call it an accident or being in the wrong place at the wrong time. The timing told me it was deliberate and I was the target. Muriel had to be behind it. Her stepfather had died that way. I called that a pattern. Muriel's alibi was a smoke-screen. She had confederates and I knew it.

I managed to scrawl something down before

sleep descended. *This is getting boring,* I thought before dropping off yet again.

When I woke up, I was still clutching the paper. It said *STEPFATH* before the letters trailed away. Not too helpful. But on the upside, my head felt much clearer. Too bad the note wasn't that meaningful.

I knew that I had to find out what was going on, and there was probably no way to do that without talking to Audra and the Snows. A small voice in my head asked if perhaps they were the same people who had been responsible for alerting the person who hit me. After all, I didn't really know anything about any of the people on Maple Street. They seemed nice, but appearances can be deceiving. Certainly Clarissa Montaine was proof of that. I pondered that and thought back. The Snows had been with me all during my visit and they hadn't known I was coming. So I didn't see how they could have made the contact. Audra was a possibility, I supposed. But she had saved my life. That didn't match up. If she had contacted someone to let them know that I was asking about the Delgados, why wouldn't she have stayed in the house and pretended to know nothing? Why would she have come to my aid? She'd called 911 and stayed with me until help arrived. Then she'd picked up my phone to reach someone who knew me.

No. It was a pretty sure bet that Audra wasn't

involved. She had asked her husband about who had owned the house after my first visit and before I was hit, so he was a possible link. Or he may have mentioned it to someone else who picked up on it. But that was getting a bit unlikely. Logic told me that the source was probably the couple back on Lilac Lane. That angry older woman who'd been on the phone when I was leaving had been hostile right from the beginning, unlike her mate, if that was who he was. What was that about?

She'd really had no good reason to take such an instant dislike to me. But they knew Muriel. Perhaps they were still in touch. Could she have called Muriel to tell her that someone was asking questions about the Delgados? If so, Muriel could have found someone to follow me. Of course, I hadn't stayed on Lilac Lane long enough after her call for anyone to arrive to shadow me. Unless the person was already there? But that didn't make sense either. What were the chances that I would have taken that approach, based on a few old city directories in the library? Who even knew that I'd done that? Somehow it didn't seem right.

So what was possible?

I drew a mental map. I had gone from Maple Street to Lilac Lane to Willows Road and then back to Maple Street. After my alarming visit to Lilac Lane there was plenty of time for someone to tail me to Uncle Mick's and then to Maple Street. And who knew if anyone had seen me on

Willows Road, where they don't answer their doors.

Muriel had intended to get me out of Vera's life. That much was obvious, starting with my sudden firing. Now there were the instructions to Kev and the signora to have no contact with me. For some reason, Vera was doing her bidding. Why? The thought that anyone could intimidate Vera was, well, intimidating. Muriel was one scary lady.

I figured it might take a while for me to figure out what Muriel would get out of it. But there was also a "how," as in how could I prove that the hit-and-run was not a random event? Could I convince the police that the driver had targeted me? To the average cop, I would sound like a nutcase. Maybe I was wrong, but the odds were I was right. In fact, it didn't seem that the cops were taking this at all seriously. I would have expected to give a statement. The cops should have asked many questions to establish links between me and whoever had hit me. Or maybe they had and I just couldn't remember.

My memories of the collision were nonexistent and my time in Emerg still flashed in my brain like a fragmented nightmare. My impact points throbbed.

Back to my problem: It made sense that there was something to uncover, something about Muriel and her family. Something that she didn't want uncovered. And that something had to do with Vera.

Questions kept rocketing around in my poor sore brain.

Whatever the connection was, it must be serious business. We all have small scandals, things we regret in our lives. But face it, in our era, there's not much that people would kill to conceal. Politicians brazen out sex scandals. Wall Street cheats never see the inside of a jail. Predatory mortgage-debt packagers ruin lives and walk free. Whatever Muriel had to hide would have to be hugely damaging to merit a murder. Muriel had been a child when she lived on Lilac Lane and Willows Road and a young woman when she left Maple Street after her mother's death. What could she need to hide? How bad could it be? I remembered my note about *STEPFATH* and pictured a young Muriel scowling as she pumped herself higher on the swings.

My subconscious had been telling me something. Was it to do with her stepfather's death? That had been another hit-and-run. Coincidence? Hit-and-run deaths happen, but both of these had a close link to Muriel. But what would she have to gain from killing me? If she hadn't gotten me fired in the first place, I never would have been snooping into her past. I couldn't believe it was my bad luck to get hit by a truck the day after I got fired.

Back to Muriel. She gave me a sour taste in my mouth. I knew little about her beyond the fact that her mother and stepfather were dead. But I was convinced she was behind my dismissal and the fact that her mother and stepfather were dead. The Snows had been evasive when talking about her mother, although at times Mindy Snow's face gave a clue that she tasted something sour too.

I needed to get back to Maple Street to talk to them. That was where I would find the answers I needed. Of course, that would involve explaining why I had lied to Audra and to the Snows and worn a disguise. Mind you, after I'd been almost killed right under their noses, I could easily claim that fear of an attack had been my motivation. Just a scared, vulnerable woman in disguise asking too many questions. Most people would believe that. Even though it wasn't true, it could have been. And I had left the Pucci scarf at the Snows', so that gave me a reason to visit them again. I was prepared to apologize to everyone.

I decided to get dressed and get going, deciding not to let a minor setback keep me down. I stood up, ready to go. Yikes. Pain city. My knees buckled and I collapsed on the bed. Maybe I wasn't one hundred percent yet. "Quite the bump on the head," the doctor had kept saying, or maybe he hadn't been repeating himself. Everything continued spinning as he gave me his little pep talk. No sleeping for longer than three hours. No drinking, no driving, and I guess no juggling chainsaws either. The deep bruises were going to hurt for a while. Keep massaging them to prevent blood clots. Lovely. He had basically sentenced me to house arrest, but that didn't mean I had to tell my uncles that.

Fine. It was hard to stay put, but I didn't want to make any of my injuries worse. The sooner I was better, the sooner I could really get digging at this Muriel problem. For sure, it would be a few days before I'd be functioning normally. But maybe I had people who could take care of some of the research for me. Turned out the usual suspects were not available. I had already texted Lance and Tiff after my accident and had no response.

Nada.

None.

Not so much as a <3.

Somehow that complete silence hurt worse than being hit by a truck. What was going on? Maybe the impact of the truck had dislodged the memory of an argument? I tried to think. But thinking hurt and now it was accompanied by a ringing in my ears. I told myself, *All right. Buck up, lady.* I've had a lot of bad stuff happen to me in my life and I've learned not to expect life to be fair or easy. Like so many other times, I chose not to waste energy on useless emotions. That was what my uncles had taught me. And according to Uncle Danny, that's a philosophy that's worked for the

Kellys ever since our Viking ancestor Olaf first arrived on the banks of the Liffey around about the ninth century. My uncles claim they get their ginger hair and matching wild eyebrows from him and also their ability to cope when times get tough or someone's in the slammer for a while. The Olaf factor usually worked for me, if only because Uncle Danny's family history "facts" always made me smile. And speaking of smiling, I did try Smiley wherever he was. No answer. I left a message. I did my best not to snivel. I knew he wasn't in charge of his schedule and he had no way of knowing what had happened to me.

"Hey, your dog misses you and, oh by the way, I've been hit by a truck. No worries, I am still in one piece, but I thought you should know." My voice cracked. Way to buck up. "It's that woman Muriel Delgado. Anyway, hope your week is going better. I'm at Uncle Mick's in case you feel like saving me from an overdose of relatives."

At least he had an excuse for being unavailable, unlike my so-called best friends, wherever they were and whatever they were up to. At that point, the painkillers were making me groggy and once again I dozed off. My injured state was nothing if not boring, I said to myself as sleep descended like an anvil in a Wile E. Coyote cartoon.

CHAPTER SIX

M Y EYELIDS FLUTTERED open to see Vera's library. It was more cheerful than usual because every surface had a potted orchid perched on top. Deep fuchsias and blues danced among white and yellow blossoms, making the library seem alive and even more of a paradise. One of the yellow blossoms in the corner grumbled at me. I tried to focus on it. It got bigger and shinier. It sprouted two large wheels out of the side of its pot.

"Crunch, crunch, crunch, Miss Bingham," it said, dryly.

Now I could see that it was in a wheelchair being pushed toward me by a dark swirling shape. The yellow orchid glowed and grew in front of me, until it turned into a pair of yellow satin pajama bottoms, with Vera and a shabby greige sweater sticking out of them.

"I clearly said, 'crunch, crunch, crunch, Miss Bingham.'" The words matched Vera's gravelly voice. I tried to make out the face of the black specter that was now propelling Vera away into the corridor. A low dark laugh floated through the open door.

"You're not welcome here anymore, Miss Bingham."

As the two left the room, all the orchids started to wilt, flowers drifting, colors draining away. Spaces began to appear on the shelves, until all the books were gone and I was standing in a room of dead flowers and dust.

I lay there shaking and had just gotten my postdream breathing under control when a large figure loomed at the end of the bed. I gasped and grabbed the Care Bear lamp to defend myself. The figure put its fingers to its lips.

Kev.

Behind him, the door to the closet stood open. The secret passages through my childhood home had been repaired. They were working fine if you knew how to use them. I did and so did Uncle Kev. This was one way to get into my room without passing Uncle Mick downstairs.

I was glad to see Kev again. He would keep my mind off my nightmare, for one thing, and I figured he could do me a favor. But first, I needed to know how he was getting away so often without attracting Vera's notice, or worse, the Malevolent Muriel's evil eye.

"It's okay," he said. "We're making a big deal about going out to get food that Muriel will eat since she doesn't eat Italian. And I need to get parts for some of the equipment that seems to have broken down." He grinned. Kev can be resourceful as well as totally frustrating.

"I don't want you to lose your job or get into any trouble because of me."

"Jordie. It's me. Kev. I'm in trouble no matter what I do or what you do. Just chill."

He was right, of course.

I laughed. Have I mentioned it only hurt when I laughed? In fact, it hurt plenty, but it hurt even more when I laughed. Worth it, though.

"Fine. Be careful."

As usual, he paid no attention. "And the other thing is, she's got me doing things you used to do."

I sat up. "Ouch." I yelped, and lay back on the bed, closing my eyes. "What kind of things?"

"Shhh!" Kev said. "You know. Book things."

"Saints in heaven save us!" I found myself channeling Grandmother Kelly. "Book things?"

"Yes."

It was the end of the world as I knew it. But it was about to get worse.

"I'm arranging to sell some of them. We're putting them on the Internet."

I didn't care how much my body screamed. I sat up again. "Sell some? Of Vera's books?"

"Don't yell. Mick will hear you!"

"But I don't understand. Are you actually saying that Vera has you selling some of her books?"

Uncle Kev was now wearing that hurt puppy

face that he does so well. "Yes. Like you used to do."

I felt my eyelid twitch. "That's not exactly what I used to do, Kev. I used to acquire books for her and sell off the previous ones at a profit to fund her acquisitions. It was all carefully managed so she could gradually improve her collection without spending a fortune. How are you going about that?"

"You know. Craigslist. Notice boards. That kind of thing."

I swallowed. "What have you sold? Not the Nero Wolfe books?"

I had worked hard to arrange for sales of some titles in order to upgrade to more desirable copies. *Craigslist?* We dealt with private collectors as well as dealers and I had been busy building a solid contact list. Selling directly to the collectors meant we, that is to say, Vera, kept a bigger chunk of change. We could apply that to the next purchase, which invariably involved more money. I couldn't believe that Vera was selling any part of her collection. Maybe the painkilling drugs were causing me to hallucinate.

"The what?" Kev said.

"The Nero Wolfe books. You know she loves them. They are Vera's current obsession." Mine too, but that was a different story.

"I never saw those."

"Rex Stout," I said.

"Oh right. I've seen lots of them. No, these were some really old books. I mean, really old. You could get them as e-books now and be way better off."

I stared at him. I could not understand how Vera—for all that she thought the world of Kev—could trust him with any part of her collection. She didn't even let him vacuum the library, after that regrettable incident with the air freshener. So what was going on here?

"Let's see if I understand this. Vera asked you to sell some of her 'old' books?"

"Well, not Vera directly."

"Explain what 'not Vera directly' means, please." Despite my condition, the shock of what Kev was saying had sharpened my thinking.

Kev said, "Huh?"

"What do you mean by 'not Vera directly'?"

"Well, Muriel, of course."

Of course? "So Muriel asked you to—?"

"Told me. Muriel doesn't ask. She tells you. You can't even ask a simple question. She's like a fire-breathing dragon in a woman's body."

"I get that. And so she *told* you to sell some of Vera's books."

"That's what I'm trying to explain, Jordan. You're being kind of slow to understand."

"Indeed I am. So then what does Vera say about this?"

"About what?"

I massaged my temple. It had begun to throb. "About Muriel telling you to sell some of the books. What does Vera say about that?"

"Nothing. Or I didn't hear anything."

"She sat there in silence?"

"Well, no. What could she say? She wasn't even there."

"All right, then. So Muriel gave you these instructions behind Vera's back and you followed them. Do I have that right now?"

"Not exactly behind her back. Vera told me to do whatever Muriel said around the house."

"Aha. Did she mention books?"

"Not as such."

"Not as *such*. Right."

Kev gazed at me, puzzled.

I said, "Is it possible that Vera has no idea that you are selling some of her collection?"

He blinked. "But I think Muriel must have gotten the idea from her and then—oh."

"*Oh* is right."

"But why would Muriel do that?"

"The first thing that comes to mind is to milk money out of the household. Those books are worth a fortune. And she can get away with it because the person who would have noticed is no longer there."

Kev goggled. "Who?"

I lay back on the pillow once again, closed my eyes and took a deep breath. "Me, Uncle Kev. I'm the one who knows about the books and how to make money reselling and how to get the best bang for the buck when buying. I'm the one who Vera trusted to do the right thing."

I lay there thinking there might be another reason: Muriel would do that just to hurt Vera. I shuddered.

Kev gasped. "I try to do the right thing." That hurt puppy was back.

"I know you do. But this is a specialized business. The same way the garden requires specialized knowledge. You wouldn't let me blunder in there with some weed killer, would you?"

Uncle Kev, no stranger to catastrophe, turned white. "You wouldn't do that!"

"Right, I wouldn't. I'm just making a point with a comparison."

"I think I get your point."

Maybe he did. Maybe he didn't. But anyway, I soldiered on. "Here's my idea. Anytime Muriel wants you to do something with the books, you say yes, of course. Tug your forelock if you must."

"Jordan!" Kev exclaimed, as though I'd said something dirty.

"Figure of speech. It means be extremely deferent or obsequious."

"What?"

"Defer to her. Be humble and obliging. And then, you bring that task to me. I'll see to it and you can pretend you did it."

"Nothing could go wrong with that, right?"

Plenty could go wrong, but not nearly as wrong as having Kev decimate Vera's collection. That would be the end of Vera as well as the collection. With his track record it might not take long. Whatever Muriel was up to, she probably had no inkling of Uncle Kev's more catastrophic abilities. I might have been really upset about my firing and at some level angry at Vera, but I didn't want her to suffer. Muriel was there to cause trouble of one sort or another. No question. But why would Muriel want Vera to experience heartbreak over her books? Was that what she was up to? At first, I'd thought she wanted to come in and take over the good life at Van Alst House; now I had to wonder.

I closed my eyes and thought about the kind of motives that Nero Wolfe and Archie Goodwin were uncovering in the books I was reading. Revenge was one solid motive. Money, of course, was another. I couldn't see that sex would figure into this particular scenario.

Uncle Kev interrupted my musing. "Could it, Jordan?"

"Nah. Nothing could go wrong. It will be all right, Kev. Just keep me informed."

"I'll pretend that I'm going to the post office or whatever. I'll let you know."

"Excellent idea."

"And you'll call me from your burner if you

need me so that no one at Van Alst House sees you've been in touch with me."

"For sure."

"I'll come by again too, Jordie. Keep you posted."

"Great. Thanks. I appreciate it. I'll have to do a bit of work myself. I'm pretty sure I won't get much from the police, although it's worth a try. I'll go see the Snows again and fess up about my disguise and all that, and I'll talk to Audra. I wonder if any of them could describe the truck and driver."

Kev paled. "You'd better not go anywhere until you're over this. Mick will hold me responsible. You stay here. I'll bring food. The signora's going to slip me some more to take to you. She's worried about what you'll get here, I think. Vera never pays any attention to anything in the kitchen, but this Muriel has a long nose and she sticks it into everything to do with the house, housekeeping, maintenance, whatever. So when the Delgado's asleep, if she ever sleeps, the signora's going to whip up some of her special meals that will help you get over your accident. She's fussing about what you'll eat for Thanksgiving especially. And she hates Muriel with a white-hot passion."

I didn't bother to respond, as I could hardly raise my head. I tried to smile at the thought of the signora's white-hot hatred of Muriel and the memory of disastrous Kelly Thanksgiving meals in the past, many involving giblets. Maybe we could all go out. Maybe we could get dinner delivered. Maybe the signora would send enough for all the Kellys, even though they'd prefer fried baloney. But I was too tired to talk. What was wrong with me? I couldn't imagine Archie Goodwin being in a fix like this. Knocked out and down for the count. No. Archie would bounce right back, suave as ever, and wisecrack his way out of the scene. His clothing would be immaculate too. Of course, Nero Wolfe had his back as a rule, even when Archie was slipped the knockout drops that time. Vera was my Nero Wolfe, although she not only *didn't* have my back, she was the reason I was in this situation in the first place. Cast out and cut off.

And Wolfe would never let Archie eat Alphagetti or Kraft Macaroni and Cheese or beans and franks. Vera had abandoned me. No yellow silk pajamas for you, madam.

I wasn't even sure why I wanted to bail her out of the trap she'd found herself in. If I could keep awake long enough to think my way through this huge problem, then . . .

Later, Kev told me I was snoring when he took the hint and left, and here I'd been thinking Kev wouldn't know how to take a hint if you wrapped it up in a big red bow for him.

IT WAS MORNING when I opened my eyes again. I was still in my childhood room and not back in my attic at Van Alst House. I had not dreamed all the things that had happened since the doorbell first rang to admit Muriel Delgado and disaster. That was the bad news. The good news was that my head felt a lot clearer. My aches and bruises would be fine with a bit of Tylenol. I got out of bed and headed for the shower.

A wobbly half hour later, I looked a lot better and felt like I could face the world.

A sleepy Uncle Mick pounded on my bedroom door.

"You got company, Jordan. At nine o'clock in the morning. Who visits this early? Are you up for it?"

"I'm back on the horse, Uncle Mick."

"Not too soon," he said. "You took quite a slam, my girl."

"Who's here? Tiff?"

A pause. "No."

"Lance?"

His forehead furrowed. "Not Lance."

"Tyler?"

"Are you trying to kill me? No cops. Thank God for small favors."

Oh right. Tyler was out of town on training.

"Who then?"

"No one I know, but they claim to know you."

"The names, Uncle Mick." I bit back Vera's comment of "and in my lifetime." I didn't want to turn into Vera and I do love my uncle.

"Snow."

"Tom and Mindy?"

"The same."

"Be right there."

Well, that was good. I didn't let myself dwell on my missing best friends. I concentrated on the positive. I'd been trying to figure out how to return to the Snows and now they'd found me. Maybe they'd rake me over the coals for deceiving them. But compared to being hit by a truck, that would be a piece of cake.

I felt my way down the stairs, wearing my favorite vintage loungewear that always makes me feel cozy: royal-blue velour palazzo pants, white-and-blue striped T-shirt and an oversized batwing cashmere sweater from the eighties. I was presentable but still would have preferred to be a bit more dressed for company. When I entered the kitchen, Tom and Mindy were squeezed around the table with Uncle Mick. Uncle Lucky loomed from the far wall. My new aunt, Karen, was sitting at the table with them, charming as always. Walter and Cobain watched from the floor.

I smiled sheepishly as I took my place.

"I guess I owe you an explanation and an apology," I said. "About the alias and all that."

They shook their heads rapidly.

Mindy said, "We feel responsible for what happened to you."

"You do?"

"Obviously, this quest is more dangerous than any of us realized. Your uncle Kevin was kind enough to call us and give us a heads-up."

Oh no.

"Was he now?"

Uncle Mick and Uncle Lucky exchanged glances.

"Yes. He told us all about the people who have been pursuing you and how you have to travel from safe house to safe house to keep from being killed. It's lucky you escaped."

No point in trying to explain that I wasn't a sleeper agent or anything else that might have sprung from Kev's fevered brain. Luckily he didn't throw a unicorn into the mix.

"I'm sorry I used a false name—"

"And a wig," Tom said. "It came off when you flew through the air."

"Of course, you were right to be wary of whoever was trying to run you down. We're glad you weren't killed," Mindy said.

"Your neatly bagged leaves seem to have saved my life."

Mindy said, "Thank heavens Tom got them back outside. He'd dragged them into the carport when it snowed. He'd just wrestled them to the curb again when you arrived."

Tom was still stuck at the wig. "Weirdest thing I ever saw. There you were shooting through the air like a cannonball and your hair flew right off your head."

"It was jaw-dropping," Mindy said. "We were so worried. It's a big relief to find you in one piece. Literally."

"Time for me to get a new wig anyway," I said with a grin. "Red is so yesterday. Black and blue are the colors of the day. But I seem to have lost the cinnamon buns. I truly regret that."

They exchanged glances and then grinned in unison. "I think we might be able to locate a supply of those," Mindy said. "Oh and I almost forgot, we brought back your beautiful scarf." She produced the Pucci scarf that I'd left as an excuse to return.

Of course, I wasn't going anywhere now and I was glad to get it back.

"Before we go too far," I felt I had to add, "you need to know that whatever happened to me has something to do with Muriel Delgado. Whoever hit me knew I was visiting you and knew I'd been asking questions about her."

"Muriel." They nodded together. "But we thought you were avoiding some kind of—"

"Pretty sure it had to do with Muriel somehow."

They sat there, mentally processing that. Finally, they both nodded. "Makes sense," Tom said.

"You don't seem surprised."

Mindy said, "Well, Muriel was a strange and angry girl. Nothing that I would find out about her would really surprise me." She paused and then added, "Well, I guess that's not really true. I think

132

I really *would* be surprised to learn she'd tried to kill you for no reason at all."

Tom said, "You can't make an accusation like that."

Mindy started to protest. "I didn't say she did it, Tom."

I interjected, "Muriel wasn't driving the vehicle. She has a solid alibi with plenty of people to vouch for her, but I do believe that she is involved somehow. She has a reason and it seems to be that I was asking about her family and her. I went to her other previous addresses and tried to find out about her, same as with you."

Tom said, "Do you mind if we ask why? I assume that it's not really a legacy, as we now know you are not who you said you were."

"You're right. It isn't. Muriel seems to have a strange influence over my former employer. She arrived at my home the other evening without warning and met with the woman who was my boss. The next morning I found myself fired. I had to move out of my quarters within hours, and the other employees were told to have no contact with me."

"I have to ask why again," Tom said.

"That's the reason why I am investigating. My employer is wealthy, although not as wealthy as she used to be. She's not well and not physically strong at all." I didn't mention that Vera was usually tough as nails and mean as a snake and grouchy as a hibernating bear or any of the other clichés that describe her. I also didn't mention she was Vera Van Alst, in case they were somehow biased against her as was most of the community—including my own relatives.

Mindy said, "That's terrible."

"Yup. I think Muriel has some kind of hold over her."

They stared at me, eyes wide. I supposed that Maple Street wasn't full of this life-and-death intrigue all the time.

I said, "I need to find out and not just for me. It's important for my employer's safety and even for your own."

They blinked.

I was betting there was a lot they hadn't told me about Carmen and Muriel. I saw no reason not to push a bit.

Tom said, "Our safety?"

"Sure. They must have seen me leave your home. Therefore you could be threatened too."

"I don't see why we would be in any danger," Mindy said. "We don't know anything."

I shook my head. Not a good idea when you're in my condition. I closed my eyes and took a deep breath until everything stopped swimming. "I think you do. I felt you were holding back about Carmen Delgado. There's something about her that you both feel should be kept secret. Or at least not discussed. I need to know what that is."

Mindy stared at her fingernails. Tom glanced around at the clock on the wall.

"It won't go any further," I reassured them. "Any idea what that hold might be?"

I could tell by looking at them that they didn't.

"It's quite serious," I said. "Any leads would be helpful."

"We know nothing at all about any of that," Tom said a bit sanctimoniously.

"Oh, for heaven's sake, Tom," Mindy said. "No one really cares about those things anymore. What harm could it do?"

Tom's eyebrow shot up.

I cared deeply about whatever it was, so I said, "You can trust me. I am struggling to understand this woman and her family. Anyway, who would I tell?"

Mindy shot Tom a rebellious glower and said, "Carmen was a bit of a—"

A warning tone crept into Tom's voice. "Mindy."

"I was going to say a beauty, Tom. Don't get all high and mighty. She was a stunning woman."

"She was a pretty girl, for sure."

"Men fell for her, in a big way. But the relationships didn't seem to work out, until poor Pete."

It hadn't worked out for poor Pete either, I thought, as he'd ended up dead in the street.

I nodded to encourage her. "The relationships didn't work out?"

"I mean didn't lead to marriage. Pete was her first husband and by then she wasn't all that young."

Tom sat there glowering at Mindy. "Well, maybe she was too good for them."

Mindy rolled her eyes. "Yes, maybe that was it. At any rate, the point is—"

I had already figured out the point, although Tom was determined to prevent that.

If Pete was Carmen's first husband, then Muriel had been born out of wedlock. She had her mother's name, not her father's. Lots of people wouldn't blink an eye over this now, and many wouldn't be scandalized, but back in the sixties when Muriel was born, that would have created quite a storm. And it must have been an awful stigma for a child.

CHAPTER SEVEN

I DIDN'T WANT Tom to leave upset and angry. And I didn't want to alienate Mindy either. I said, "So Carmen kept the child. That news must have spread like wildfire."

They exchanged glances.

Mindy nodded. "She did and it did."

"Well, more power to her. I imagine it was quite difficult. Did her family support her decision?"

They glanced at each other and shrugged. "We've never met anyone. I don't remember Pete mentioning any either. They had a small wedding at City Hall. No one else attended. We went and so did Muriel. But in those days a wedding wasn't a lavish affair."

I said, "Well, it gives me an idea that Muriel had to build backbone to survive if she was an illegitimate child and with no relatives to make her feel wanted and support her, except her mother. My mother died when I was young and I can't imagine growing up without all my uncles to protect my interests and build my confidence." And give me an unusual set of skills and a great set of lock picks.

"There were lots of babies born out of wedlock

even back then," Mindy said. "Most of the girls dropped out of sight. Gone to an aunt's, we used to call it. They didn't keep their babies. They put them up for adoption. They wanted it kept secret." She sighed heavily.

Tom said, "Must have been hard on them giving away those children." He really was an old softie. I liked his sweet, sad face more by the minute.

Mindy said, "For sure, life wasn't easy for them either. You had to sympathize. People seemed to know about the pregnancies, and there was gossip as well as the heartbreak of losing a baby. But Carmen was different."

"Different?"

"Yes. Carmen didn't care what people thought. She never did. She wanted what she wanted and that was that." Hmm. Sounded a lot like Muriel to me.

I said, "You knew her back then?"

"Oh yes, we were all at school together. She had all the boys in the palm of her hand, but she had a reputation for being pretty fast, so most of the mothers made sure she didn't end up with their lads." The glance at Tom told me there was another story there.

I said, "Even though she didn't care what people said about her, back then it must have been hard. Carmen didn't marry until Muriel was in her teens, so how did she make ends meet?"

Tom squinted. "I think Muriel was about sixteen.

I realize now that they lived in abject poverty early on. I think the two of them had a room and a shared bathroom over in a boardinghouse on Willows. Carmie's parents disowned her. I don't really know how she survived or how the child did. I feel terrible that I never tried to help her."

Mindy rolled her eyes again. She must have been training for some sort of eye-rolling competition. "Your mother would have had your head on a plate if you had."

Tom got a faraway look in his eye and said, "Then Carmie got work at the shoe factory and was able to move from Willows over to Lilac Lane. She stayed on there until something happened."

"What?"

"I don't know. But by the time she moved to Maple Street, she hadn't worked there for a while."

I thought about it. What could have happened at the factory that would have given Carmen some power over the Van Alsts? Did she uncover something illegal? A death that would have been the responsibility of the Van Alst family? Something she could use to extort some money?

Whatever, an unemployed single mother wouldn't be buying a house on Maple Street without some ace up her sleeve.

"Thanks for this," I said, "It does help me understand Muriel a bit. I guess she comes by her forceful personality honestly."

"I guess," Mindy said.

"Carmie adored her," Tom said. "So Muriel didn't have a hard time at home."

But she would have in her neighborhood and at school, I thought. There would have been slurs, remarks, all kinds of digs. There would have been shoves and pushes when teachers weren't watching. There would have been hair pulling and shunning. Muriel must have learned to stand her ground at school. I thought about her scowling and resolute presence.

Mindy spoke up. "It would have been horrible for her, Tom, even if Carmen was too clueless to realize it."

"Well," I said, "you two have helped me understand quite a bit. I know it wasn't easy for you and you are not gossips, so I appreciate knowing this background." I paused. "I guess Muriel didn't inherit her mother's beauty."

Mindy snorted and looked embarrassed. Tom said, "Not a bit. Carmie was slender but—"

"Curvy," said Mindy. "Carmen had the kind of figure that men notice."

Tom agreed. "And poor Muriel was large and awkward. Carmie had a beautiful, sweet face and a smile that could light up a room."

"And she knew how to wear makeup and clothes that flattered her too, although they were always too tight in a way that suited her," Mindy said a bit snappishly. I was predicting a chilly ride

140

home for the Snows today. "Muriel was so ungainly and so plain, it was hard to believe they were related."

What did that mean? Was Muriel someone else's child? Was Carmen merely pretending to be the mother?

"But they were related? For sure?" I said. I couldn't think of too many circumstances where an unmarried woman in the early sixties would pretend that someone else's child was hers, particularly when there was no money in it.

"Of course," Tom said. "You could see it in their features. The only thing was on Carmie, those features looked good. But now, Muriel is what they call a handsome woman. Imposing and . . ."

Well, imposing, scary, but not plain. "Handsome" might have been pushing it. *You could carve a roast on that face,* I'd heard Kevin say.

"You've seen her lately?"

"Just a glimpse on Bridge Street last week. We didn't speak. In fact, I wasn't sure it was her in the beginning."

I stuck in a question before we lost the thread. "So you don't know what Carmen did at the shoe factory?"

Mindy glanced at her watch. "Look at the time!"

Tom stared at his shoes as if they'd betrayed him by not carrying him from the room. They both looked so guilty that I knew I'd hit on something big with that question.

"No," they said.

As if.

I mean, they could have been off the hook if they'd said, *She made shoes*.

"She worked in the factory, you said earlier. Who did she work for? Maybe I can follow up with that person. This must have been when, back in the late sixties, early seventies? That person might still be alive."

"He isn't," Mindy snapped.

"Mindy!"

"Well, he isn't, Tom. So let's leave it at that."

Mindy closed her mouth and gave the impression she was going to keep it that way.

I had no intention of leaving it. I had two choices. One, head to the library and comb through the local archives for information on the Van Alst Shoe Factory. Or two, push for an answer here so I didn't have to collapse in front of Lance's blue-haired groupies. As my uncles have taught me, when in doubt, bluff. I had a hunch and I hoped it would pay off. I thought I knew what they were trying to keep from me.

"So, Carmen Delgado went to work for Mr. Leonard Van Alst. Am I right? No point in hedging. I can always find out."

They didn't have to tell me that I'd gotten it. The answer was written on their faces.

I decided to push it one step further. I knew plenty about Leonard Van Alst, the third generation of the Van Alsts to run the shoe company and the man generally believed to have run it into the ground, bringing economic disaster to Harrison Falls and the surrounding communities. He was reputed to be a vain, impulsive and silly man. Just Carmen's type.

He was also Vera's father.

Now there was a juicy tidbit.

I gave it one more push. "And then one thing led to another. A beautiful, voluptuous woman with a child to support snagged a wealthy factory owner and started to move up in the world. Did Leonard Van Alst buy her the house on Maple Street?"

Tom said, "Everyone's tongue was wagging and poor Carmen was shunned by the community. I don't want to gossip."

Mindy said, "Oh, for heaven's sake. Of course, he bought that house for her. Everyone knew it."

Tom glowered. "She was trying to do the best for her child and make a decent life."

Mindy muttered, "Maybe 'decent' isn't the right word. He was a married man and a father."

My turn. "And then the factory closed down."

Mindy said, "So many people lost their jobs and homes. And yet Carmen kept on living in her pretty little house. He saw to that. It didn't endear her to people who'd lost everything, including some of our neighbors who had to sell their homes when their jobs disappeared."

143

Tom scowled. "It was terrible. Carmen was harassed on the street. She stopped leaving the house. Muriel had to take care of everything, get groceries and run errands. People were cruel to her too. And she had nothing to do with any of it. She was only a kid. It makes you despair of your fellow man."

"She was always odd, though," Mindy said.

"Doesn't excuse it. People should have been ashamed of themselves. Bullying, plain and simple. We tried to be nice to her."

"But she was definitely peculiar, different, as I said before." Mindy wasn't letting go of that.

I said, "If I remember the family history, Herman founded the factory. By the time the grandson, Leonard, took over, things went downhill fast. Money was squandered on art and trips and extravagances even though the factory was in trouble. So if he bought a house for Carmen, of course, that must have upset people."

"Oh, it did. And it didn't help Carmen's reputation in the community any that he made sure she got her house in his will."

"He did?"

"Yes. He took care of her." There was still an edge to Mindy's voice, and I couldn't help but notice that Tom had turned away from her slightly. Gone was the cozy affection that they'd brought with them.

I hoped that Tom and Mindy made up soon. But

even more, I was hoping they'd leave soon. As much as I liked them, my head was swimming with this new development. Any more and my brain wiring would start to smoke. Muriel's mother had been Vera's father's mistress. Even though the family fortune was sinking, Leonard Van Alst had left a house to Carmen Delgado. Everyone in town knew that, apparently. Did Vera know it? If so, why would it make her defer to Muriel? I would have expected anger or even contempt. Disinterest at the least. What was I missing here? I needed to sort it out. And in order to do that, I needed a bit of privacy.

When I started to sway, Uncle Mick declared the session over, and the Snows were on their way, a lot cooler than when they arrived.

I was hustled back upstairs and told to settle down. I couldn't even resist.

But I also couldn't sleep. I had finally realized the hold that Muriel had over Vera. If Muriel's mother had been Vera's father's mistress for many years, that would leave a cauldron of motives. More than that, I pondered Tom's comments about the length of the relationship. I was no math wizard, but it seemed to me that Carmen had worked at the shoe factory after Muriel was born. Leonard hadn't inherited the family factory at that point, and he had his own family to support. How could he manage to buy a house for his mistress at that point? All this information cleared up some of the strangeness but still left a lot of questions.

My brain ached, but I tried to remember when Leonard Van Alst had taken over from his late father. Vera was in her early teens. I knew that much from what I'd read. Vera was never keen to discuss that period. From then on, it had been a fairly steep decline for the Van Alst family, the factory and the town. From what I'd heard, more of that could be attributed to Van Alst than to the changing economy.

A strange and horrible thought occurred to me. How long had the affair gone on? When had it begun? Could anything from so long ago be worth killing for?

CHAPTER EIGHT

T HE POLICE ARE at the door."
These are probably the worst words that any Kelly could ever hear. The Binghams share that view, although I am the only Bingham that I know.

"What did you say?" I opened my eyes after my morning nap.

"Police. At the door," Uncle Mick said with a spasm in his jaw.

"Why?"

What had my uncles been up to? It was always better not to know. But really, since the events earlier this year (and we were still finding bullet holes) there was nothing, and I mean nothing, that remained in our home to implicate them in anything.

Uncle Mick was not too happy. And there was the fact from time to time that a great deal of material passed in and out of the back door for "projects." It would be less than good if any such material was on the premises when the cops showed up, not that I would know anything about it anyway. Still, I thought I might wake up and panic.

"They're here to see you," he said. "Shall I tell them you're unconscious?"

"But I'm not unconscious."

"They don't know that."

"What do they want?"

"To talk to you about your hit-and-run."

"I don't really remember anything about it, but I'll talk to them. Maybe they'll be able to tell me something. Don't you think it's a good thing if they get on it and find out what happened to me and why?"

I could tell that he disapproved of this police business, despite the fact it made complete sense to use their expertise.

"It's okay, Uncle Mick. I am sick of being in bed and I'm going to get up again and get going. Is it Tyler Dekker?" I knew that Tyler was probably not back from training, but I could always hope.

"Never saw this guy before. And I don't think you should get up, my girl. You're awful pale and a bit shaky."

"Oh. Well, give me a few minutes." I didn't want to meet him looking like I'd been fished out of the garbage, although I guess I had been.

AS COPS WENT, my interviewer seemed to be a one-off. True, he was middle-aged and kind of handsome in a slightly weary way. He was also pale and light on hair. His was almost translucent and buzzed close to his scalp. I figured he had it cropped short so people might not notice that there wasn't much of it. It was a good haircut, though. I also would have guessed he was about six days from retirement. He hadn't figured on having to waste any of those days on the hopeless job of interviewing me about a hit-and-run there was little chance of solving.

Although he didn't seem too involved in the entire activity, he did manage to keep a wary eye on Uncle Mick all the time he was interviewing me. Uncle Mick returned the favor. He kept his arms crossed in front of his chest. Every ginger chest hair seemed dangerously alert somehow. Walter and Cobain were quite unimpressed with the detective as he didn't appear to have any treats.

His name, if you can believe it, was Detective Jack Jones. He was a snappy dresser from the black cashmere blend sport jacket to the charcoal shirt and tie and the knife-edge crease in his pants that drew attention to his polished cordovan tassel loafers. No wedding ring or any pale indentation to show he'd recently had one. My guess was no wife and no kids in college equaled money for decent clothes. He sat down in the chair Uncle Mick had reluctantly provided, opened a small white notebook and clicked his pen.

He was not the stereotypical cop, but then again who is? In my experience, there's no one type and you can't go by experiences. I have yet to meet a police officer who's in the least bit like Rex Stout's Inspector Cramer or Sergeant Purley Stebbins. Nero Wolfe routinely made fools of the two of them. He might have had a harder time with some of the officers I'd met in real life. By way of background, as you know, my family attracts a lot of attention from the forces of law and order and so I have firsthand observations. For another thing there was the slightly bashful and occasionally blushing Officer Tyler Dekker, a sweetie if ever there was one. And not a fool.

But even if Detective Jones wasn't a buffoon like Cramer could be, that didn't mean I couldn't finesse him for info. Certainly Archie Goodwin always managed that with Cramer and Stebbins. And I suppose I should admit that Wolfe did too.

I said, "Do you get a lot of fatal or near-fatal hit-and-run incidents here in Harrison Falls, Detective Jones?"

He stifled a yawn and shook his head. If I'd had any doubts that he was going through the motions, the yawn would have put an end to them.

I was pretty sure he wanted to say that he got to ask the questions. Cops love saying it and I've been on the receiving end of that comment more than once. But I was pretty pathetic with my bandaged head and pale face. The décor in my room would have added to the pathos. Anyway, the man was tired and looking forward to sleeping in for the rest of his life, starting soon.

"So that's a no?" I asked.

"No," he said, his eyes fixing on Care Bear.

"It's not a no?"

"Yes, it's a no," he growled.

"I wondered. I've heard of another one and—"

He glanced at me and said, "Another one of what?"

"Another hit-and-run."

"Here?"

"Yes. Well, not in Harrison Falls, but over in Grandville."

He shook his head. "First I've heard about it."

"Well, it was a while ago."

"How long?"

"Nearly forty years."

He laughed, and not in a nice way. "Before my time."

I bet it was not, I thought, but of course, I didn't want to alienate him.

"Before my time too," I said. "But I wondered if maybe it might not be connected." I tried to bat my eyelashes, but it made me feel nauseated.

He really shouldn't have scrunched up his face that way. It was not at all becoming and just had to be hard on the skin. I kept my beauty advice to myself. After all, I wasn't doing too well in that department lately.

"Not every crime over a forty-year time frame

is connected, miss. Maybe you've been watching too much television."

"I'd rather read mysteries than watch TV. I'm more Nero Wolfe than *CSI*."

He snorted. "Oh well, that will give you all the right answers."

"My taste in entertainment aside, I feel that there is something worth checking into."

He shrugged, yawned again. "There won't be."

"Well," I said, "but some of the same people are involved."

"Here's an idea," he said. "How about I ask you some questions about your hit-and-run here in this town two days ago and we deal with that? Let someone else deal with the forty-year-old crime."

"Fine. But then, can I—"

"Back in the hospital you claimed to have no knowledge of who hit you. Have you changed your mind about that?"

This gave me something new to think about. For instance, I had no recollection of talking to the police at the hospital. I mentioned that. He didn't respond.

"As I said, I don't remember talking to you or any other officers at the hospital, although I remember being there. I recall nothing about being hit. Of course, people who've been whacked from behind by a truck often don't notice all that much."

"How do you know it was from behind?"

My turn to blink. "Oh. Well, if the truck had come from the front, I'm sure I would have seen it coming. That's the kind of thing you notice, a truck hurtling toward you. As it was, the other reason I know it was a truck is that other people witnessed it. And I can't imagine they'd make that up. So I accept it, unless of course, it's not that I didn't see it, but I don't remember it."

"So who do you think hit you?"

"I can't be sure. Like I said before."

"Any enemies?"

I hesitated.

He leaned forward. "It's a good idea to share that kind of thing with the police after someone's tried to kill you."

"Well, who doesn't have a few enemies, what with the Internet? . . . Anyway, the one person I could describe as an enemy has an alibi."

"No offense, but we're usually the judge of all that alibi stuff."

"I realize that. But people I trust say that this person was at home when I was hit."

"Who was it?"

"Let me start from the beginning." I filled him in on the arrival of Muriel at Van Alst House.

"Van Alst?" he said. "Like Vera Van Alst."

"None other."

"Huh. Not too popular around these parts."

I couldn't help thinking this guy was a bit of a jerk.

Uncle Mick had an expression on his face, like maybe he'd swallowed a toad or something. I attributed this to the fact that he was in agreement with a police officer. That was obviously too weird for him.

"So," I said. "I worked for Vera. I liked the job; I was good at it and it paid well. Until we had a visit the other day from this Muriel Delgado. The next morning I was out of a job and then Muriel moved in."

"She took your job?"

"No, she didn't. She doesn't appear to be doing anything except sponging off Vera. She made sure that I was out of the way. There must be some reason for that. My best guess is that I would oppose whatever it is she wants to do to Vera."

"Doesn't sound like that has much to do with our investigation," he said. "Unless she was driving the truck that hit you."

"She wasn't. In fact, she's the person with the alibi."

"So why are you wasting my time with this little fairy tale?"

"Because there was another hit-and-run involving the same family some years back."

"But—"

"Muriel's stepfather was killed by a hit-and-run driver outside the Grandville hospital back in the seventies. The case was never solved. I was hit by a hit-and-run driver on the street she used to live on while I was there visiting her former neighbors and asking questions about the Delgados."

"And?"

"*And* I think that's too much of a coincidence to ignore."

That didn't impress Detective Jones. "Maybe. Why would she want to harm you?"

"Like I said, I was asking people in her old neighborhood about her. And bam, I'm almost a hood ornament."

He smirked.

I said, "I admit it's a bit of a stretch. But I think she wants to damage Vera, maybe even take over her life and her home."

"Let me remind you: Real life has to make sense."

"It does make sense to me."

"Can you prove that Muriel . . ."

"Delgado."

". . . Delgado is involved?"

"No. I'm not the person who finds the proof. I'm just the person who was hit by the truck. And if I hadn't landed on those bags full of leaves, I would probably be dead or in a vegetative state. You asked me if I had any enemies. I believe that Muriel Delgado is my enemy and she has some reason to want me out of the way."

"What reason exactly?"

"I thought I made that clear. Because Muriel's

trying to take over my boss's life and I was digging around in her past."

"Pretty unlikely motive. Anything else?"

"Yes. Did you talk to the Snows? And Audra Bennacke?"

"We talked to all the witnesses. They weren't able to identify a driver, but they said the vehicle seemed to head right for you."

"And did they say that vehicle was a green truck?"

He hesitated. Finally, he said, "A truck, but not green. The witness saw a red truck, and she also said it was driven by a male. There may have been a passenger and the truck may have had some kind of commercial decal on the side."

"Oh."

"You seem disappointed."

I was. I'd been hoping for the same green truck that had delivered Muriel's belongings. That would have established a link. I was disappointed in myself that I hadn't grilled the Snows a bit about who had hit me. Instead I'd focused on the Muriel and Carmen questions.

"I am, I guess. A green truck delivered Muriel and her belongings to Van Alst House when she moved in. I thought it might be the same one."

He scratched his nose. " 'Course, there's more than one green truck in this world. Half of Williams County drives trucks and there's plenty of green ones."

"I guess you're following up."

"We're following up on *red* trucks. So do you have anything else to add?"

"Aside from the connection to Muriel Delgado and the other hit-and-run, no."

He snapped his notebook closed. "We may need to talk to you again."

"I won't leave town." As I was sitting there with my head still bandaged and my bruises threatening to bloom, I grinned facetiously.

"We don't actually say that," he muttered.

"By the way," I said, "I have a good friend on the force."

"Who's that?" he said, taken aback.

"Officer Tyler Dekker. He's only been here for less than a year."

"I know Dekker. Good cop. On his way places."

"I guess that's what all his away training is about."

Jack Jones raised an eyebrow. "Training? I don't think there's any training going on this week."

My battered face must have fallen. He said, "But I'm probably wrong. I'm tied up with my re—other things lately."

That would explain it. Jack Jones was putting in his last bit of time, probably not checking into what the young folks were doing. I hoped that was it, because if Tyler wasn't training, why the heck wasn't he around and why would he have lied to me?

But I didn't want to think about Tyler Dekker right at that moment. Whatever else came out of this unsatisfactory interview, I hoped at least that someone on the Harrison Falls Police Force would take a close look at Muriel Delgado.

Otherwise it would have to be me. And I was in rough shape.

"Are you sure you won't verify this possible connection?" I said, with what I believed to be admirable restraint.

"We *will* investigate the incident involving you. As for the other thing, I doubt that much will come out of it, but I'll make a note."

I said. "Fine, I'll take it. Pete Delaney. Married to Carmen Delgado. Died in 1974."

I was no fool. Eighty percent of this man's mind was on his postretirement lifestyle. The other twenty was facing a mountain of paperwork to allow him to get to that Nirvana. Like he'd care about a forty-year-old hit-and-run. He'd put more thought into his lunch order.

He said, "Don't get your hopes up."

Who said anything about hope? "Forget the ancient hit-and-run. Maybe consider that someone else might be in danger from this woman."

He opened the notebook again.

He raised an eyebrow. It seemed like even that effort was almost too much for him. "Who?" he said when I had given up on any kind of reaction.

"She's delicate and—"

158

Apparently he had a weakness for delicate women, although I bet it wasn't someone like Vera that he'd pictured. "What's happening to her?"

"Well, this Muriel Delgado has moved in and is separating her from her friends and all support systems." I felt a bit guilty in not mentioning the signora and Uncle Kev and poor Eddie wherever he was, but it was in a good cause. "I feel strongly that she will start to plunder the estate and—"

"I need a name. We'll get someone on it."

"It's my boss. The same person we've been talking about. Vera Van Alst." I watched the expression change on his face. "I know that you're not a fan. You made that clear earlier, but she's a vulnerable person and she deserves to be protected."

He put down his pen. "My father worked at that factory, until it closed."

"Oh."

"They ruined this town."

"Um, did your father find another job?"

"No. He didn't. He died."

Oh, dirty pool. There wasn't much I could say except, "I'm sorry."

"Heart attack at forty-two, but we all knew it was stress because the factory closed."

"Yes. People suffered. Must have been awful for your family."

He nodded.

I gave it one last try. "But Vera had nothing to

159

do with the closing of the factory. She was a kid."

"She's one of them, isn't she?"

What could I say to that?

He said, "They only think of themselves. Still got that big mansion and the car and all the servants?"

Servants?

I didn't really think of the signora and Uncle Kev and me as *servants*. Staff. Yes. The signora was close to being family. "Vera wasn't responsible for any of it. Sins of the father. Vera's stuck in a wheelchair in an empty old house in a town full of people who despise her. All she really has are her books and her cats."

"If you say so."

"I do say so." I felt myself getting quite huffy. "And this situation needs to be looked into, whether you like the potential victim or not."

"I hate to break it to you, but we don't investigate ideas that people have about things that *might* happen to other people. We don't interview people that you've taken a dislike to merely because you say so. The police need evidence, something to go on. You come up with something like that in the next month or so, call the station."

Huh. I was pretty sure that he'd be gone and I'd be starting from scratch.

"I will."

"Good luck with that." With a nod to me and one

to Uncle Mick, he got to his feet and tucked away the notebook again. Another twenty minutes closer to his new life.

Uncle Mick was still seething when he came back after seeing the detective out.

"It's not my fault that the police came to your house, Uncle Mick," I said, "if that's what you were thinking. I got hit by a truck, remember?"

"Remember, my girl? How could I forget? If it takes cops to find that person, so be it. It's not that, it's that I don't think we have the benefit of the best the Harrison Falls police have to offer."

"I hear you. This guy's at the end of his career. He's practically phoning it in. He wasn't interested in helping Vera at all."

"The thing is, my girl, that he won't be alone in that. Most people around here would share his opinion, including the people he works with. Except for maybe the younger ones. Like your friend what's-his-name."

Uncle Mick knew perfectly well what Tyler's name was and most likely had investigated him and his family without mentioning it to me. But I didn't want to think about Tyler Dekker, who was perhaps not on training after all. Wherever he was, he wasn't here, checking on my recovery. And he was not available to help Vera escape from the clutches of the dreaded Muriel.

"I know. It's down to me, Uncle Mick."

He drew himself up to his full five foot ten and puffed out his splendid ginger chest. "Indeed it is not down to you. You are getting your rest. You heard the doc. You've had a shock and you shook up your head. You have to let things take their course. Kev's over there, so nothing can really go . . ."

"Exactly."

"Even so, you can't go mixing it up. Too risky. Let yourself heal."

How to explain? I needed to get some kind of closure. Someone had intended to kill me. Someone *had* killed Pete Delaney. Someone who had a connection with Muriel Delgado. Muriel Delgado had it in for me. *I'd* be on my guard. But for all her tough bluster, Vera wasn't really in the best shape to defend herself against any murderous attempts. Although if anyone could kill you with a sharp tongue, it would be Vera. But now, she seemed to be totally under La Delgado's thumb. I thought back to Muriel fondling the Rex Stout books and Vera's reaction. Did she want Vera's home and possessions or was it sheer vengeance?

It didn't matter how bad I felt, I had to do something.

"I have to help Vera. Even though she's a Van Alst, you were starting to like her. Remember?"

"*Like*'s a bit strong," Mick said. "We do care about our favorite niece, though."

"Your only niece. You wouldn't want anything bad to happen . . . to either of us."

His freckles darkened in defeat.

I had him there and we both knew it.

OF COURSE VERA was the only one who really knew what was going on. I needed to talk to her. I absolutely had to find a way to confront her and get some answers. As she'd already fired me and I'd been hit by a truck, there didn't seem to be much for me to fear in the confrontation. I thought about how I'd do that. I'd been following my favorite private detective and learning some key lessons. Never fail to meet someone's eye and ask them the hard questions were two. And another, make sure you look debonair while you're doing it. Archie didn't articulate these tips, but he lived them.

First I called Uncle Kev and tasked him with getting Muriel out of Van Alst House long enough for me to get in there and ask Vera a few tough but essential questions. I set about becoming respectable. I slipped into last year's herringbone tights and my knee-high riding boots (a steal off Kijiji), all topped off with a little cashmere shift that had been my mother's. Nothing beats an outfit that costs almost nothing but would knock the socks off any stylist in SoHo. I'd gotten rid of the bandages. I felt confident and classy despite being both broke and broken. I snatched one of

Mick's old fedoras, lest anyone gawk at my scratches and bruises.

UNCLE KEV AND I were lurking behind Vera's bank, beside a cable installation van. The wind had died down, so we no longer had to hunker against the brick wall.

"You sure you know what you're doing here, Kevin?" Despite the frigid November temperatures, a prickle of sweat formed on my lip. Kevin always *thought* he knew what he was doing. He was giddy with excitement, rubbing his mitts together like a kid on Christmas.

"Oh, I know what I'm doing, Jordie. Trust me, Cherie has never let me down."

His eyes twinkled in a way that gave me pause as to what Cherie's line of work might be, whoever and wherever Cherie turned out to be. That was before I remembered that Cherie was the cable installer who had so taken Kev's fancy after rigging up Van Alst House. Why was I surprised?

The cable repair van rattled as the person atop the telescoping ladder adjusted position above us. The cold metal pinging sent another chill up my back. Perhaps my gorgeous but uninsulated knee-high riding boots were the wrong choice. Even in this crisp sunshine, I was freezing.

Kev looked down at my shifting feet through the puffs of our breath. "What have you got on your feet, girl? Those aren't practical." He shook his head like I was the silly one in this family, and I was about to say something about that when a nasal but pretty voice filled the alley.

"Why hello, ma'am." A sweet southern drawl continued, "I was wondering if I could speak with Miss Vera Van Alst. It's Amy calling from Upstate Trust and Financial regarding the cash withdrawal she requested." There were at least four syllables in "Amy."

I craned my neck skyward to the person on the ladder, who was clearly a cable repair gal. Frosted blue eye shadow, ringed big blue bedroom eyes over a dainty nose and pouting hot-pink lips. Blond springing curls bursting out from under a white hard hat caught the light like an angel . . . an angel from Kevin. She wore a navy-blue pair of coveralls cinched impossibly small at the waist and, speaking of strange choices in footwear, high-heeled Timberlands. She spoke into a red retro phone receiver clipped into a panel of wires at the top of the electric pole. Cherie was idly wrapping her finger around the red spiral cord, completely at ease, like she was relaxing on her bed, chatting to a girlfriend . . . in nineteen eighty-one.

"Well, I promised Miss Vera I'd have her withdrawal ready for pickup as usual by herself tomorrow morning, but I had no idea the bank would be closed then because we are finally painting over this gawd-awful beige paint. You'd think after twenty years . . ."

Bank closed for painting? I tore my gaze away from the angel in the sky who was spewing this BS. I stared into the beaming face of Kevin. "See, she's hooked directly into the phone line from the bank, so when she calls Vera's house, that's what's gonna show up on the Caller ID."

". . . oh dear. Yes, I do know that Miss Vera is not entirely mobile . . . Well, I'm so, so sorry for the inconvenience. Is there any way I could make . . . ?" Cherie tapped her long nails against the side of the receiver, to sound like typing.

"I see a Mr. Kevin Kelly is also authorized to pick up on Miss Van Alst's behalf."

Even from twenty feet below I could hear the bitter tone of Muriel's voice chastising and intimidating Cherie.

"Why, no, I would not want to be responsible for an old woman not getting her medications! But . . . but . . . oh no, please don't call my manager! I'm still on probation and . . ."

Cherie was getting squeakier by the second; she glanced down at Kev, who shot her a thumbs-up and a grin.

"Perhaps you could come to the bank today and get Miss Van Alst's funds on her behalf? If you brought a letter of . . . Oh no! I'm not trying to make this difficult . . . Yes, I do realize this is my mistake . . . Well, I'm here until twelve fifteen, ma'am, and then I'm gone for the day. No, no. No letter required for you, ma'am."

"Wow, she's good, Kev." I was astounded at the Oscar-caliber performance from the retro lady at the top of the ladder.

"I've got Muriel's number, Jordie. I knew how she'd play this. Any chance to get in with the bank, you take it."

"Nice work. I have to admit it." I don't think I'd ever been so proud of Kevin. Especially not for arranging a con. Usually, I am opposed to those. But I had to admit, this was a really great scheme to get Muriel out of the house and maybe even catch her trying to commit fraud, although, considering our little ruse, maybe that wasn't a stone we wanted to cast. I didn't really care about that part anyway. This was about getting access to Vera and trying to show her she was in danger financially, and maybe otherwise, as well as squeezing a bit of truth out of her.

It was also about protecting my friends. And if protecting my friends happened to coincide with mealtime at Van Alst House, well, that was a happy accident. My stomach gurgled in approval.

Kev watched Cherie sashay down the ladder. I'd never seen anyone sashay on a ladder. I would have bet against it being possible, although I would have lost that bet. Kev had an entire galaxy twinkling in his eyes.

"Well, what's a girl gotta do to get a hug around here, Mr. Kelly?"

In response to that challenge, Kev rushed forward, picked her up and swung her in circles in the alley. Something told me that Kev and Cherie had been in touch between the cable installation at Van Alst House and this latest bit of trickery. Cable wasn't the only possible hookup. Of course, not really my business.

KEV'S PHONE RANG. Muriel. I could hear her blasting away at him.

Kev said, "I'm downtown getting some stuff for the signora. But I'm on my way back, Muriel. What? What bank? Sure, I can meet you there at noon. I don't know what you're talking about. No need to talk to me like that. I'll wait for you there. Sheesh. What's wrong with your car? Oh. Flat tire? Really? That's too bad." He turned and winked at me. "Okay. I'm coming to get you right now."

Okay, I figured I had enough time to get out to the Van Alst place and confront Vera before Muriel, dragging Uncle Kev, arrived at the bank to find out that no withdrawal had actually been requested nor was one ready. Then I'd have to get out of Van Alst House before Muriel returned. Unless, of course, I was able to prevail on Vera to see reason and give the swirling black vision the boot.

I dropped by Uncle Mick's on the way. He'd agreed to come with me, in case I had trouble with wooziness. We took one of his cars, so I could take it easy. That didn't mean he was in a good mood about it.

I'd given up on getting Uncle Mick to smile as we swung down the long driveway to Van Alst House. He was visibly disapproving of my plan and also deeply distracted by whatever it was that was deeply distracting him lately. My head was spinning and I didn't feel much like talking anyway, so that worked. It was barely a ten-minute drive to Vera's, so I didn't want to squander any energy arguing that it was a trip that I shouldn't be taking. Instead I stared out at the flock of wild turkeys in the chilly and bare farmers' fields that bordered Vera's property.

The signora answered my knock on the back door and began one of her strange little dances. I made the international sign for *shhh*. "I need to see Vera. Don't let her know I'm coming."

Mick was behind me to catch me if I tumbled as I walked resolutely down the long hallway to the office. I managed to keep myself upright, but my head was swimming. Even the scent of old books was no comfort. I needed to hold it together long enough to tell Vera what I now knew. That was all.

I knocked firmly on the office door and Vera barked, "Oh, for heaven's sake, Fiammetta, why bother to knock? Why not crash in like you usually do?"

Grumpy, yes, but despite the harsh words, without Vera's usual bite.

I opened the door and stepped in.

She was at her Edwardian desk surrounded by stacks of paper. She glanced up and did a cartoon double take. Next she managed to simulate outrage.

"What are you doing here, Miss Bingham? You have been specifically asked to leave these premises." Vera's halfhearted outrage masked something else. Unless I missed my guess, that something else was fear.

"I did leave and now I'm back," I said.

I wobbled over to the desk and pulled up a chair. I sat without being asked. It was that or fall down. This postcollision thing was getting old.

"Well, you will have to leave again. At once."

"Not yet, Vera. I have something to discuss with you."

"I said at once and I meant that. It's called trespass in case you weren't aware of that, Miss Bingham. It means being unlawfully on someone's property."

"Don't worry. Muriel's not here, Vera."

Something flickered over her face. Relief?

"And I won't stay long."

The door opened again and the signora teetered in with a tray containing coffee, cookies and sandwiches with rustic Italian bread. I wondered if she could conjure these things up in seconds by some sort of magic or if Kev had warned her I was coming.

"Get that out of here, Fiammetta," Vera growled in her growliest voice. "Miss Bingham is just leaving and you are not to let her in again. I have explained that to you in terms that even you can understand."

"I no hear you, Vera. Sorry sorry. Eat!" I loved the way she pretended not to hear Vera. Perhaps she'd missed her calling as an actress.

"No, not eat. Forget sorry, just do what I tell you for once!"

Vera may have shouted but the signora danced around as if she hadn't heard a word. I had to admire her imperviousness to Vera's instructions. I reached for a sandwich. Why lose the opportunity?

"Miss Bingham, I will be picking up the phone to call the police. I will tell them that you are on the premises against my instructions and you are threatening me."

"Go for it. I won't stop you," I said. "By strange coincidence, I was talking to the Harrison Falls police about the fact that I'd been hit by a truck driven by someone intent on killing me."

Vera's hand reached for the telephone.

I continued. "During that conversation, I suggested that you might be in danger from Muriel

171

Delgado. I offered some reasons why that might be and do you know what the officer said?"

"The point, Miss Bingham, and in my lifetime." She sounded her usual imperious self, but I couldn't help but notice a nerve jumping under her eye.

"He didn't say that. He left me with the impression that there are still plenty of hard feelings about the factory closing and if there was a complaint from you, it had better have some formidable facts to back it up. Not much sympathy, I'm afraid, Vera."

Of course, that wasn't exactly how my conversation with Detective Jones had gone. But I needed to make the point. I added, "Perhaps Tyler Dekker will come out to arrest me. He likes you. Although not nearly as much as he likes me."

Vera's hand pulled back from the phone. "What do you want, Miss Bingham? I no longer employ you and that isn't likely to change."

"You wouldn't be able to afford me for much longer, Vera. I think you are about to get fleeced and that includes your precious collection. I don't wish you any harm, but can you say the same for Muriel?"

Vera clutched her cherished copy of *The Red Box* in her brittle, white-knuckled hands.

"Your Rex Stout books seem to be vanishing. Let me guess why."

"My *guest* is entitled to borrow them, Miss

Bingham. Your concern is unwarranted." Her pinched face said otherwise. I knew I'd touched a nerve.

"I know that Muriel's mother and your father had what used to be known as an arrangement and I believe she is holding that over your head."

Her eyes burned into mine. "How did—?"

"A lot of people know, Vera. It's a different world now. People don't care. And even if some do, it's hardly worth losing your home over."

Vera narrowed her eyes.

I kept going. "I suppose it's the family image, but any minor or even major indiscretions are nothing to people these days. They remember the factory closing, but nobody has any more than the mildest of interest in some scandalous fling forty or fifty years ago. You have to admit that I'm right."

Vera sat there in her wheelchair, calm and quiet, before she spoke. "I am glad you weren't killed by the unknown person, but aside from that I take no joy in your company, Miss Bingham. Our association is finished."

I said, "But—"

"But nothing. You are wrong in your assumptions, Miss Bingham. And you are even more foolish than I thought you were. Muriel is not here because of some imagined extortion about my father's flings, which were quite open. Her mother was one of many. She is here at my invitation and you are not. It is time for you to go. Otherwise, I will take my chances with the police and their long memories and your besotted young officer. The last I checked, they still had to uphold the law. For the ultimate time, I am asking you to leave."

Foolish? That stung. But it wasn't the biggest shock. I couldn't believe that Vera was going to stick to her story. My jaw was slack. I hoped I didn't drool.

"I won't tell you again." She was pale as ash and she seemed to be shrinking in her chair.

I felt Uncle Mick's hand on my shoulder and heard the signora skittering around bleating erratically. I rose and turned to leave the room. Had I been wrong? Despite her bluster, Vera's haggard face told me that she was afraid of something. Was it me? That didn't make sense. Ditto for Uncle Mick and the signora.

Vera made a furtive glance toward the window. Wondering what? If her nemesis was about to return? To catch me in conversation with the former lady of the manor? That glance revealed a lot.

"It's not the end, Vera," I said. "I have your back."

"And I'll see yours as you depart," she snapped.

As we exited the house, Uncle Mick holding my elbow, the signora dashed after us with a tin of cookies and a plastic storage bin stuffed with sandwiches.

In the car, Uncle Mick refrained from comment. "Thank you for not saying 'I told you so,'" I said. "Much appreciated."

"Wasn't easy, my girl."

"But we're not done."

He jammed down the accelerator and we shot along the driveway, spraying gravel. A pair of idling turkeys scattered. Once out the ornate gates and speeding along the road, I spotted a speck in the distance. The speck became a vehicle driving erratically. I bent down out of sight.

I said from my squat on the floor, "Is it Kev?"

"It is, my girl."

"And is Muriel with him?"

"If by Muriel you mean a biddy with a face like thunder, yes."

I raised myself and watched through the rear window as the car made a sharp right turn at sixty miles per hour and rocketed down the approach to Van Alst House.

"A close call," Uncle Mick said. "I thought Kev was supposed to keep her away a bit longer."

I said, "She's as easy to resist as a tsunami. There is no standing up to her. I mean, you saw Vera."

"Yes, and I never would have believed it. There's something dark buried between those two old ladies."

Archie Goodwin whispered in my ear, *That hit the nail on the head.*

Mick was still shaking his own head when we got back to Michael Kelly's Fine Antiques. He didn't say another word. That was fine. I had plenty to think about.

Vera was afraid of Muriel. Perhaps not for the reason I'd thought, but there was something. Vera didn't care much about public opinion or she never would wear those disgusting old sweaters. But she cared deeply about some secret and Muriel knew it. That was dangerous for both of us.

I hadn't figured out what the secret was yet.

CHAPTER NINE

WHEN WE GOT home, Uncle Mick wasn't having any arguments. Afternoon or not, I was to rest. I was back in my bedroom, feeling like a bad little girl with only Walter and Cobain and the signora's sandwiches (prosciutto and cheese) and almond cookies to keep me company. Good thing, as that turned out to have been lunch. Uncle Mick had places to go, people to see, equipment to move. None of those things were my business and I preferred it that way. He left me with instructions not to get in any trouble. What trouble could I possibly get into in my pink-and-white pony kingdom? Tell me that.

Walter and Cobain took more than their share of the bed, and they also demanded a lot of head-scratching and patting. Life with the uncles had helped them develop their entitled side.

A word of acquired wisdom: If you ever find yourself faced with a double-barreled problem like how to prevent someone you care about from being fleeced, or worse, while you recover from a car accident, you will not find your My Little Pony collection much help. The same might be said for any dogs lounging in your recovery area.

I needed people to talk to. People to bounce my ideas off. People to make helpful suggestions. But all my people were unavailable. My first inclination was to whine. But who could I whine to? The dogs were no help. They whine when they want food or a trip outside. I was good for both.

Luckily—and there always seems to be a luckily—it took more than that to keep this girl down. After all, hadn't I had my heart broken, my savings eviscerated and my credit cards maxed out by the man I thought I loved? I had survived. I owed a lot of that to the much unloved Vera Van Alst. Of course, Vera's unavailability was the crux of the problem. I'd always had the unwavering support of my uncles. They'd helped me get back on my feet then, although they were too busy now. I'd had the best friends ever in Tiff and Lance. I'd been falling in love with Officer Smiley; there was nothing he wouldn't do for me. Until everyone made themselves scarce. Of course, there was no point in comparing the state of my life one week earlier with now.

At least my fictional mentors Archie Goodwin and Nero Wolfe helped keep me afloat spiritually. I'd certainly gotten a sense of Wolfe lately: the massive ego, the great creative mind and the need to be physically pampered and to have his staff at his beck and call. Not perhaps the right role model for my circumstances, except in one way. Wolfe never left the house. Okay, only under the direst circumstances. He used his big brain to make connections, to examine facts, to assess suspects, to see patterns and determine motives. He knew how to get people to come to him and sit in a nervous circle in front of him in his office. He could read people. He could exploit their greed, weaknesses and lies. He was audacious and fearless. He could stare down the forces of the law, if they got through the front door of the brownstone. He was a puppet master.

All right, so I wasn't a genius, but I had enough smarts to get myself through college and much of it on scholarship. I might not always have the best judgment when it came to other people, but I could see patterns. I was observant and I could read people. Perhaps I could play Pied Piper and get people to come to me. I was at least charming, something that Nero Wolfe couldn't put on his résumé.

Wolfe had even more going for him: He had the great Archie Goodwin, as well as the lesser lights Saul Panzer, Fred Durkin, and Orrie Cather, on call as his operatives. He had people to investigate, to shadow and to watch from shadowy corners. He had Archie to keep the cops from the door and to evict any unruly clients or witnesses. I might have been a bit light on allies, but as Archie's great admirer, I could try to approach things from his perspective.

I might have to be my own sidekick. I still

needed to find out who'd helped Muriel move.

I figured I'd gotten everything I could out of the Snows. And Audra didn't know much anyway.

So that left . . . I glanced at the dogs again. I couldn't think of a single way they could help, although they were a great comfort.

I was stuck. I wasn't quite making the cut as a mini-Wolfe or a female Archie. I was on my own, with not a single person I could count on. It was a lonely feeling. But it was time to pull myself together. Yes, I might have had lots of support in my life, but I could also stand on my own two feet and face life head on.

Or I could fall asleep.

WALTER NUDGED MY arm. Cobain did the same. They had their walk faces on.

All right. Not like I was getting anywhere on my own.

I glanced out the window, half hoping to see Uncle Kev climbing in. No such luck. You know you've hit rock bottom when you view Uncle Kev as a possible solution to anything.

The trees were swaying and leaves blowing wildly. It was getting nippier too. I bundled up in my red wool cape and put Walter's fleece-lined hoodie on him. Cobain's own coat of fur was thick and shaggy. He didn't need extra gear, but I tied a jaunty red scarf around his neck so we'd be matchy-matchy and he wouldn't feel at a fashion disadvantage next to Walter.

And we were off. I was still a bit lightheaded but the brisk autumn air helped to clear my thinking. The dogs were in heaven, stopping by every bush. This was about the pace I could handle. I had the phone with me, in case, but I wasn't expecting any problems.

We didn't go that far, a couple of blocks tops. As we began the bush-by-bush return to Michael Kelly's Fine Antiques, a funeral procession drove slowly down the street. I stopped respectfully, as I had been taught to do. There went someone who'd had worse problems than I had. The funeral procession consisted of only three cars, including the stately hearse. The person's problems had gone past being ill and dying. There weren't many to mourn. Naturally, my thoughts turned back to Vera. With the antipathy from the people in Harrison Falls, aside from me, my relatives and my friends (wherever they were) and Eddie and the signora, who would mourn her passing? Muriel? I thought not. In fact, I was still worried that if something happened to Vera, Muriel would be the cause.

It seemed unbearably sad to me. Was there nothing I could do? I shook myself. It's not like me to be morose. I needed a new plan. But what?

Perhaps Vera wasn't in any kind of real danger. Perhaps I could find another way to reason with her. Perhaps . . .

By the end of the walk, I was back to feeling lightheaded and even the dogs were happy to return to a warm house. But I still had no brilliant ideas on how to deal with Muriel. I had to do something and I couldn't bear being back in my bedroom for another minute. Wolfe liked to fiddle with paper on his desk. Why not?

I SAT DOWN at the kitchen table to make a few lists. I figured they'd help. When I was done, I had the following:

What I Know
Muriel is dangerous
Muriel has control over Vera
Muriel is cutting off Vera's support
    systems

I stared at the sheet.
I didn't really know these things. But I believed them. It wasn't at all the same thing. I went back to the list. I did know (and also believed) some other things. I added them.

Muriel's mother had been single for a
    long time before she married Pete
Muriel's early life was spent in poverty
Muriel had a hard time in school and in
    the community
Muriel's mother died of an illness

Muriel's stepfather was killed in a hit-and-run

I was injured in a hit-and-run

A green truck delivered Muriel to Van Alst House

Another truck with lettering on the side was spotted by a witness. Coincidence? Wrong color—but connected? Same company?

Muriel has a solid alibi for that time

Vera is worried about something

What I Think I Know

Muriel's mother had a long-term affair with Vera's father

Muriel is trying to take over Muriel's money, home and possessions

I was targeted because I'd been asking questions about Muriel

What I Don't Know

Why would Vera roll over and play dead?

Who drove the green truck that delivered Muriel's stuff to Vera's place?

Was it connected to the truck that hit me?

Who drove that truck?

Did Pete Delaney have life insurance? Who inherited from him?

Where has Muriel been in the years since she lived in Harrison Falls?

What exactly does she want from Vera?
Who let her know that I was asking
questions about her?

I supposed there was a lot more I didn't know
about this situation, but I didn't even know what
that might be. My uncles like to say, what you don't
know *can* hurt you. I decided that just because
my friends and family were AWOL, that didn't
mean I was helpless. There must be someone who
could help. I started another list:

Allies
Uncle Kev

Whoa. That was grim pickin's. Having Uncle Kev
as an ally is like playing catch with a grenade. Fun
while it lasted, and sometimes not even that long.

I added the signora to the list, because you never
know.

And then *Cherie????* She had a lot of question
marks, but she also had a lot of nerve. I wanted to
trust her fully, but I'd been burned recently. Kev
was the only one to vouch for her and that was
more of a recommendation from his libido.

Finally, I added Detective Jones. He hated Vera,
but he didn't hate me, although he seemed to find
me boring so I figured if I approached him with
any new info about my hit-and-run, he might help
a bit.

And that was it.

I sat morosely staring at my lists. The dogs lay at my feet. Walter snuffled in sympathy and Cobain moaned. I didn't take much comfort in it. This was not a time for moaning and snuffling. This was a time for doing. But doing what?

I considered making a list of lists, but soon discarded that idea for what it was: a bit of procrastination.

I went up and down my pathetic lists hunting for the best place to start. The truck seemed like the obvious place. What could I do?

Had Muriel moved from another location in Harrison Falls? I'd have to assume that until I had different intel. Not great, but the best I had to go on. Harrison Falls was a pretty small place. It wouldn't take forever to drive around snooping for a green pickup with lettering.

It wasn't like I had anything better to do.

I FOUND MY handbag, located my keys, fixed my face, fought my way into a pair of dark skinny jeans and a chunky cable-knit sweater and headed out for a drive. I took the dogs. I had to lean against the door for a minute until I got the dizzy thing under control before leaving, but that wasn't so bad. It felt good to go for a spin. I started from the farthest end of town and began a systematic slow check up and down each street. Luckily much of Harrison Falls is laid out in a grid pattern, but some of the more recent subdivisions have a lot of circles, crescents and dead ends. Never mind. I crawled along curbs, stared down driveways and speculated about what was in garages. It was one of the most unproductive evenings I'd ever spent.

Two dark, truck-free hours later, I was starting to get bored. The dogs, however, were still thrilled at the outing as evidenced by the stinky dog breath fog building up on the inside of my window.

"Time to go home," I said at last. I glanced at the gas gauge. Bad news. I was nearly out of fuel. The Saab had its charms, but good gas mileage wasn't among them. As we pulled into the first service station, I noticed three trucks at the pumps. Right. Chances were the movers' truck would need a top-up sooner than later.

There were a lot fewer gas stations than houses in Harrison Falls. And I was already sitting at one. I needed to dream up a story. It didn't take that long.

I headed in to pay.

The guy behind the counter gave the impression his life had been one long sad story that was getting sadder by the day. I hated to take advantage of him, but you know how it is.

"So," I said. "Don't suppose you'd happen to know a guy who drives a green truck with some kind of decal on the side."

He shrugged. "Lotta trucks come in here."

"I bet. These guys are movers. Like I said, had a logo or lettering on the side. Sound familiar?"

He shrugged again.

I began to spin a yarn in the hope it would lead somewhere. "Anyway, the guy driving it lost an envelope with some cash. Quite a bit. I could give it back to him and he could be grateful, if you know what I mean, or I could turn it over to the police."

He stared at me.

I stared back.

He said, "Or you could keep it."

"I could, but that would be, um, against my religion." For some reason, I wasn't actually struck by lightning.

This time he shrugged and stared. He had a talent for it. But I didn't think he had a matching talent for deception. I concluded that he didn't know anyone with a green truck well enough to angle for a cut of the reward.

Just to be on the safe side, I sat in the Saab in a slightly out-of-the-way spot and pretended to talk on my cell while watching the clerk. He didn't pick up a phone or do anything much at all. Probably still shrugging and staring.

Disappointing, in fact a total flop. Not, however, a fiasco.

I could see as I left that my routine needed work. I have never been afraid of work. And that gas station wasn't the only game in town.

I had no luck at all on the west side of Harrison Falls.

Three service stations later, I finally got a nibble. Archie would have been proud of me. The guy behind the counter had one of the last surviving mullets in the region. I tried not to stare at it. I met his slightly spacey blue eyes instead. I imagined that the particularly vague expression was not being faked but was the result of years of dedicated marijuana use. A decade of supersized fries probably accounted for his jowls and the strain on his Rush T-shirt.

"Hey man," he said. "Can I help you?"

"Yeah, um, man," I said, and launched into my found-money routine. It was pretty pat by now. Repetition can do that. "So," I said, finishing up, "if you know this guy, it would help."

"Uh, what guy?" Puzzlement settled on his pudgy features.

I resisted the urge to snap. I was, after all, lying my sore and damaged head off. It wasn't this guy's fault. "The movers with the green truck?"

"The green truck?"

"Yes. The guy with the green truck who dropped the envelope with the money in it. He was helping a woman move out to the Van Alst place the other day."

"Uh-huh."

I waited and then, when more was not forthcoming, added, "I would like to get the money

188

back to him. I do not want to contact the police as I don't consider them to be friends."

"You want to give it back?"

"Yes."

"And he doesn't want to take it?"

Maybe I'd been inhaling a bit of that ganja because like a fool I said, "Who?"

He stared at me, probably thinking I was the stupidest person he'd seen since whenever.

He said, "Can't help you. But I know some guys who have a truck and do a bit of moving as a sideline."

"Does their truck have writing on the side?"

"Well, yeah."

"And what does the writing say?"

"It's their landscape business. It's just letters."

I knew that trucks with lettering on the side couldn't be scarce in our part of the world, but the moving connection was also interesting. It wasn't like I had anything else to go on. "Letters? That could be them. Could you give me a name? I'd recognize that, I think."

He said, "Frankie?"

"Frankie? Right. I think that might be his name."

"And he don't want this money back?"

"Oh, I am sure he does. I can't remember where, um, he lives."

He nodded. Sagely. He got that.

"Do you know?"

"Not exactly."

I blinked. "Not exactly?"

"Well, like, not the exact address or anything."

"Right. Um, well, what do you know about where he lives?"

"He don't have an exact address, I don't think."

"He's homeless?" That was bad for many reasons, none of them including compassion, as we *were* talking about the guy who hit me.

"Not exactly homeless."

"What then?" That came out a bit sharper than I'd intended.

The mullet guy looked kind of hurt.

"Sorry," I said. "I'm nervous knowing I have this money and all."

"You got it on you?"

"No, no," I said hurriedly. "It is in a very, very, very safe place until I find Frankie. Wherever he is. I am sure he'll be grateful to you for any help you give me."

Fear fluttered across his features. No question about it.

"Don't tell him I told you where he lives."

"But you didn't."

"Didn't what?"

"You"—I pointed at him to ensure he'd know who I was talking about—"didn't tell *me* where *he* lives because you *don't* know."

"Right, that's good then."

"You suggested that Frankie didn't have an address."

190

"Yeah, yeah. That's right. That's good."

So far it sounded like Frankie was dangerous enough.

I decided to try a Wolfe-like trick: "You suggested that I could find him if I went to—"

"I never mentioned Sullivan's." His hand shot to his mouth, but too late to stop the words.

"Who's Sullivan?"

"I can't tell you."

"Why not?"

"Man, Frankie and Junior won't like that if I talked about them. They'd . . ." His voice trailed off. His hand shook a bit.

Frankie and Junior. Two dangerous dudes. Now we were getting places.

"Sorry," I said, "I couldn't hear you. And if I did, I wouldn't remember."

He stared. I guess that was too subtle. "Remember what?"

"Hey," I said. "Let's pretend we never had this conversation."

He nodded, loving that idea.

"I'll never mention it unless you talk to Frankie about me."

"I wouldn't do that," he sputtered.

"How do I know that?"

"Because I wouldn't know what to say about you. You're acting kind of weird."

"Head injury. Just forget you ever saw me or I'll tell Frankie you told me where to find him."

He shook his head hard enough that it must have messed with his brain. I fished in my bag and pulled out a twenty. I handed it to him. "Is this for gas?" he said.

"I didn't get any gas. I don't even have a car. It's for you. Keep quiet about what we talked about."

"Is there really an envelope full of money?"

"What do you think?"

"I think I screwed up again. I'm always falling for stuff."

"Well, your secret's safe with me. I don't even know your name."

"It's Steve," he said. "And you're not the only one who doesn't tell the truth."

I figured that if she hadn't died of a broken heart, Steve's mother probably worried herself sick over him. A couple of twenties and a Klondike bar and this guy would be under your control.

"What do you mean?" I said.

"About what?" Steve said.

"Not being the only one who didn't tell the truth."

"You said there was a lot of money and then you admitted there wasn't."

"Agreed. But what didn't you tell the truth about?"

A sneaky look slid across his face. I fished out five dollars, held it out of his reach and said, "The truck." My heart sank. All this for nothing? "What about the truck?"

"It's not green."

"It's not green? The green truck isn't green?"

"The truck that went with that woman to the Van Alst place wasn't green."

"What color was it?"

"Red."

I shivered. "How do you know it was the same truck I'm talking about?"

"Because they told me they were moving someone to the old Van Alst place and there was this big scary lady waiting for them in her Grand Prix and yelling orders at them while they were filling up their truck, like she owned them. She gave me the evil eye too. I was just minding my own business here at the cash. She gave me the creeps."

I saw then that I'd been asking the wrong questions. And been given the wrong information. There was only one truck and it was red.

"And Frankie and Junior were in the truck?"

"I'm not telling you that. Do I look crazy? Keep your money. It's not worth it. Can you go now?"

"But I'll find them at Sullivan's?"

He went white before my eyes. Even his mullet seemed to lose its color. "I never sent you!"

"And we never had this talk," I said.

He agreed.

I left the service station and headed in the opposite direction to where the Saab was tucked out of sight. Fear makes people do funny things and I didn't want to take a chance that Steve wouldn't call Frankie or Sullivan, whoever he was, and tell them I was asking questions about an envelope full of money that had fallen out of a truck accompanying a big scary lady on the way to Van Alst House.

I walked around the block and headed back to the car, keeping well out of sight of the service station.

A red truck. Something new to think about, if Steve was actually telling the truth. But how could Kev have been wrong about the color?

SO, SULLIVAN. WHO was that? The second guy in the truck? Or was that Junior? Were Frankie and Junior couch surfing at this Sullivan's place?

I figured it wouldn't take too long to find a guy named Sullivan in a place the size of Harrison Falls. I headed home to my computer. My head was spinning slightly and the last thing I wanted to do was to crash the Saab. Didn't want to run over anyone either. I'd been on the receiving end of that. No need for anyone else to suffer.

AFTER WALKING THE dogs and feeding them, I had a solitary dinner of the signora's food. The kitchen was empty and echoing without my uncles. The dogs helped but they weren't that good at small talk. Time to get to work.

It sounded like Frankie was the owner of the red truck, if indeed it was a red truck. Judging by my gas guy's reaction, Frankie was not to be trifled with. So time to find this Sullivan. There were ninety-seven listings for Sullivan in the Harrison Falls area on 411. There was no Frank, Frankie or Francis. No Junior either, and I assumed Junior's given name would be Francis too. I spent a bit of time at the kitchen table combining Sullivans. It was still a long list and no guarantees. I left aside the Sullivans in Harrison Falls East and Harrison Falls South. I'd try them if I had to. But as I was in Archie Goodwin mode, I settled in to do the grunt work.

It wasn't eight thirty yet. Most people with day jobs would be home from work, finished with dinner and errands and not yet hitting prime-time television.

"Hi there, trying to reach Frankie. He there by any chance?"

"Wrong number."

"Hello, looking for Frankie. Is he at your place?"

"Frankie who?"

"Oh hello. Did Frankie drop in tonight? I need to speak to him."

Click.

This went on. By the thirty-fourth call I was getting discouraged. I reminded myself I didn't have anything better to do and anyway, this was the easiest form of detecting there was. Archie would never have given up and he would have made little witticisms after every call.

Of course, there was always the chance that Frankie had been alerted that a strange woman was trying to reach him, but I decided not to worry about that. There was no way he could have figured out who I was as I made the calls from this burner. I sighed. For all I knew, Frankie was on his fourth boilermaker at the local bar.

Wait a minute. The local bar? There was something familiar about that.

I would have smacked myself on the head, but that would have been a bad idea. I did go back to 411 and checked out "Sullivan" under businesses.

Sullivan's Bar and Grill.

Bingo.

Jackpot.

And all that.

I'd never get that hour of calling back, but now I had something to get my teeth into. If I remembered correctly, Sullivan's was a rough-and-ready joint in the same area of town as Willows Road.

What now?

I didn't want to go walking in there asking for Frankie. The situation obviously called for a ruse. But ruses usually require a confederate and mine were, as previously mentioned more than once, MIA. Except of course for the most unpredictable one.

Kev.

But Kev was trapped at Van Alst House. That left nobody.

I stared at Walter and Cobain. They could be recruited for undercover work and had been, but somehow I didn't think they'd make the cut for the trip to Sullivan's Bar and Grill. The cats were beautiful, but useless in a ploy, unless your name was Kevin Kelly, but that's an old story. Let's not go there now.

What would Archie do?

Archie might make a deal with a little number. I had an idea who that little number could be. Minutes later I had a deal that Archie might be jealous of. The only problem was I needed to wait until the next day for the dame to be available.

Maybe that was just as well, as my head was throbbing and my knees were wobbly again. My girlhood bedroom and all those ponies beckoned.

"WHAT?"

A garbled blithering emerged from the phone. The blithering was compounded by being whispered. It might have been funny except for the only word I could make out: "kill."

I tried to break in: "Eagle, I can't hear you. You are whispering and I can't understand."

The blithering took on a higher tone, still unintelligible.

"Please don't panic, um, Eagle. Take a deep breath and tell me what is going on."

"Kill them."

Okay, two words now, but I was no further ahead. As they say, consider the source. The source was Uncle Kev so it could have been nothing at all. Or, given the circumstances, it could have been big news. "Kill them" sounded more like big news.

"Kill who?"

"I can't talk."

Now that was clear. "Don't leave me hanging. Kill who?"

"I'm coming over."

"What? It's two in the morning!"

"Life or death. Wait for me."

"Tell me what's going on. Should I call the police?"

"No police. Don't open the door to anyone else but me, Bo Peep."

"But—"

"Shh."

"Is Vera all right?"

But of course, he was gone. Fine. He always did have a knack for keeping people on their toes.

I couldn't concentrate much for the next hour or so. I jumped at every noise. None of the noises were Kev. I had fallen asleep on Uncle Lucky's sofa surrounded by dogs when Kev hammered on the door. The dogs set up a ruckus as I opened it and he tumbled in, dropping a squirming object in a large gray blanket.

I stared. "What is—? Oh no, Kev. What are you thinking?"

Two Siamese hunkered down in terror. One yowled. The other raked my ankles.

Walter and Cobain were silent for a shocked second. That was all it took. The next second the air was full of shrieks and barks and, yes, snuffles.

When I managed to corral the dogs and check Cobain's bleeding nose, Uncle Kev was on the floor trying to entice the cats to emerge from under the sofa. A sharp-clawed paw emerged and Bad Cat gave Uncle Kev something to remember him by.

I barely managed to say that he had it coming and by the way, had he lost what little mind he possessed?

"What is going on? Make it good."

"She was going to kill them. I told you." Kev staggered to his feet. I closeted the dogs in the antique shop and returned with a roll of paper towels. I handed Kev a sheet of paper towel to staunch the bleeding. From behind the shop door the dogs set up a chorus of complaints.

"Who was—Oh. Muriel? She was going to kill the cats? Really?" Now why was that so hard to believe? I had no trouble suspecting her of doing Vera out of her property and perhaps her life. I was certain that Muriel was behind her stepfather's killing and the hit-and-run attack on me. But who would hurt a cat? Would Muriel do that?

"Really. She was. She is. She was about to feed the kitties poison. I spotted her putting rat poison on their food when the signora wasn't watching and Vera wasn't around."

"No!"

"Yes."

"That would be a terrible way to go. Poor cats," I said. As my feet and ankles were safely off the floor and tucked up with the rest of me on the sofa, I could afford to attract their attention.

"No kidding."

"But they didn't eat it?"

"No. I phoned her cell phone number and she went to see who it was. I grabbed the cats and put them in the Caddy."

I should actually have figured that out by the scratches on Kev's hands.

"And how did you explain their disappearance?"

"I pretended that they had dashed by me and run away."

"As if they would do that!"

"They would if they were chasing those wild turkeys."

"Good Cat and Bad Cat are spoiled indoor pets. Those turkeys would eat them for breakfast."

"I don't think Muriel knows anything about cats. She believed me."

"She doesn't know much about turkeys either, I guess."

"What did you do with the poisoned food?"

"I dumped it in a bag and got rid of it."

"Where did you put it, Kev?" This would be one of those Kev loose ends that could cause grief down the road. "The dogs could eat it, if they come across it."

"It's not here, of course. What do you think I am?"

I didn't answer. No point in hurting his feelings. But I made a note to find out.

"And she didn't figure it out?"

He shook his head. "She thinks they ate it all."

"They never eat all their food."

"You know that. I know that. Vera knows that. But Muriel didn't. She hates the cats and she never goes near them."

"I guess that's a good thing."

"Won't she wonder why they didn't come back?"

"I offered to 'look for them' and she said not to worry about it. They'd return when they felt like it. She said that we shouldn't pamper them."

"Bit late for that," I muttered.

There was a yowl from under the sofa.

I added, "So she thinks they're out there, dying from the poison in the woods or something?"

Kev nodded. "Yeah."

"Vera is going to be devastated. Oh. Do you think that's why Muriel did it?"

"Poisoned the cats?"

"Yes, Kev. Poisoned the cats. That *is* the topic of our conversation."

"She might have done it for that reason. Vera loves them and it would hurt and distress her."

"Exactly, and Muriel would enjoy that or use it to her advantage. It would lower Vera's resistance even more."

"Or she might have done it because she got a scratch or two."

"I know how that feels."

Kev said, "Quite a few actually. From Bad Cat. Ankles."

"Well, Muriel brought it on herself. She moved into their home and upset their lives. Who can blame Bad Cat for scratching her?"

"Sure, but it could have gotten them killed. Maybe it still could." Kevin was still white-faced and almost trembling.

"She won't find them here tonight, Kev. I doubt if even Muriel would storm this place seeking revenge because you saved the cats' lives."

"Did you think she'd have you run down by a truck?"

Sometimes Kev hits the nail on the head. I said, "You're right. We have to make sure that she doesn't know they're here. Or alive at all. We'll find a better place for them in the morning. You should make sure that she doesn't catch sight of your sweater. It's covered with cat hair."

"Oh yeah, I couldn't avoid it. Even though I was saving their lives, they put up a lot of resistance."

"No need to tell me about it. I know what they're

like. And as for the scratches on your hands and arms, how will you explain those?"

"I'll think of something. Maybe I can say I was stung by bees."

"It is getting close to the end of November, Kev."

His face brightened. "I know. I'll say I was checking for the kitties in the yew hedge at the back of the property and I got scratched by the needles."

"That could work. If you don't complicate the story too much. Remember the rules for lying."

Kev went back to his hurt expression again. "I'll put some bandages on and tell them that story before anyone asks about the scratches and I'll ask Fiammetta for some ointment or something. She'll have a cure."

"Right. Probably something involving food and possibly alcohol. Not that there's anything wrong with that."

"Better idea!" Kev jumped to his feet.

I waited, and finally said, "What is it then, Kev, this better idea?"

"Turkeys! They're vicious. Muriel is afraid of them. She'll fall for it hook, line and sinker."

People falling for things hook, line and sinker is a favorite thing in our family.

"Why not," I said. "No worse than any of the other ideas. I'll get you some bandages. Because anyone with a brain in their head would not think these were turkey scratches."

When I returned with five bandages for Kev's hands and arms, he slipped into a morose mood. "The signora is really upset about the kitties. Maybe I should tell her the truth."

I bit my lip. I didn't want the signora to be unhappy, but if she thought the cats were alive she would never be able to contain her jubilation. I imagined her round little body spinning with joy. Muriel might catch on and Vera certainly would.

"That's kind, but a bad idea, Kev. You really should wait. It's awful, I know. But the signora's not the best one to keep her feelings hidden. Then Vera would figure it out. Of course, that could be a good thing. If Vera knew this, maybe she'd turf Muriel out of the house and we could all go back to normal." I thought about it. "On the other hand, we don't really know what hold Muriel has over Vera. Shouldn't take a chance."

"This is a nightmare," Kev said. "But at least you can keep them safe here until this is over."

"What? The cats can't stay here after tonight. Are you serious?"

"Where else could they stay?"

"Well, it can't be here. You saw how the dogs reacted."

"Lots of dogs are friends with cats. These guys have visited Van Alst House. They should be used to the idea of the kitties."

I was tired of biting my lip. I rubbed my temple.

"That isn't likely to happen in this case. Either a cat will be hurt or a dog will be hurt."

"But," Kev said, "they can't go back home. Muriel's going to kill them." Or an uncle will be hurt.

"If she knows you know, then—"

"No, Jordan. If she knows I know, then she'll know I saved them and then I'll be gone and who will be there to keep an eye on Vera and the signora? They have to stay here."

"There must be more than two places for cats in this world," I said reasonably.

"Name them."

I thought fast. Normally, I'd rely on Lance and Tiff. But they were incommunicado. I briefly pictured them riding a unicorn together on a rainbow. Okay, maybe I'd spent a bit too much time in the pink pony room. Back to the cats. Even if Mick and Lucky were around, the dogs were already in their homes, so that wouldn't work. Karen no longer had her own place.

It was obvious that I needed some new friends. Or some old friends to step up.

Kev said, nervously, "Whatever you decide, they can't go to the pound."

"Never in a million years," I said. "There has to be a better way. Hey, what about Cherie? I'm seeing her later tomorrow, although I guess that means today. She's always up for a challenge and—"

"Um. She has met them and it did not go well."

"Right." Of course, it didn't. What was I thinking?

In the end, we agreed to confine the dogs to Uncle Mick's side of the building, where coincidentally, my room was. The cats had been enticed into Uncle Lucky's living room downstairs as well as his bedroom and bathroom upstairs. After five minutes, they were the newly established rulers of Lucky's kingdom.

I was back in the kitchen, having given over Lucky and Karen's comfy living room to the cats. I would have been happy to take Good Cat with me, but the dogs remembered Bad Cat and I didn't think that would lead to a happy ending. So I kept the door closed to the new cat area. Walter and Cobain were parked next to it, sniffing. Walter did an excited little dance, snuffling. I took that to mean: *Just let me at those cats! They'll make a good snack.* Cobain began to whine. I took that to mean: *It's the end of the world as we know it. The cats are massing and we are doomed.*

They had my sympathy. I felt like whining too.

Of course, it seemed almost cartoonish, this situation, but it wasn't. Muriel was evil enough to try to poison the cats for whatever reason. Maybe there was no reason at all, a cruel woman who enjoyed spreading misery. Born bad.

My fears for Vera grew.

• • •

I HUSTLED ABOUT getting food for a pair of pooches who had apparently not been fed for years, if their early-morning performance was anything to go by. If I hadn't given them a regular supply of food and treats, I might have fallen for it.

Meanwhile over in Cat City, the Siamese were getting restless. I wasn't sure if they were actually hungry, as they would consider it beneath them to reveal that. I did get the sense that they'd like to get over to the dog side of the dwelling and give Walter and Cobain a few things to think about. I needed to make sure that didn't happen. Once the dogs were falling into their dishes, I took the small container of special cat food that Kevin had left with me, found two small bowls and made my way to Uncle Lucky and Karen's quarters. I put my high boots on first and my leather gloves. If I'd owned a goalie's mask, I might have worn that too.

The dogs and I escaped the feeding of the felines without incident, except for a minor scratch on my forearm. I was sure it would heal in time. I got the heck out of there. Somehow my investigation into the shadowy drivers of the red (formerly green) truck seemed a lot less dangerous than hanging around my uncles' house while the cats prepared for war. You could almost hear the distant drums.

After the care and feeding of cute but needy animals, it was time to make some progress. I decided to head over to Maple Street to talk to Audra and the Snows. I chose not to let them know ahead of time, not wanting anything to impede that progress.

Mindy and Tom were home and seemed happy to see me, although Tom said he didn't think I should be out and about so soon.

Mindy said, "Shhh. The poor thing must be stir-crazy."

Tom redeemed himself by saying that Mindy had just finished baking a couple of apple pies. Of course, I'd been well aware of that from the moment I approached the front door. As breakfast had been fast and furious and not that great, pies sounded perfect.

"I like to have a few in the freezer for emergencies," she said. "Tomorrow, I'll make the pumpkin pies for Thanksgiving."

I beamed at her.

Tom said, "Mindy always likes to test the first pie to see if it's all right."

That sounded good to me. "Happy to help."

We resumed our places around the small pine table. As Mindy served up the pie (which smelled out of this world), she asked if I wanted ice cream with it.

You bet I did. *Try and match that, Archie Goodwin,* I thought.

Once all the pleasantries, concerns for my well-being and serving were taken care of, I said, "I'd like to talk to you about the truck that hit me."

They both nodded earnestly.

"Did you both see it?"

Mindy said, "Tom did. I was behind him but not quite out the door when it happened."

Tom said. "It was a blur but I saw it all right."

"Great. What color was it?"

Mindy rolled her eyes, for the first time on this visit.

Tom looked sheepish.

Mindy said, "You're asking the wrong person."

"But I thought you said you were still in the house?"

"I was. The color-blind person was outside."

Oh.

"Sorry," Tom said. "I only see shades."

I said, "But red and green, would they be quite different, um, shades?"

"Not really."

Mindy said, "It's quite common in men. Of course, they don't like to let on."

"All right, then, that's not too serious. Did you notice any writing on the side of the vehicle?"

"Everything happened so fast. I wasn't really paying attention to the truck. I was waving goodbye to you when all of a sudden it shot down the street, hit you and you went flying."

"Right into the leaves," Mindy said. "That's when I walked out the door."

"Okay."

Tom said, "I'm not much of a witness. I don't notice details."

"Would you recognize the driver?"

He shook his head. "Didn't even see anyone. The police asked the same thing. I feel really bad, like I'm letting you down."

"You are not letting me down. I really appreciate that you were there for me. You made sure I got help. And you raked your leaves like a good citizen and that saved my life. This apple pie's a lifesaver too, Mindy."

I figured Archie would have been proud of my schtick, although I have to admit, it was sincere.

I was sent off to talk to Audra with a pie for her family and one for me to take home. Tom came with me to Audra's and he waited while I tucked my apple pie in the Saab first. I figured he was making sure I didn't get zapped by any red or green trucks this time.

CHAPTER TEN

THINGS WEREN'T QUITE as serene in Audra's home. Even though it was only mid-morning, Audra's hair had escaped her ponytail and she had a collection of mismatched stains on her shirt. The children were peevish. Nap time perhaps.

"I won't take long," I said. "I can see that you're busy."

She smiled. "It's always busy."

"First, I wanted to apologize for misleading you."

She nodded. "I understand from Tom and Mindy that you were avoiding some dangerous people."

"Not well enough apparently," I said with a sheepish grin. "But I'd also like to ask a quick question: Do you remember the truck that hit me?"

She stared. "Yes."

I nodded encouragingly. "I'm looking for details. There was lettering, I believe. What did it say?"

She said, "Shouldn't you be, um, I don't know, letting it go?"

"I am trying to identify that truck because I think it's linked to two other incidents." Of course, I meant Muriel's arrival and her stepfather's death. That reminded me: I had forgotten to ask Mindy and Tom about Pete. I'd have to go back and have another slice of pie and information.

I smiled at Audra.

She didn't smile back. "I told the police everything."

"I appreciate that, and thank you for calling 911 and for calling my uncle for me."

"Anyone would do that."

"Maybe, but I'm still grateful."

She gazed at me with exasperation. "The police should take care of this. My husband has told me not to talk about it, in case we are vulnerable."

I was a little taken aback by her attitude. People are not usually exasperated with me. It gave me a sense of what it was like to be Uncle Kev.

She said, "I have children to think about."

"Oh. Sorry. Of course, you have to be careful. But as you've already told the police what you saw, it shouldn't endanger your adorable children if you describe the truck. I'm not going after those guys, you know."

Cross your fingers, Archie whispered.

I said, "I don't have much faith in the cops and I can't remember anything, so I also am pretty vulnerable. They know what I look like but I don't even know what color truck to avoid."

Heavy-handed, but it worked.

She nodded slowly. "It was red. I don't remember

what was written on it. And if you're going to ask me if I would recognize them, the answer's no."

"Them? There was more than one?"

"Please, I don't want to talk about it."

"No need, then. I'll take that as two men in a red truck."

Her eyes filled with tears. She clutched her green-eyed, curly-haired toddler in her arms.

Wow. She was really rattled. But I knew more now than when I came in. I gave her a break. "So you wouldn't recognize them because it all happened so fast."

She sagged in relief and nodded. I knew that was not true. But the time wasn't right to push it. I really didn't want this kind, lovely woman to be distressed. I had enough to go on at this point.

I headed back to the Snows'. I did check over my shoulder in case a truck was hurtling toward me, but the coast was clear. I picked up the pace anyway. I had a lot to do before we got to the bottom of this Muriel Delgado business. But I also had an idea to explore and I figured the Snows would be able to help.

"Sorry, Tom," I said when he opened the door, a quizzical half smile on his face. "I don't need to come in. I apologize, but I have another question. I forgot to ask you earlier."

He waved away my apology. "Perfectly under-standable under the circumstances."

Right. Whatever Kev had said those were. I

added, "And I forgot to ask you something." I pointed to my head, still covered with Mick's fedora. "A bit woozy from that truck incident."

"Of course."

"Did Pete Delaney have a life insurance policy?"

He stared at me, shaking his head in bewilderment. Mindy appeared behind him. I repeated my question.

Mindy didn't hesitate. "Of course, he did. It was a hefty one too. A million dollars. That was a lot of money in the midseventies. More than enough to take care of Carmen as long as she lived, even if she needed private nursing and expensive therapy."

"Of course, she didn't live long."

"No. She lasted just six months after Pete died. To tell the truth, I didn't expect her to survive as long as she did."

"She must have been devastated by his death."

Mindy said, "Devastated? No. Sad, yes. She missed him, of course. But she wasn't devastated over *his* death. Not like—"

Tom turned to glower at his wife. She lifted her shoulders. What else could she do?

"So she had been devastated over Leonard Van Alst's death."

I thought Tom's eyes were going to bug out of his head.

Mindy said, "Much more so. Come on, Tom. You know it was true. But she got over it in time, more or less, and married Pete."

"She really cared about Pete," Tom said with dignity.

"Yes. I think she did, but she was devastated by—"

I said, "I'm sorry to have asked these questions. I don't really want to cause trouble, but I need to get to the bottom of this. So, after Carmen died, did Muriel also inherit the house?"

"Yes. Muriel got everything, well, what there was. The house and whatever Pete left to Carmie and the insurance of course, all went to her. She sold up and left. She didn't even say good-bye to anyone. Mindy was good to Carmie. But Muriel didn't even take time to acknowledge that."

"You were good to her too." Mindy put her hand on Tom's arm.

"Poor girl," he said, and I knew he didn't mean Carmen. "But don't go getting ideas that Muriel did her mother any harm. She didn't. She adored her mother and she was pretty cut up about Carmen's death. That was sincere, at least."

I couldn't really imagine Muriel being cut up about anyone's death, but I was willing to accept that she cared for her mother. "And they never found out who hit Pete?"

"No, they didn't. But it wasn't Muriel, was it, Mindy?"

"It wasn't. Some people thought it might have been Muriel, but it turned out she had an airtight alibi." I could have sworn that Mindy was more than a bit disappointed in that airtight alibi.

"Oh. Interesting. And what was that alibi?"

"We never found out. There was never anything in the papers. We heard that she was with a credible witness. Tom knew someone on the Grandville police force and that's all he would tell us about the crime. But the investigators believed Muriel and the witness."

IT WAS AFTERNOON before Kev called, worrying about "the kitties." I had to reassure him before I could get the information I needed.

"Kev. The guys with the truck. You said there were a couple of guys." I whipped out my notebook on the off chance that Kev might come up with something useful.

"Just a couple of guys, Jordie."

"Close your eyes and think. Were they young?"

I imagined Kev closing his eyes and scrunching up his handsome face. "The young one was."

Of course, this wasn't going to be easy. "One was young?"

"Yes, Jordan. The young one."

I put down the notebook to massage my temple. "How young?"

Kev would be adding a shrug to the scrunching. "Twenties maybe."

"What was he wearing?"

"The usual."

I kept calm. "And that was?"

"Jeans, work boots, gray hoodie, over a T-shirt."

"Okay. Anything special about them?"

"No, just what you'd expect."

Be cool, I told myself. "And what would you expect?"

"Bit of mud on the boots, same with the jeans."

"Any logos?"

"Oh yeah. Metallica on the T-shirt. The hoodie was open. And he had a plaid jacket over it."

"Was the hood of the hoodie up?"

"No."

"Wonderful. And what color was his hair?"

"You know, that nothing color of brown." Kev's hands would be heading up to stroke his own splendid Kelly ginger hair.

"Light brown?"

"Yeah."

"Long? Short?"

"Almost not there."

"You mean bald?"

"The ways some of the young guys buzz their heads. His was due for a fresh buzz, but what was there was kind of brown."

I wrote down *kind of brown buzz.*

"Tall or short?"

"Depends on what you mean by tall or short."

Not to be hindered, I said, "Was he taller than you? Close your eyes and think about it."

"He was. I'm five ten, so maybe six feet."

"Now we're getting somewhere. Now, about the other guy."

"The other guy?"

I imagined Kev thinking hard with his eyes closed and his mouth open, looking quite deranged.

"Uh-huh. The older one. Listen to me," I said, to stop the next foolish question. "Let's talk about him."

"Okay, you don't have to be mean, Jordie."

"What was he wearing? Try to picture him."

"Let's see, he was wearing, jeans."

"And?"

"Work boots."

"Muddy?"

"Yeah they were, now that you mention it. The signora made them take off their boots when they got to the door. Vera didn't say anything, but they did what the signora asked. Muriel was really cheesed off about it."

"Good to know."

"The kid had on gray work socks and the older guy had red ones."

I was pretty sure the socks wouldn't help us much to identify the driver of the red truck and his helper, but I didn't want to make Kev nervous. He was bad enough when he wasn't. "Okay, and what else was the older guy wearing?"

"Plaid work jacket over a hoodie. T-shirt underneath."

"Same rock group?"

"Nah, this was an old band, Steve Miller."

"All right then. And how old do you think the older guy was?"

"Maybe fifties. I thought he might have been the dad."

"Hair?"

"Yes."

"Color? Style?"

"Hard to tell. He was wearing a baseball cap. Wait. It had a logo."

"Great. What logo?"

"Didn't mean anything to me. Some letters. *L-S-W* maybe. Or *S-W-L*. Or . . ."

"Keep imagining that and maybe the image will come back to you. So you couldn't see any hair?"

"A bit curling around his ears. He had curly hair. Gray. Look at that. I'm pretty good at identifying suspects."

"Amazing, Kev. Now was he tall?"

"No. He was shorter and stocky. Maybe five seven or eight. Muriel towered over him. He was built like a fire plug."

"Who was driving the truck?"

He'd be back to face scrunching. "You know what?"

I took a deep breath. "I don't know what, Kev."

"It was the young guy. He was driving."

"Very good. Now think about the truck."

"The green truck?"

I had a pretty good idea why Kev had had so much trouble in school. "Yes, the green truck."

"What about it?"

"What size was it?"

"It was a big pickup."

"Big how?"

"Big cab, would seat four, I guess."

"So it wasn't a cube truck?"

"No. It had a cab on it and a cover."

"Is that where the trunks and boxes were?"

"Yes."

"And was there lettering on it?"

"I think there was."

"We're getting somewhere. What did the lettering say?"

"Same as the hats."

I had already written down *L-S-W* and *S-W-L* in the hat description. I drew an arrow from that to the truck info.

"In my limited experience, I've found that movers usually have cube trucks or vans, not pickup trucks. Did they look like movers to you, Kev?"

"No."

"And try to remember the company name of the moving truck."

"I don't think it had one."

I didn't want to insist that it had, as it would just make Kev worse. "The initials, Kev. Try to remember what they were."

"Just a jumble, Jordie. Sorry. Can I open my eyes now?"

"Okay, Kev. Open your eyes and tell me one more thing."

"Sure, Jordie."

"Do you have any trouble telling red from green?"

"Well, I think everybody does."

I sighed. "No. Everybody doesn't. So is there a chance that the truck that delivered Muriel was actually red?"

I waited through the long pause before Kev said, "There might be a chance."

Better late than never. I said, "Okay, Kev. I'm looking for a red truck. And if you get a flash of any kind of memory about the letters on it, you have to let me know."

"I will. Absolutely. You know me, Jordie. You can always count on yer Uncle Kev."

Right.

IT WAS PAST five o'clock and Sullivan's was dark and gloomy. Although no one had been smoking there for years, the miasma of old cigarettes still clung to the walls and the worn seating. The tired-looking man behind the bar was polishing glasses. I didn't hold out much hope for the results from that particular cloth. He seemed to be keeping a sharp eye out on the place.

The clientele was mixed. I spotted hardly any

women. A couple of guys in suits sat at one of the wooden tables, heads bent almost together in intense, whispered conversation, but mostly there were working men. Farmers, construction guys, factory workers. I listened to the occasional bellow of laughter and slap on the back. With the exception of mine, most eyes focused on the massive flat screens mounted at each end of the bar. A faraway game of football was somehow fascinating.

There wasn't much to like or admire about the place, although I had spotted a fantastic vintage jukebox off to the side that I would have killed to own. However, I had to stay put and keep an eye out for the guys from the truck. I wore an army cap, baggy wool pants and a Penguins jersey. It was a sacrifice that I'd had to make. My pal Archie had to don disguises from time to time, like the time he dressed as a funeral director in *The Golden Spiders*. He kept his sense of humor and so would I. After all, I was as incognito as I could get and I hadn't had to dress as a funeral director. My job was to sit, watch and fade into the grimy woodwork.

Of course, no one was looking at me because any eyes that could still focus and were willing to stray from the blaring television screens were on my companion. Cherie was way beyond splendid in skinny jeans that had that sprayed-on look. They were tucked into a pair of over-the-knee black leather boots. Her blond hair was a wild tangle of curls, her eyeliner dramatic and black, her lips glossy and smiling. Her cleavage kept trying to escape from her sparkly top.

We found a spot in a corner where we each had a back to the wall and a good view of the bar. As mentioned, most of the customers were men, no big surprise. At the end of the bar, an older guy was slumped on his bar stool, his head resting on the surface, his glasses askew. Clusters of guys sat in groups of two, three or four. Voices were raised, laughter loud and maybe just a bit artificial. You could just about smell the testosterone. My friends didn't know what they were missing.

I did feel tension in the air. Perhaps the crowd was less relaxed than usual because of Cherie. That girl could shake a place up. On the other hand, I didn't know what usual was for Sullivan's and I was glad I didn't.

Cherie ordered us club sandwiches, fries and gravy and a pair of Coronas to wash them down with. My idea was that we would sit there in the hope that somehow we'd find out something about the people who'd been in the red truck. By osmosis maybe. We engaged in desultory conversation and did a pretty good job of feigning a total lack of interest in anyone on the premises. Our waitress plunked down the drinks with a sneer at Cherie and a nothing for me. My invisibility was working well.

Five minutes later, the clubs arrived. Of course, I was starving. However, I was also worried that a bite at Sullivan's might lead to food poisoning. But the fries were hand-cut, hot, fresh and just salty enough. The club had real chicken. The bacon and the lettuce were crisp. The toast was toasty. It was hard not to wolf it all down in four bites. I managed, but only barely. Cherie kept tossing her hair and ignoring the world. The world was not ignoring her, though.

From my invisible station, I scanned the crowd. No one there really fit the description that Kev had given me of the two men who'd delivered Muriel's belongings and who'd probably run me over.

After a half hour, it seemed like every man in the place had sauntered past, giving Cherie the eye. She managed to seem supremely unaware and at the same time utterly flirtatious. I wondered how she did that.

I was beginning to give up when Cherie beckoned to the waitress (who had taken quite a dislike to her) and ordered a caramel cheese-cake and a piece of lemon meringue pie without consulting me. I wasn't going to tangle with her about which one I'd get, but luckily both suit me. I got the pie as it turned out.

Cherie got the cheesecake, a dirty look from the waitress and a lot of lingering glances from the guys in the bar. We made short work of the desserts.

So far, except for the food, we'd come up empty.

"What are you so worried about?" she said as I fussed a bit in my seat in the corner booth.

"Well, it's not like we can keep coming back until they show up, is it?"

"Isn't it? Why not? We're just a couple of friendly girls who heard the food was good here."

"It is," I said.

"You betcha. Seconds?"

What would Archie do? He wouldn't worry about a silly thing like calories. Live while you can, I decided.

"Oh sure."

Periodically, the door would open and a cluster of new people would arrive or one of the existing groups would depart, stumbling, but always with a backward glance at Cherie.

Cherie signaled for the waitress and ordered the same thing again with another beer each. I figured we'd switch and compare the desserts. I didn't think I could manage the dessert and the drink, and the dessert won hands down. It wasn't the worst way to spend an hour, but I did feel that we had to come up with something concrete soon. Maybe Sullivan's was going to end up a waste of time. And time was in short supply if we were to help Vera before Muriel plundered her and Van Alst House. Of course, I also had the motive to get my job back. Although a bit more self-serving, it was still a reality for me.

My pants were feeling a bit snugger when I finished the second dessert. Cherie still looked the same size, which was amazing as she'd polished off her cheesecake and my beer.

"I can eat anything and not gain an ounce," she said.

"Wait until the signora gets her hooks into you," I commented.

"Looking forward to it. Here's a couple more. Get a look at them."

A man in his twenties had arrived, accompanied by a fiftyish fellow who must have been a relative. Perhaps it was his father, because there was a strong resemblance. Both of them were wearing baseball caps with the letters *FXR*. They both had mud on their work boots. Instead of a hoodie the younger guy wore a Carhartt jacket.

The younger guy bellied up to the bar and nodded to the bartender. He immediately produced their brew of choice. For sure, they were regulars. He carted the two large foaming glasses to the seat the older man had selected.

Cherie took this opportunity to stand up and stretch, a vision that would have to be seen to be believed. If there had been a testosterone-o-meter in this particular bar, it would have hit the top range. Cherie sauntered past the newcomers to ask the bartender a question about a certain cocktail. I thought I heard her mention Sex on the Beach, but I really hoped I had imagined that.

On the way back, the younger, taller man removed his hat, revealing a short buzz cut. We had scored. Our red truck guys were right in front of us. I headed out to the parking lot. I wasn't worried about anyone noticing me because Cherie was now checking out the jukebox. She had to bend over slightly to do that. I hoped there were no heart attacks following that.

Toward the back of the parking lot, I located a red pickup truck with the letters *FXR*. Right. Under that it said: "Landscaping and Snow Removal." Of course, that explained the mud on the boots.

The phone number was a help too. I wrote down the name, although I was unlikely to forget it, and added the phone number. There was a black tonneau cover on the bed of the truck, so you couldn't see the contents. I checked the front of the truck and sure enough found a mud-covered license plate and a dent on the right front side, where it would have struck me. It doesn't take much to make a dent these days. It wasn't the only dent by a long shot. I hoped these guys were better landscapers than drivers. All of a sudden, I shivered. Maybe I wasn't the only person they'd hit.

Next, I walked around to the back of the truck, where that license plate was also obscured by mud. Apparently that mud thing was a way of life for these two.

I looked around for something to wipe it off. No luck. But I really wanted to know that plate number, so I took off my jacket and used the lining to wipe the plate. I was glad I was wearing the hokey disguise, as I wouldn't likely have done that with one of my good jackets. I wrote down the number, shuddered and put the jacket back on. At least I had some information that might confirm our Muriel connection and something concrete for the police about my hit-and-run.

After Sullivan's and this mucky business, I looked forward to a nice shower and then a visit to the cop shop. Of course, my family might disown me for that, but I thought it needed doing.

A new addition preceded me through the door of Sullivan's. He looked slightly familiar, but I couldn't see his face and his overcoat was nice enough but not one I recognized. It did cross my mind that Sullivan's wasn't a classy-overcoat kind of joint. Plaid shirts, insulated vests, hunting jackets, yes. Cashmere overcoats, no. As I sidled past the bar, I kept my face turned away. I was able to watch a bit in the mirror as I headed back to my safe corner seat. I couldn't see the new arrival's face, but I did get a gander at his shoes. Glossy cordovan tasseled loafers. I may have actually gasped. I covered the gasp with a cough and one of those "Excuse me, it's just allergies" comments. No one paid attention. Not even Cherie.

She was still at the jukebox, this time asking for suggestions for the next tune. Someone shouted out "Stairway to Heaven." Cherie made that selection before sauntering back to join me.

"And?" she said.

"I got the plate number."

"That's wicked."

"And there's a dent in the front."

"Hey! Look at you go!"

"I'm betting it's the truck that hit me and as far as I can tell, these are the same guys that Uncle Kev described, the ones that delivered Muriel's stuff."

"It's all coming together." Cherie's giant baby blues sparkled. "Do you think we should do a citizen's arrest?"

"Nope. I think the police need to take care of it. But there may be a bit of a snag on the police side. Give me a minute, will you? And create a bit of a distraction. There's a cop at the bar and I don't want to run into him just yet."

"Why not?"

"Because he is going to want to know what we're doing here in the same bar as these suspects. At least I hope they're going to be suspects soon enough."

"It's a free country."

"No argument on the free country side, but I, as you know, am disguised to look not at all like myself. That will make him very suspicious."

She sniffed. "It's your party. We'll do things your way. One distraction coming up."

I left Cherie to do her magic and I headed back outside. I reached the Eagle on the cell.

"Bo Peep?" he said.

"I found the truck that hit me. I know where the driver is and where his buddy is too. I'll let you know how this next bit plays out before we find the right cop to talk to. In the meantime, see what you can find out about FXR, a landscaping firm. Where they're located for starters, plus anything about the people who own it."

"Wait a minute, Bo Peep! Where are you? Can I come? I'll be right there. Don't keep me away from this."

"Sorry. Bad reception here. Breaking up. Hello, hello, Eagle?" I hung up. As if I would invite Uncle Kev to this covert op.

I hustled back inside and stopped in my tracks. The two guys were gone. My face must have fallen.

"We've lost them," I said, slumping in my seat.

"You may have lost them, but I don't lose men," Cherie said. "Not ever, sweetness."

"Except this time," I said bitterly.

"Stop fussing. They've just gone to the gents', not that anyone's a gentleman here. They'll be back. And guess what I have?"

"I don't know."

She slapped a business card on the table.

FXR LANDSCAPING
Frank Riley, Owner

I felt my excitement mounting. We had a phone number now, and better yet, on the bottom was handwritten in messy uneven uppercase: *CALL ME. FRANKIE.*

I had to hand it to Cherie. She was irresistible. She wanted to talk about Uncle Kev.

"That Kevin," she said fondly. "He's special, isn't he?"

"He is that, all right." I had a feeling that we each meant something different by "special."

She leaned forward, revealing spectacular cleavage. Her large baby blues were shining. "I never met anyone quite like him."

"Oh, I can believe that."

"He has so much energy."

Hmm. I didn't have the heart to tell her that Kev's supercharged energy levels, comparable to a six-pack of Red Bull, could wear on you, and I didn't intend to let him derail this mission.

Part of me thought, why not let them have their moment? After all, Cherie was like a secret weapon. But the thing was—and you can call me manipulative—I needed her on my side as everyone else in my life had gone AWOL. Without her and unpredictable Kev in limited doses, I'd be pretty much alone to solve the riddle of whatever was going on with Vera and Muriel. And of course, I was alone with a pair of dogs and two highly unpredictable Siamese and uncles that came and went like will-o'-the-wisps. That thought gave me a little shock. I wasn't used to being in charge of all those animals on my own without so much as a wandering uncle. I glanced at my vintage Bulova.

I was pretty sure that the dogs would have their legs crossed and the cats might shred Uncle Lucky's new sofa if I didn't get back soon.

"I think it's going to lead somewhere," Cherie said.

"Which one is Frankie?"

"The old one. I'd say he's the dad. They both have the same little piggy eyes. Did you notice?"

"I did. And what's the son's name?"

"Junior."

"That's excellent. We need to learn more about this Frankie and Junior, especially their connection with Muriel."

Her eyes sparkled. "That Kevin. He's very sweet."

"Oh right." Special I could understand, but sweet? But again, not up to me. She'd find out in time. In the meantime, we needed info.

"And Frankie?"

To my relief, Frankie staggered back out from the men's room, adjusting his very large jeans as he walked. The younger man swaggered behind him.

"Can't you just let the police know the license

232

number? They can check the vehicle and see if there's evidence that links it to you."

By now, I'd had enough of a look to be certain that the police officer at the bar was who I thought he was.

"I'd feel a bit better about that if I didn't see the lead detective in the case sitting right over there at the bar."

"What?"

"That guy at the bar. That's Detective Jack Jones. The local guy in charge of the investigation into my hit-and-run."

"What's he doing here?"

At that moment, Jones got off his bar stool and sauntered across the room, pausing to exchange a few pleasantries with Frankie and Junior. "Good question."

Cherie said, "Do you think he's investigating our landscapers? Perhaps he's on to them."

"Maybe. He seems awfully friendly with them, don't you think?"

"He does, now that you mention it. He's sitting down. Look at that. They're buying him a drink. Could it be a setup?"

"I don't like this at all. Harrison Falls is a fairly small community. It wouldn't be surprising if Detective Jones knew Frank Riley at least. They look about the same age, midfifties. Maybe they went to school together or something or played some kind of sports."

"So you'd better get your ducks in a row before you go to him with your suspicions."

I nodded. "Absolutely. I'll need some kind of proof before I do, and I'm beginning to conclude that Detective Jones isn't the person to present that proof to."

"Who would be?"

Tyler Dekker would have been nice, but he was out of reach. "I don't know yet. And I think I'd better find out."

"What do we need to do next?"

"We need to find out more about them. We need to know if they have police records. If there's a connection between them and Muriel, or between them and Vera. Or all of the above."

"I could try a date with Frankie."

I bit my lip. "I don't know. These guys are really dangerous. I wouldn't want you out on a limb."

She laughed. A long, low throaty laugh that attracted quite a bit of male attention everywhere in the bar. I slumped down in my chair to make sure none of that attention came to me. Cherie had no known connection with Vera, Muriel or anyone else in our current drama. I did. And Detective Jones could easily recognize me if he took a good look. But it was fine. No one in Sullivan's showed the slightest interest in *me*.

"The date could be somewhere fairly public."

"And if he's not happy with the outcome of it?"

"He won't find me."

"But he'll have your name."

"You don't actually think he'll have my real name, do you, sweetness?"

"Even so. We have to figure out what you'd learn from him that would make it worth the risk."

"Risk? I don't think there'd be much risk for me."

"You are talking to a person who never even met him, let alone tried to 'manage' him, and then ended up facedown in a pile of leaves before being hauled off to Emergency."

"But you weren't expecting trouble."

"Apparently I was asking for it, though. And you would be too. Don't take a chance. We'll think of something else."

"Like what?"

By now, Jones's and the two landscapers' drinks had arrived. The hilarity level at the table had gone up. Lots of backslapping. Way too much. Although this gave me a sinking feeling, I was glad I had seen him. Otherwise I would have gone straight to him with what little I'd learned about them.

Cherie tilted her head and regarded our suspicious backslappers."We need to learn more about them."

"I already put Kev on it." Of course, I wasn't too hopeful that would get us anywhere. So many tasks with Kev end up with zero results.

"That's awesome. And I can also check them out online and see what I learn."

"Sure thing. Then if we need to, and I hope we won't, you can call him and we'll set something in motion. Maybe if we could get a photo of them."

"We can do that now."

"What? Don't—" But of course, it was too late. Cherie was heading back to the jukebox, iPhone in hand. She made quite a show out of getting a selfie with the jukebox. Then followed it by a pout. She sashayed over to the drooling Frankie and his son and a bemused-looking Detective Jones. I heard her ask if Frankie could take a picture of her.

"I love this old jukebox," she gushed. "Love it to bits. Do you mind, darlin'?"

Frankie didn't mind as it turned out. Cherie's poses were provocative to say the least. I had to smother a grin as every eye in the place was on her. "Why don't you get in the picture too?" she cooed. "You're doing all the work."

Detective Jones took advantage of the interruption to slip from the bar and vanish through the front door. In the meantime, Frankie practically tripped over his own feet getting up there. "And Junior too. Do you mind taking a couple of shots of us?" she asked the server.

It was quite obvious that the server really did mind. But there wasn't much she could do. Once she handed the phone back to Cherie, insult was added to injury as Cherie checked out the results, frowning prettily. Eventually, she pronounced herself satisfied and swayed back to rejoin me.

"Got 'em," she said.

"Can you send them to me? I'll print them out and show them to the witnesses. I hope they don't find you too distracting," I said with a grin. "I'm heading out now, so I need you to create another of your little diversions until I get in the car. I'll wait for you. I'll get a shot of the truck too. Not sure why I didn't before."

Once again, Cherie was the perfect accomplice. I slipped through the door like a noodle down a hungry throat. My heart almost stopped as Detective Jones stubbed out a cigarette and headed back in. I scuttled past him, head down, hoping he wouldn't see my face and make a connection with the hit-and-run victim he'd interviewed.

I kept looking over my shoulder as I snapped the photos of the red truck. Why had I insisted on telling that cop about the other hit-and-run? If there was a connection between him and the Rileys and between the Rileys and the old hit-and-run, he'd know about that too. I shook my head. Junior wouldn't have even been born back then. But Jones and Frankie, they were tight.

I was chewing my lip five minutes later when the door to the bar opened. Cherie turned around and waved back to someone, then hurried over to my car.

"Did you get it?"

"Yup. Lots of them." I patted my phone.

I gunned it and we spun out of the parking lot.

"He's still sitting there with them. Every time I went over, the conversation stopped. I thought I heard your name, though. Couldn't be positive. Does he know where you're staying?"

"The cop? Sure he does. He interviewed me at Uncle Mick's."

"Perhaps you'd better stay somewhere else."

"Where? I can't go to Vera's. I can't go anywhere, really. He's a cop. If I check into a hotel he'd be able to find that out."

"Stay with me. None of these people know my name or where I live."

"You're pretty identifiable. They could find you."

"Trust me. They couldn't find their noses on their faces."

"I guess we should keep moving before it's too late," I said.

"Don't forget my offer," Cherie said.

My head was beginning to swim. I asked myself how well I really knew Cherie. After all, she just showed up out of nowhere and now she was like family. I'd been had before by sudden intense friends. Could I trust her?

On the other hand, she had helped out hugely. I was probably just being paranoid. But as we say in our family, just because you're paranoid doesn't mean they're not out to get you.

I said, "Tonight I'm going to sleep in my own bed. Uncle Mick and Uncle Lucky will be back. I just need to relax. I'm safe there. Once you and Kev find out more about these guys, we'll figure out what action to take. I mean, if they turn out to be criminals with a mean streak, we'll factor that in."

"Killjoy," Cherie said.

CHAPTER ELEVEN

F ROM THE TIME I got home, walked the dogs, dodged the cats and climbed into bed, maybe twenty minutes elapsed. I didn't even read the first page of *Champagne for One* before conking out. I did have a fleeting thought that "champagne for one" sort of described me in my abandoned state.

The next thing, it was daylight and who knew what Archie Goodwin had gotten up to in that book. I crawled out of bed feeling like I had been hit by a truck. Oh right. I had been.

Two dogs looked at me with great interest. Was I thinking about food?

But before there was any food, we had pressing business to attend to. I slipped my jacket on over my pink plaid flannel pajamas and stuck my feet into the first pair of kicks I spotted and headed out with the dogs. The brisk fall air helped to clear my head. Perhaps I was starting to get back to normal. I didn't run into any neighbors, of course, because our part of the street is entirely made up of buildings owned by my uncles, including the flagship Michael Kelly's Fine Antiques. The other buildings, purchased through the miracle of shell companies, were either rentals or empty. The garages were particularly useful for the storage of the many unofficial Kelly vehicles. Mick and Lucky had recently acquired the former dress shop across the street. No one had mentioned what they'd acquired it for. I didn't ask. I didn't want to know. Whatever the purpose, it had a particularly vacant look today with the forlorn "FOR RENT" sign in the shop's front window. With the economy the way it was, there wasn't much hope that anyone would actually try to rent it.

Maybe someday, Karen would be able to get her mystery bookstore business up and running again. But Karen still had lingering memory and energy issues from the attack on her the previous spring. Plus she was now living happily ever after married to Lucky. It occurred to me that I might get my own little business going there. The location would be right. There was a space upstairs that might make a wonderfully chic loft apartment. It would be close to my uncles. I was sure that they would cut me a deal on the rent. This made an entertaining daydream any time I was walking the dogs, but I really wasn't ready to give up on my last job. Nor was I ready yet to toss Vera to the wolf that was Muriel Delgado and her vile Riley accomplices.

So, back to work.

First, I fed the dogs. Apparently they hadn't had a bite to eat in a couple of years. Then I took my chances to give some food to the cats.

Unfortunately, we had run out of their food. How had that happened? You can't really count on Uncle Kev for anything and so, naturally, he had rescued the cats, but hadn't brought enough of the food they really liked. Not, as you might expect, caviar or peeled shrimp or catnip-infused tuna, but Blue Wilderness brand, specifically duck flavor. Oh, *pardonnez-moi*. Decadent and not easily found, I grumped. They had started looking at me like I'd make a nice tasty snack.

I did think they might carry Blue Wilderness at the Poocherie in their Famous Felines section. Of course, the shops weren't open yet to check. I tried everything I could think of. They turned down my offering of other treats. Finally, I had a vague memory of Uncle Kev once enticing them with Cheez-Its. Naturally, there were Cheez-Its in Uncle Mick's cupboard. I listened to their complaints and tried to explain that (a) I would pick up more Blue Wilderness and (b) it shouldn't be long before they were back to being kings of the castle at Van Alst House and (c) I really hoped Cheez-Its weren't bad for them, even if they had survived when Uncle Kev had offered them.

I don't know much about cats or their diets and after all it was the kind of household where Cheez-Its could make a human meal and I'd be most likely having sugary cereal myself.

I tossed the Cheez-Its toward them and was surprised to see them pounce.

"I hope you enjoy them, at least. Sorry they're not served in a crystal bowl."

It sounded like they said "yada yada" in response to my comment. But that might have been my imagination.

"I know you're missing company," I said, extending my hand, intending to stroke Good Cat. Good Cat likes a bit of human contact. Everyone knows Bad Cat doesn't care for people except for Vera, so I quickly withdrew to get yet another bandage and a bit of antiseptic. He has quite the reach.

As I settled in to my own breakfast—the last of the Sugar Frosted Flakes combined with the dregs of the Count Chocula added up to one bowl. I wondered what they were having at Van Alst House. A mountain of pancakes with high-grade maple syrup? Fluffy scrambled eggs with chives and a towering plate of hot buttered toast? A Dutch baby with fruit and whipped cream? It didn't bear thinking about, but it did increase my resolve.

As I had all that increased resolve, it was time to get going. I wasn't the only one getting going. Although there was no word from Uncle Kev (maybe he knew I'd be upset about the cat food situation), Cherie had been busy. She'd sent me the series of photos of the Rileys, smiling like fools. In the pix where Cherie had also appeared, she seemed to have Photoshopped herself out of the picture.

Good thinking.

One of the photos had the Rileys appearing to be reasonably somber. Their pudgy faces in repose still managed to look dangerous. I printed five copies of that one as well as the silly smiling versions. This was a big step forward. I hurried upstairs to get dressed for the day. The dizziness I'd been experiencing since I'd been hit seemed to be gone. I was feeling good again. In fact, I was in Archie Goodwin mode. He'd be on the case if he were me. He wouldn't be sitting around feeling sorry for himself and reading mysteries, not that I had been. Okay, maybe a bit. He'd keep hitting the streets to see what he could find. And he would look damn stylish doing it. I would stick to the basics, black turtleneck and tight well-worn jeans, my plaid coat and oversize deep orange purse.

I needed two things besides cat food: First, I wanted more dope about the Rileys. Second, but more important, it was past time to find what linked Vera and Muriel. Archie wouldn't let a single encounter with another human being pass without getting some information and neither should I.

So who would know something about Vera and Muriel in high school? Their friends, of course, but who had they been? With the exception of Eddie, I'd never heard Vera mention even one friend from her past. In fact, she never mentioned Eddie either. He was the one maintaining that one-sided friendship. Certainly, she had no friends outside of me and my family and the signora in Harrison Falls.

Mindy and Tom were the people I'd found who were closest to Muriel. That wasn't very close. They had told me about the hit-and-run death of the stepfather, Pete Delaney. I was grateful, but at an impasse.

Vera was fifty-five. Muriel about the same, I figured. I could talk to people that age and see what turned up. I knew from conversations with Vera that she had gone to private school in Switzerland but had returned to graduate from high school in Harrison Falls. That must have been a rough ride, I'd thought at the time. I figured the time frame was when the Van Alst Factory was failing at the hands of Leonard Van Alst. Vera had adored her father, but the rest of the world seemed to think he'd been a fool when it came to running a business. Now that I knew he'd also had a mistress on the side and that mistress was Muriel's mother, the plot was thick all right.

So they both had gone to school in Harrison Falls, even if Vera had only been there briefly. I'd have to talk to people in that age group. How hard could that be? As I've mentioned, Harrison Falls is a small place and people have long and bitter memories.

I paused and my eyes opened. Detective Jack Jones. He was also in his midfifties, unless I missed my guess. I'd figured back in the bar that might explain his chumminess with the Rileys, as Frank had probably been at school with him.

What to do next?

Of course. Archie would go find a teacher. He'd charm that teacher (almost certainly a woman) until she was ready to tell him anything.

I would have to do the same. Naturally, anyone who'd been a teacher when Vera and Muriel were in attendance would be long retired. Maybe even long, long retired. But how to find out who?

Was it merely a coincidence that Walter picked that moment to nudge my leg and look at me with googly eyes?

"What?" I said.

Walter did a little dance.

"It's not like you would know any retired teachers, Walter. So are you just angling for a T-R-E-A-T? You haven't had one since we walked down Main Street."

Walter looked so disappointed that it was all I could do not to laugh. "Who do you know, Walter? You say you're friends with anyone who has food, like Lainie and Phyllis? Oh, Phyllis was a teacher. Nice one, Walter." Walter just kept dancing; it was almost like he really knew what I was talking about. Cobain looked on from his position on my bed, hope gleaming in his liquid brown eyes. "Okay, fellas. Let's go downtown. And no drama when I pick up cat food."

Both dogs were ready. Cobain lumbered to his feet and both of them stood wagging at the door, promising to be good, until I hooked up their leashes.

First, we strolled over to Bridge Street to the Poocherie to fulfill my promise to the cats, before I started my detecting duties. I was glad to see Jasmine and her pink-tipped hair and metallic smile this time. Walter and Cobain were thrilled to be there. The place was an olfactory paradise for them. While I was talking to Jasmine, I could hear Cobain's tail thumping. Walter's tail doesn't reach to the floor, but it was wagging. Hope springs eternal if you're a dog in a store full of treats.

"What happened to you?" Jasmine squeaked.

"What do you mean?"

"Your face."

"My face?" I didn't expect to be insulted and, while I may not be the reigning Miss Universe, as a rule people don't think there's much wrong with my face.

"Bruises."

"Oh. Right. I got hit by a truck. Did you hear about that on the news?"

"I never listen to the news. But bummer. Are you okay, Jordan? Except for your face, I mean."

I glanced around for a mirror, but as it was a pet store there weren't many, except for the one in the parrot's cage and I wasn't desperate enough to try that. I had to let the bruise comments go and seize the opportunity.

"Yes," I said. "Not that the cops have been any help."

"I'm not surprised," Jasmine said. "They just try to keep us down."

I chose not to explore where that might lead. Once I'd purchased a couple of bags of Blue Wilderness, I showed her the picture of the Rileys. "I think these are the guys who drove the truck that hit me. Do you know them?"

She stared at the printout and scratched her pink-tipped head. "Yeah, they do look familiar. I've seen them here on the street. Not long ago."

"Really? They drive a red truck with *FXR* on the side."

The door opened, the bell over it jingled and the store filled with chattering dog walkers. Jasmine glanced at them, just as the tail of an energetic golden retriever knocked over a display of cans. I'd lost her.

As she headed over to redo the display, I wrote down my cell number. "Please call me if you remember. Any time of day or night. I'd appreciate it. They're dangerous."

"Sure thing. Grab a couple of treats for your pooches."

I had to leave the dogs outside the Sweet Spot while I popped in. I told myself not to be over-whelmed by all the wonderful candy and chocolates and fudge. The owner's name was Rachel and she was far too polite to mention my bruises. I did tell her that I'd been hit by a truck and showed her the photos. She shook her head when I showed her the photos of the Rileys. Rachel was probably in her late thirties. She'd come to Harrison Falls with her husband. I figured she wouldn't know either Muriel or Vera. I did ask anyway.

"I wish I could help. We live over on the other side of Grandville. I don't know many people outside the shop. But Phyllis Zelman at the Food Drop knows everyone."

"We're on our way there next. I'd like to get some of that fudge. Might need to give someone a little gift."

Rachel wrapped up the fudge, walked to the shop door with me and produced a couple of dog treats from her pocket. "Good doggies, waiting so patiently outside."

"Oh, they've already had—oh well."

All I heard was a pair of gulps.

Next stop, the Food Drop.

There was no sign of Phyllis, but I walked through calling out her name. Walter galloped ahead and stood by a closed door and tried to wag himself airborne. Finally there was a rustling and what sounded like muffled swearing from a back room. I stuck my head in and spotted Phyllis wrestling with a large garbage bag filled with canned food.

Her round black-framed glasses had slipped down her nose and she uttered an expression not really suited to a retired teacher running a food bank.

That took me by surprise and I'm afraid that I laughed. I also offered to help.

"I wish people would use their brains," she said. "Boxes are a lot easier."

"Right." I helped her wrestle the bag of cans over to the nearest shelf.

"What happened to your face? And what does the other guy look like?"

I was getting used to questions about my bruises. If this was the price of information, so be it. I whipped out the photos of the Rileys. "They look like this."

Phyllis pursed her lips. "It figures."

"You knew them?"

"I knew the father. He was a hell-raiser in school."

"Did you teach him?"

"He didn't last that long. But he was always a bit of a thug. Had a few brushes with the law. Not a nice man, and as they say the apple doesn't fall far from the tree."

"I'm looking for information about either of them. I know they were driving a truck that hit me. That's why I have a bruised face and it's lucky for me that I'm not dead. The one witness is afraid to come forward."

"Yes. If they'd hit you with a truck, what else would they do? Be careful who you talk to about them in this town."

"But what can I do? I need to find out about them."

"You can offer to help me a bit more."

"Done. I only have a few minutes now, but I'll give you whatever time I have before Thanksgiving."

"Good. Now help me move those boxes. They weigh a ton. You'd think we could get a few men to help around here."

I had an idea that she'd driven some volunteers away, but thanks to Vera, I was used to ignoring the rudeness of grumpy people. It just rolled right off. You had to see the person underneath. In this case it was a grumpy person knocking herself out to provide food for people who needed help.

"Will do," I said, "But I do need a favor."

"Make it good. You're interrupting my work."

"It is important."

"Fine. Don't waste time. Out with it."

"I am looking for someone who might have been on the staff at Harrison Falls High School when Vera Van Alst went there." I had already decided that I wasn't going to toss Muriel's name around because I knew the hard way that could lead to trouble. Of course, I trusted Phyllis, but who knew who she'd talk to.

"Why? Is it about Frank Riley again?"

251

"No, it's someone else. It's . . . I need to find out something. It's important."

"Then why don't you just ask the Van Alst woman herself?"

This was my opportunity to say that I couldn't because I'd been fired, but I didn't think that would help my case. "It's a surprise." That was true. If I found out any useful information and used it to liberate the Van Alst legacy, that would be a very nice surprise.

"A surprise?"

"Yes." I put on my most honest look; after all, I am going straight. "Trust me. She'll be very happy."

"If you say so. I never taught her."

"Of course not. You're not old enough. I thought you might know some of the older teachers who were there back in the seventies."

"Are you trying to get on my good side? Because it will take a lot more than that." She pushed the round black-framed glasses back up her nose for the third time.

"I'm sorry. I . . ."

She glowered.

I finally got it. "You mean you *were* there?" Apparently, Phyllis was older than I thought. I'd put her in her late sixties and in good shape at that.

"Don't look so surprised. It was easier to get a job then. I was a young graduate and thought I'd give teaching a try. I started at Harrison Falls

High and I ended up retiring from there thirty-five years later."

"Wow. I mean, that's great."

"Not really. I didn't have the adventures I might have had if I'd gone further afield or continued my education."

"But you made a difference for a lot of kids."

"If you say so."

Oh boy. Vera liked to use the same expression. I gave my usual answer. "I do say so."

I thought I saw a small twitch at the corner of Phyllis's mouth. "So do you remember Vera as a student?"

She rolled her eyes. "What do you think?"

"Um, right. Hard to forget even then?"

"Oh, nothing like she is now, of course."

"Have you seen her recently?"

"No. We don't move in the same social circles."

"Well, Vera doesn't really move in any social circles. She stays home. She's stuck in that wheelchair and her interactions are either with the staff or with people selling or buying books."

"Sounds dreary."

"It works for her. It's kind of fascinating. I must say I like the book collecting world too. But anyway, you haven't been in touch for a long time."

"Can we hurry this up? I have a lot to do. Boxes to move and all that."

"I am helping you. Just let me make sure the

dogs don't escape. So, back to Vera, what do you remember about her?"

"Very intelligent and way ahead of the others academically. Socially? An awkward girl. They wasted their money on that Swiss finishing school if you ask me. She had trouble fitting in. Of course, people hated the family like poison."

"No big surprise. That must have been tough. Do you remember if she had a friend called Muriel? Muriel Delgado?"

Phyllis paused and put down the box she'd picked up and glared. I found myself rubbing my forehead as her eyes bored into my head. But I didn't want to give up. "Do you remember Muriel?"

"Another one that you couldn't forget if you tried."

That was still true. However, I wasn't sure that Muriel would have had a profile like the prow of a ship, eyes like a hawk and the power to intimidate back then. I doubted she'd swanned through high school in a swirl of black garments, sowing fear in her wake. "What do you remember about her?"

"Not that she was a friend of Vera's. That's for sure because—" She stopped abruptly and said, "That's really enough."

"Enough? Why enough? What bothered you about her?"

"It's none of your business, that's what. It was

all just rumors. I can't be bothered with rumors."

Phyllis always was one to play it straight. As much as I admired that about her, I found it inconvenient in this case.

"Did you actually teach Muriel?"

"I didn't. She was Murphy's cross to bear." She snapped her lips together in a straight line. Not a word would escape. She narrowed her eyes at me, knowing I'd caused that to slip out. *Murphy's cross to bear.*

I smiled.

"At any rate. Enough about all that. I'll see if I can drum up some more volunteers, but everyone I know seems to have pressing business elsewhere. I'll be at your disposal all day on Thanksgiving."

Her eyes were still narrowed. "Why are you standing at an angle?"

"Hmm?"

"You're . . ."

It was hard to hear her because my head was spinning. With a thump, I found myself sitting on the dusty floor. Phyllis was bending over me. Concern had replaced suspicion and disapproval.

"Not to worry," I said. "Like I said, I was hit by a truck and there are some, um, lingering after-effects. They've been telling me to take it easy, but I got horribly bored. And I was feeling pretty good."

"I understand that. I had the same reaction after my heart attack."

"Oh. Heart attack? I'm sorry. Should you be doing all this?" I didn't know much about heart attacks. Although most of my family should be prime candidates, to my knowledge there's no history of them in the Kellys. I'd always thought of heart attacks as being fatal. Apparently, Phyllis didn't share my view on this.

"I'm right as rain now. Quadruple bypass made all the difference. And may I remind you that I'm not the one who collapsed on the floor."

"Point taken," I said.

Walter licked my ears and Cobain laid his head in my lap. I found myself perking up immediately. I said, "That's quite something to recover from."

"It was a hurdle," she said.

"Did you have lots of help and support? Relatives nearby?"

"I have no relatives, but my friends were there for me."

Somehow I hadn't thought of Phyllis as a person with a lot of friends.

She must have read my mind. "The Retired Teachers' Club is a great source of friendship. Do you think I spent my time alone here because I don't have a friend in the world?"

"What? No. I just wondered. Maybe because my own support system seems to have evaporated. Not that I want to sound whiny. I had a dizzy spell. You had a quadruple bypass."

She snorted. "Well, my friends were great. We meet every Sunday for brunch at George's Diner. They'll be there now. I'm too busy this month, but I'll be back to it as soon as Thanksgiving's over. And most of them will help with the dinner, before, after or during."

That was excellent. I'd be on my way.

"Can I drive you home?" she said. Underneath the crisp and crusty manner, she was a softie who didn't want the world to know it.

"Thank you, but I really need the exercise to clear my head. And there are the dogs. I'm looking forward to Thanksgiving now. I wasn't before. I realize that I am lucky in so many ways."

I took my time walking home, with the detour to George's Diner. It was one of those old-fashioned types, with good predictable food and servers who have been there for thirty years and know your name. I have a soft spot for establishments with bright neon signs on the windows.

Dogs weren't allowed in, of course, so I hitched my two to the bench right outside and told them to behave.

Flo was the server. Flo was somewhere in her midfifties, but she wasn't taking those years lying down. Her hair was an unlikely bright copper and she still had the wings and mall bangs and two swoops of glittery eye shadow in a style she'd probably been wearing for decades. It didn't look remotely natural, but it suited her. She was a naturally pretty woman with an air of kindness. Sure enough, Flo didn't know my name yet but was pleased to help anyway.

"I'm looking for the retired teachers," I said. "I need to speak to Miss Murphy."

She pointed to the left-hand side of the restaurant, where raucous laughter rose from a long table at the end. "I think you might mean *Mr.* Murphy, hon," she said. "Unless our Ed's been keeping secrets."

I couldn't help laughing. "I don't know him. Just assumed I was looking for a woman. Would you mind telling him I need to speak to him?"

She hesitated. "I don't want to interrupt. They're vicious if you interfere with their fun."

I liked Flo. "Well, it's a matter of life or death, if that makes a difference."

"Wait here."

A minute later a man in his seventies made his way toward me, guided by Flo. He was pleasant looking and must have been handsome in a Kennedy-like way in his younger years. He could still turn heads and the cane didn't seem to make a difference.

He looked at me quizzically. "Life or death?" He raised his eyebrows. "You seem a bit young for that."

"It's not my life that's at stake. And it's a bit tricky too. I hope you can help."

He nodded. "You have my attention and my curiosity."

"I am investigating"—I put a slight emphasis on the word "investigating"—"a situation between Vera Van Alst and Muriel Delgado." His head jerked. He knew them both, no question, and he was uneasy as soon as he heard their names.

I plowed on. "The situation is taking on dangerous aspects and I need to ask you some questions."

Mr. Murphy turned to where Flo was standing, quite obviously listening to our conversation. He cleared his throat and Flo must have suddenly remembered that the salt and pepper shakers on the neighboring tables needed to be filled. She skittered away.

"I can't speak about either of them," he said.

"Why not?"

"They were minors. I was a teacher. It would not be ethical."

"But there was something serious that happened. I can tell by looking at you."

"It's a long time ago. It's not my affair."

"Well, it's mine. Muriel has moved in with Vera Van Alst. She has separated her from her friends and employees. Does that concern you? I am probably the person who cares most for Vera Van Alst except for her cook. I have been fired. Vera is in bad health and vulnerable."

He blinked. And I knew it did concern him. He shook his head. "I can't help you. If this is true and you are worried, I advise you to go straight to the police."

Did he emphasize "true" just slightly? I didn't want to say that the police had been useless. In retrospect, maybe I should have. I also didn't mention my hit-and-run. He didn't comment on my bruised face.

Mr. Murphy turned and walked back toward his laughing colleagues. I stepped up behind him and said, "As long as it's not on your conscience."

He stopped, his back stiffened. Then he kept walking.

I probably slumped as he continued without looking back.

Flo drifted over, brimming with sympathy, her blue eyes bright. She glanced back toward where Mr. Murphy was taking his seat. He wasn't smiling.

"He won't tell you. He's a by-the-book guy. Straight as an arrow."

I stared at her. Of course. She was the right age. And she was very interested in our conversation. If there's one thing I know it's that nosy people can be great sources of information. I learned that at my uncles' knees.

Speaking of uncles, mine might have been conspicuously absent but they still could come in handy. After all, the ladies loved them and this was exactly their kind of place. Hot chicken sandwiches. Mmmm.

"By any chance," I said, leaning forward in a friendly manner, "do you know my uncle? I'm sure he's mentioned you."

Her hand shot to her copper wings. A small smile hovered around her mouth. "Who's your uncle?"

"Mick. Mick Kelly. Michael J. Kelly is the official title, but everyone calls him Mick." Except the police, of course, but I didn't want to dwell on that.

"Oh, Mick! Of course, I know him. He mentioned me, hon?"

"Sure, that's why I came here."

"You said you were looking for—"

"Mr. Murphy, yes."

"Actually, you said Miss Murphy."

Caught. Oh well. "I might as well be straight with you. It was just because I need to get some information about two women and I heard that one of them was, and I quote, 'Murphy's cross to bear.' I just assumed Murphy was a female teacher."

Flo snorted. "Sounds like Phyllis Zelman with a remark like that. She always calls him Murphy."

I said, "But of course, he couldn't answer my questions. Confidentiality and all that. I have to respect it, but it leaves me in a bit of a tough spot."

"Hmm. How is Mick? We haven't seen him here in a while."

I laughed, despite the pang in my heart. "Join the club. He's very busy. Got a big project going."

"Something to do with antiques, I imagine."

I hope not, I thought. "Most likely," I said. "Anyway—"

"So tell him I say 'hi' and mention that we have a fish and chips special tomorrow. Even more special for our friends."

"Right," I said. "So—"

She glanced over toward Mr. Murphy, who wasn't taking part in the lively chatter at the table. Instead he was gazing out the window with a furrowed brow, oblivious.

"You sure got to him."

"I didn't mean to. I just mentioned Vera Van Alst and Muriel Delgado and asked about their relationship in high school. That's all it took."

"Why do you need to know?"

I hesitated. I didn't know Flo except I was willing to bet she couldn't keep a secret. "It's complicated," I said. "And sensitive." Of course, I didn't want to alienate her. I added, "Did you know them? I think they're quite a bit older than you." Another thing I'd picked up from the Kelly uncles: shameless flattery will hardly ever fail you.

She laughed and gave me a playful tap on the arm. "I can tell who you're related to and yes, I did know them."

"Muriel and Vera?"

"Yes, we went to school at the same time, not that either of them gave me the time of day. But I saw things."

"Did you?"

"Oh yeah. I might not have been a brain like that Vera Van Alst, but I wasn't stupid."

"And you probably had lots of friends."

"I did. People liked me, which is more than you can say for either—"

"I bet they did. Here's the thing. I used to work for Vera Van Alst, but a few days ago, Muriel Delgado moved in and I was fired. So I'm—"

"What?"

"I was fired."

"You said that Muriel Delgado moved in to Van Alst House." Flo leaned against the counter and stared. "I can't believe it. Did she have a gun?"

"A gun? No . . . oh, you're joking."

"I guess that wasn't funny."

"I think Vera is in danger, so can you tell me why you reacted that way?"

"Because they hated each other, at least at first. Well, Vera just had her nose in the air. She probably didn't hate Muriel, but she wouldn't give her the time of day. Mind you, she didn't give anyone the time of day. I guess that changed afterward and they became friends. Muriel was a strange girl, and what a little snob that Vera was! And that was after the factory going under all because of her father and his mismanagement."

"She hasn't changed much."

"You worked for her?"

"I did. And in spite of her, um, personality traits,

I'm really fond of her. She was a good boss. She's also a lonely soul. Now I am worried."

"You should be. Muriel was a piece of work."

At that moment a cluster of retired teachers got up and signaled. Flo made her way to the cash register.

I ducked outside to check on the dogs, who were happily cadging treats and getting ear scratches from everyone who walked by. "Won't be long, lads," I said. "I think I'm onto something."

I headed back in and looked around for Flo. She was bending over listening intently to Mr. Murphy. I waited until the bills were taken care of. When I approached, she didn't make eye contact. Bad sign.

"You were saying?" I gave her my most encouraging smile.

"I can't really remember much. It's been a long time since I saw either one of them. We were stupid kids. I'm sorry if I gave you any other impression."

I felt a tingle on my neck. I turned to find Mr. Murphy's eyes on me. There was no point in attempting to bully poor Flo. She was obviously fond of the former teacher and he'd given her a hard time.

CHAPTER TWELVE

OUTSIDE THE HUDSON Café a couple of the regulars thought they might have recognized the Rileys. They didn't remember where or how or why they recognized them. As I was finishing my questions, Lainie rushed out of the restaurant and gave me a huge bear hug. "I heard."

"Heard what?"

She blinked, brushed back her elegant silver hair. "That you'd been hit by a truck, of course. Oh my God, your poor face! Those bruises."

"Was it on the news?"

"I didn't hear it on the news, but Jasmine from the pet shop came in for a cake a couple of minutes ago and she told me. She said you'd been in this morning."

"Right. I went there before I saw Phyllis at the Food Drop."

"Should you be walking around?"

I said with a grin, "A slice of your caramel cheesecake might make everything better." For a moment I debated picking up a couple of double-chocolate mocha brownies with truffle icing, the signature treat at the Hudson Café. So many treats, so little time.

"I shouldn't have said that about your face, Jordan. I was just alarmed about the bruises. You're as pretty as ever and the blue will match your eyes. And I will prove that I am sorry by giving you the entire cake."

"What? No, Lainie. How are you going to make a go of it if you give away your cakes?"

"We love you. You bring in your friends. You get hit by trucks. We want to keep you alive."

Lainie was so warm and charming and we were so lucky to have her in our lives. I smiled. "Well. I guess I could accept *some* cake in that case."

"You have to take it all. No more arguments. Save it for what matters."

She took my arm and propelled me, arm in arm, into the café. I tried not to think that I was usually there with my best friends, now among the disappeared. Still, I had friends left, like Lainie.

"What's that?" She gestured to the photos I was carrying.

"Oh, almost forgot. Do you know either of these guys?"

She squinted and paused. "I think I do. They look like a couple of landscapers who did some work for my neighbor last summer. Why?"

"They may be the guys who hit me."

She bit her lip. "Whoa. Maybe you shouldn't be flashing their pictures around. Did you tell the police?"

"I'm not sure I trust the police."

Her eyes widened. "But aren't you dating that cute blond officer?"

"He's out of town. I'm on my own except for my uncle, who is like having the Three Stooges conveniently colocated in one body. Oh, and I have the dogs too." I didn't mention Cherie. She was too hard to explain.

"The Three Stooges in one man?" Lainie hooted with laughter before turning to a pair of passing servers and asking me to show the photos.

They both shook their heads.

Lainie looked worried as I left with my entire—that's right, *entire*—caramel cheesecake. "Please be careful. I will talk to my neighbor. If I remember correctly, it wasn't a happy situation with them. I'll call you with whatever I find out."

I gave her my cell number and a thankful hug. I promised to come in for a meal soon. Then I collected the dogs and headed home, not much wiser than when I left.

I was stepping out of the restaurant, carrying the cake in a large cardboard box and wondering how I could manage to carry it home while hanging on to two uncoordinated dogs of different sizes and traveling speeds. Just out the door, I spotted something that made me gasp. I stepped back into the restaurant and bumped into Lainie again.

"What is it?" she said. "You're white as a sheet."

"There's a cop working his way down the street." We peeked out, just in time to see Jones enter the Poocherie. "He's the one who gives me really bad vibes. I think he might be connected with the Rileys. I don't trust him at all."

Lainie stared at me. "Really? Like a crime show on television when there's a corrupt cop and nobody knows?"

"Except this is real. Don't tell him I was looking for the Rileys."

She put her hand on my shoulder and looked me straight in the eye. "Maybe you shouldn't be looking for them. Maybe you should find a friend and just go visit for a while. Out of town. You're in between jobs. Take advantage of it. Fly, little birdie."

"Well, I would fly but now I have this big cake to eat. Afterward I'll be too heavy for liftoff."

"Cute." She chuckled. "If you won't be sensible, be careful. And remember, you're not alone with just your Stooge uncle. You can call me any time."

I felt tears welling. I hate that. "Thanks."

Lainie's patients must have been very lucky when she had her practice in Manhattan. Now we were fortunate to have her healing presence and her great food in Harrison Falls. I got out of there before I started to blubber.

The dogs and I turned the first corner we could and scuttled back to Michael Kelly's Fine Antiques. Once there, I put the cheesecake in the fridge and gave the cats their Blue Wilderness. I thought I heard them ask for Cheez-Its, but surely not.

I made sure the cats were contained on Uncle Lucky's side and then left the dogs in charge of security. I made tracks for Maple Street with my photos.

I CALLED UNCLE Kev. He answered immediately in a whisper.

"Bo Peep," he said.

"How are things?"

"You mean how are things, Eagle."

I sighed.

"Not so good. The signora is in a bad state. She's cooking all the time, but you know that Muriel won't eat Italian food. The freezers are jammed and the signora's still at it. Even the freezers in the kitchen refrigerators are stuffed with ravioli. The good stuff! Muriel won't even look at it and I heard her complaining to Vera."

"Well, we're working on the Muriel problem and I need you to do some—"

"Anything you need. I'm yer man."

"Right. So just please listen to me and don't inter—"

"I never interrupt."

I rolled my eyes. "I need you to go to George's Diner and talk to a waitress called Flo. Try to find out what happened between Muriel and Vera back in high school. Flo was there at the same time. And make sure that you get her alone. There's a retired teacher named Mr. Murphy who knows something. He says it's unethical for him to talk about them. He doesn't want Flo talking either, so stay out of his sight."

"The diner's not that big. If you're there, you're in sight, Jordie."

"Yes, I found that out the hard way. Stay sharp."

"I have an idea."

My common sense told me not to let Uncle Kev go with any of his "ideas," but as they say, beggars can't be choosers.

"Just find out what people said about them. Gossip is fine. We want to know if Muriel had a hold over Vera. Apparently, at first they hated each other, oh, and Vera was a snob."

"There's a shocker," Kev said with a chortle.

"Dig deep, Kev. We need to uncover what explains this bizarre hold Muriel has."

"Will do, Bo Peep. Over and out."

"Wait a minute! While you're there, ask around about the Rileys. Did you get the photos from Cherie?"

"She's great, isn't she? In fact—"

"Kev? Focus. We're pretty sure the Rileys hit me with their truck. I'm *really* not going to feel safe until I know where these guys are."

"On it!"

"And Kev."

"Yes, Jor—Bo Peep."

"Be careful."

．．．

TOM WAS PUTTERING outside when I arrived. As usual, the Snows' yard was immaculate. He seemed thrilled to see me. I sauntered over, keeping an eye out for rogue trucks as I went.

"Mindy will be thrilled. She's just made a big batch of pumpkin spice muffins for Thanksgiving. Cream cheese icing too. They're the best things ever, except for her pies. Why don't you come in for a bite?"

Ha. I'd barely had time to drop off the cheesecake. Was it my day for baked treats or what? If I hadn't thought my life was in danger, I would have been a happy camper. I cheerfully followed Tom.

I was disappointed that neither of them recognized the men in the photos.

"I don't think so," Mindy said, frowning.

"Can't be sure," said Tom. "The truck was moving so fast and we were just coming out the door. What we saw was you flying through the air. Want to try the muffins? They have dried cranberries and candied pumpkin seeds."

Mindy said, "Everyone loves them so I have to bake a lot for the holidays."

Tom glanced at her. A look of intense sadness passed between them. What was I missing?"

"One or two?" Tom said to me. I noticed that he patted Mindy's shoulder gently as he spoke.

Who was I to say no?

It was a different story at Audra's house. The

kids were playing happily with her kitchen pots when she answered the door. Her smile faded when she saw me.

"It will just take a minute," I said. "No pressure. I've been to see the Snows. They sent you these amazing pumpkin muffins. Can I come in?"

In spite of the muffins, I sensed she wanted to say no. I solved that problem by stepping through the door, smiling broadly and trying to give her a hug. "I owe you so much."

She dodged my hug. "Mindy's always sending food. She's such a good cook and it's a real shame that—"

"What?"

"You know." She glanced at the beautiful children who shared her green eyes.

"I don't know. Please tell me so I don't put my foot in it when I'm talking to them. I really like them."

"She's always preparing for visits that never happen. They've a boy and a girl, both high flyers. Both married. No one made it for Thanksgiving last year. Or Christmas. They just let them think that they'll make it this time and then something 'comes up.' Last year Tom and Mindy invited us at the last minute because in the end they had an empty house. Nice for us, but it's heartbreaking." Her voice cracked. "I can't imagine that as a parent."

"I'm sad to hear it. And I'm sorry to trouble you with these photos. Do you recognize these men?"

I pulled out the photos and slid them on the hall console, even as she began to protest.

Audra barely glanced at the photos. "No." She shook her head a little too emphatically. "I've never seen them."

"Sure they weren't in the truck that hit me?"

"Yes."

Her knuckles were white as she gripped the table edge. She wasn't good at lying. "Good luck with your search. I have to get back to the kids now."

I headed for the door and she was right behind me, shutting the door so fast it almost clipped my butt. It didn't matter. Her reaction confirmed it. She'd seen the Rileys in that truck. She was too scared to admit it. She feared for her children and she knew these men were capable of killing. I couldn't blame her.

Whatever was going on between the Rileys and Muriel, it was dangerous.

AFTER MY VISIT to Audra, I sat in my car thinking for a bit before I sent a text message to Tyler Dekker.

> If anything happens 2 me, check out
> Muriel Delgado + Det Jack Jones
> Audra Bennacke is lying. She's scared.
> Retired teacher Mr. Murphy knows
> something–ask Flo at George's.
> Wish U were here.

I added, Miss U ☺

That was true. His absence had made my heart grow fonder, as inconvenient as that was. Still, I couldn't count on him to solve the crime against me. I'd count on myself and Uncle Kev and possibly Cherie; time would tell. My role model, Archie Goodwin, wouldn't allow a lack of facts to dampen his spirits. That would be my approach.

I had barely sent the text to Smiley when my cell phone rang. *The Hudson Café* showed up on the screen. Lainie's call reinforced what I already knew: The Rileys were like unstable bombs.

"I don't want to alarm you," she said, somewhat breathlessly. "But I talked to my friend about those landscapers, the Rileys. They're a father and son. She said to tell you to steer clear. She said she found them very intimidating and became frightened in the end. They did a shoddy job and she's probably going to have to pay to get it redone. She was terrified to take action against them. The father threatened her and she took it seriously. They're a couple of thugs. Please be careful and let the police handle it, Jordan."

I finally got a chance to break into the conversation to thank her.

"I appreciate this, Lainie. Don't worry. I won't confront them."

"Perhaps you shouldn't be going around asking questions about them. You wouldn't want them to get wind of it."

"You're right. I don't want them to get wind of it. They've already tried to kill me."

"Will you stay away from them?"

"Yup. Thanks so much for this." I decided not to mention that Uncle Kev, one of the least careful people on the planet, was at the moment nosing around Bridge Street at George's Diner and would be asking about them.

"I'll see if I can learn more about them. I have no connection to them, so that's probably a bit safer."

"Thanks. I'm going in a different direction anyway. I've got a line on some other stuff."

"Other stuff?"

"It's ancient history, well before your time here in Harrison Falls."

"Please try to be careful. And remember that I am just a phone call away."

I was still smiling before I hung up. I was glad to have Lainie in my corner. At least I had a friend. Poor Vera couldn't even say that. I'd thought of myself as her friend, and where had that gotten me? Uncle Kev could be viewed as a friend, but you couldn't count on him to succeed in helping. Eddie, the now-retired postal carrier, was devoted to her, but he was in Florida. I would have been happier with Eddie around. He was timid, but he was intelligent and he cared. How long was that cruise going to last? I wasn't even sure when it had started. Eddie ate like a bird and was allergic to alcohol, so what kind of time would he have been having on a cruise? He'd be missing Vera. Eddie had been besotted with her since school. Vera had only gone to school in Harrison Falls for a year. The chances were very good that Eddie would know about any relationship, positive or negative, that Vera had with Muriel. Maybe he'd even know what hold Muriel had over Vera.

Was there a way to reach Eddie?

There had to be.

Eddie was always lurking about Van Alst House. Vera wouldn't have had his telephone number, if he even had a cell phone. There was no need. Kev and Eddie had mainly ignored each other in the quest for Vera's affections, so he most likely wouldn't have it either.

Perhaps the signora would. Somehow they'd managed to communicate, and Eddie often hung around the kitchen with her.

I'd never seen the signora use a telephone, but Eddie used to pick up things at the grocery store for her. Did she call him?

Worth asking.

Kev would be the person to try to get the phone number out of the signora.

As I drove home, happy with this new line of inquiry, I was passed by an ambulance and two fire trucks heading along the river and out of town. A pair of police cars followed, roof lights flashing and sirens wailing.

At least they were all heading away from

George's Diner, where I knew Uncle Kev could inadvertently do a lot of damage.

Unfortunately, two minutes later, another fire truck thundered past me heading in the direction of Bridge Street, raising the worry quotient.

In my family we have a little saying: Where there's smoke, there's Kevin.

"NOT MY FAULT," Kev said. "I was just trying to blend in by helping in the kitchen. Some of that cooking oil has a real low flashpoint."

I rubbed my temples.

Kev burbled on. "Anyway they got it out soon enough, although Flo is a bit upset with me and she won't be talking too much."

"Oh great. So a waste of time and a threat to life and limb."

"What? It wasn't a waste. I got a great lunch there. Big fries, hand cut. Flo said it was on the house."

"But the information, no go?"

"It was a go."

"Just tell me," I snapped. I try to be gentle with Kev because he's a delicate flower, but really, sometimes that's too hard.

He sniffed.

"I'm sorry. What do you mean it was a go?"

"She knew them all right."

"Great. Did you get any kind of hint about the hold Muriel had over Vera?"

"No. Except that maybe Vera's father had a thing going with Muriel's mother. But that wasn't new. Vera would have known that. Everyone did. So it couldn't have accounted for the change."

"What change?"

"Something happened and they started to get along. Be friendly. Then almost as suddenly, they weren't friends again."

"No clue what it was?"

"Well, we were just getting to it when the thing with the oil happened, so it kind of ruined the talk with Flo."

"I bet it did."

"But there was something else before I forget."

"What?"

"Trying to remember."

"Was it something Flo said?"

"I think so. It was important. I know that."

"Keep thinking. About Vera? About Muriel?"

"No and no."

"About Mr. Murphy?"

"No."

"About Muriel's stepfather?"

"No."

"Vera's father?"

"No."

"Call me when you think of it." How important could it be?

"I remember. Those guys."

"What guys, Kev? You mean the Rileys?"

"Yeah!"

"What about them?"

"They were there."

"At George's?"

"No, at the school at the same time."

"What? That's not possible."

"It is, Jordie. Flo looked at the picture I had and she knew them right away."

"But Junior's in his twenties, Kev. He couldn't have been at school with Vera."

"Not him, silly Jordie. But the other one, the father. They all knew each other. Except for Junior, who wasn't born yet."

"Thanks, Kev. Good work."

Except for the kitchen fire.

"You know what?"

"What, Kev?"

"Flo thought there was a thing between Muriel and the older guy."

"Frank?"

"Yeah. Frank."

"Could be really important. Wow. It could mean that if they had something going, maybe Frank was involved in the hit-and-run of Muriel's step-father."

Kev said, "Frank couldn't have been committing hit-and-runs all the time. Sooner or later, even the dumb cops here would pick him up."

I cleared my throat.

"Sorry, Jordie. I didn't mean your dumb cop.

He's not that dumb, but you know, the rest of them."

I wasn't even bothered with Kev's dig at Smiley, because he had identified two major connections. The friendship between Vera and Muriel was important especially since it ended abruptly, and the fact that Frank Riley had been at school and had a "thing" for Muriel was bang-on.

"You hit the nail on the head."

Kev blinked. "I did?"

"Twice. Frank most likely doesn't go around committing hit-and-runs or whatever the expression is. He's a thug, but he only gets really down and dirty when Muriel's around. First her stepfather was killed, which worked out very well for her. Now this week, there's another one when she's back in town for the first time in nearly forty years and determined to get control over Vera and get rid of Vera's allies; that's me."

"But why would he do it?"

"I don't know. Money? Love?"

"Couldn't be love. She just gives me the shivers."

"Speaking of weird love, can you try to get Eddie's phone number from the signora?"

"Eddie's . . . ?"

"Yes. Eddie has known Vera since high school, so—"

"He'll know these guys too."

"And maybe he'll know what happened back then between Muriel and Vera."

"Wow. But I'm not sure that—"

"Just do it, Kev. And call me as soon as you have it."

I DROVE HOME worrying about how we could reach Eddie and whether I was ultimately responsible for any damage at George's Diner and what Muriel could get up to before we managed to get rid of her.

Once there, I did my best to reassure the cats that the supply of new food wouldn't run out and in any case, they would soon be back terrorizing everyone at Van Alst House. I assured the dogs that the cats could not unlock the door from Uncle Lucky's apartment and take over Uncle Mick's and my side. I sounded more confident than I felt.

I reheated a nice selection of the signora's food and made myself a late lunch. All those treats had given me an appetite. After that, I enjoyed a slice of caramel cheesecake and one of the pumpkin muffins. Didn't want to show favoritism to either Lainie or Mindy, two of the loveliest people I knew.

Maybe it was a sugar overdose. Or the lingering results of my collision with the truck. I soon began to think that maybe I shouldn't have ignored the doctor's warning about not doing too much. Another bout of dizziness and fatigue set in fast. I didn't even make it upstairs to Ponyville. The stairs were simply beyond me. I crashed on Mick's comfy old sofa, with two dogs vying for the small leftover section.

My last waking thought was that Archie would be disappointed in my lack of stamina.

When I woke up, the sky had taken on a late afternoon gloom. The day was disappearing. The dogs hinted at walks and meals missed, although it was just after four. There was a distant yowl of dissatisfied Siamese.

I sat up and my head spun. It also throbbed. I felt like hell. I managed to get the dogs around the block. The bracing cold air helped a bit. This wobbliness was very bad just when I needed to get cracking on the Muriel situation. We wobbled back to the house and I gave myself a good talking-to.

Uncle Mick wasn't around, but his solution for when you felt bad was always grilled cheese sandwiches with Velveeta. I tried it and it made all the difference. I contemplated having a couple of desserts as they were temptingly available, but decided to forgo the sugar buzz and think.

I went back to my piece of paper and began to make lists again. I updated my notes:

Muriel and Vera had been enemies
They became friendly
Don't know why
They fell out of friendship again
Don't know why

Muriel has something over Vera
Don't know what
Frank Riley was at school at the same time
Muriel had an alibi for the time of the hit-
and-run that killed Pete Delaney
Could Frank have killed him for her?
How to find out?

I SAT THERE chewing the end of the pencil and listening to Cobain's tail thump on the floor. I thought as hard as my fuzzy head would allow. There was something else flickering at the edge of my consciousness. What?

Something to do with police.

I felt a little tingle as it came to me. Detective Jones. Wasn't he the same age as Vera and Muriel and Frank Riley?

Was the fact he was "on" the case and doing a terrible job of investigating my own hit-and-run more than a coincidence?

I added Detective Jack Jones to the list.

The phone rang and jerked me out of my deep, dark thoughts.

"Bo Peep?"

"Yes."

"I found Eddie's number in Florida. He left it with the signora in case of emergency. I guess this is an emergency, right?"

"If it's not, I don't know what would be," I said.

"You should call him. If I call from here and

he's not there, he might call back. We wouldn't want him phoning and Muriel picking up."

"I'll do that. But I need you to do something too."

"Anything!"

"Can you find out from Flo if Detective Jack Jones was also in high school at the same time as Vera and Muriel?"

"Oh boy, Jordie, I mean Bo. I don't think that will work. Flo's a bit upset with me."

"Of course, she is. Silly me. But maybe we can put your friend Cherie on it."

"That's a great idea. I'll get in touch with her. She can do anything."

"And you trust her, right?"

"With my life," Kev said.

Well. It wasn't like we had every option in the world.

I got Eddie's Florida number and the Eagle went off to track down Cherie.

I WAS HOPING that Eddie and his mother were back from their cruise and kicking myself that I hadn't paid that much attention to the details when he'd told us about it.

No answer. I got one of those pre-recorded messages that mean you can't tell if you've reached the right person. Naturally, it didn't reveal Eddie's whereabouts or his return date. Never mind. I took a chance and left a message telling

Eddie we urgently needed his help. I was very clear that Eddie (if it was Eddie) was to call me on my cell. He was not to call Vera first under any circumstances. I added mysteriously that this was all for Vera's safety. I would explain why when we spoke.

I hung up and thought about it. Eddie and I had shared some cryptic exchanges since we'd met last spring, but now I worried this one had too little detail.

I called Eddie back and left him a longer message with the full story: I told him how Muriel had moved in and intimidated Vera. I emphasized that Vera was being cut off from her support system and that we feared for her well-being. I explained that we needed information. I mentioned Jack Jones too, just in case.

I got myself another piece of caramel cheese-cake and turned on the regional news to see if there was any mention of the kitchen fire at George's and specifically any mention of Kev. Because that might take some dealing with, as the aftermath of Kev's activities so often did. Even the radio announcer's solemn, deep voice didn't prepare me for the shock of the breaking news.

The bodies of two men have been retrieved from just outside Harrison Falls by emergency personnel this afternoon. The men, a father and son, are believed to have drowned. They died when their truck left Long Boundary Road and plunged through a guardrail and into the river. Their names have not yet been identified, as the next of kin have not been notified. Police believe that another vehicle may have been involved in the crash and are asking anyone with information to come forward.

CHAPTER THIRTEEN

TWO MEN IN a truck, dead. A father and son. The Rileys?

Had they tried to run someone else down and ended up in the river? I pushed the cake away and headed back to the sofa. The dogs were pleased but I was very troubled. What were the chances that the father and son in a truck were anyone but Frank and Junior? In this part of upstate New York there was no shortage of trucks with fathers and sons riding in them.

But if it was the Rileys, I had a pretty good idea who might have caused their deaths: Muriel Delgado. Had Muriel learned I was still asking questions about her all over Harrison Falls?

Ideally, I should have taken my suspicions to the police. But what would I have said? That Muriel Delgado may have thought they could link her to not one but two hit-and-runs? I had nothing aside from the fact that she and Frank Riley had been at school together. We now had Detective Jack Jones in the mix. He'd seemed to be hot on my trail this morning on Main Street. And he showed a bias against me for sure.

The dogs snuggled up and Walter snuffled in my

ear. I think that meant a walk would be good. But it could have meant, *Please let me eat that cake or chase those cats.* Cobain is always more mellow and a bit sad. I wasn't sure what he wanted, so he got a scratch on his ears. I wasn't going anywhere until I figured out what to do next.

I leapt to my feet when my phone rang.

Eddie?

I sure hoped so.

"Bo Peep?"

"Kev, I'm trying to stay off the phone in case Eddie calls back."

"Okay, but I'm going out of my mind here. Muriel's been driving us crazy for a day."

"Has she gone out at all in the past day or so?"

"Are you kidding? The signora and I would be celebrating if she'd even leave us alone for fifteen minutes."

"Okay. Thanks. Gotta go, Kev. I'll be in touch. And by the way, have you heard from Cherie?"

"Nothing. Oh no, here comes Muriel. I can't even use the phone without her appearing out of nowhere. Every time I try, she's right there. Bye."

"Wait! You're sure she hasn't left Van Alst House?"

"Darn sure. I spent the past day and a half trying to stay out of her way. It ain't easy, Jordie."

"So then she couldn't have killed the Rileys."

Kev said, "What? You mean those guys who delivered her stuff?"

"I think they're dead, Kev. I doubt that it was an accident. And if I'm right, that means things are ramping up. Muriel's getting rid of them because they were weak links. They were stupid and obvious and I was asking questions about them. They could lead back to her so they had to go."

"But she couldn't have killed them, Bo Peep. She never left Van Alst House."

"Fine, like in the other cases, she made it happen. So you know what this means, don't you, Kev?"

"No. What?"

"That the Rileys were killed and Muriel was in full view of witnesses, making sure that you were all aware of her presence. Same tactic as the other hit-and-run. That means she has someone else working with her."

"Who?"

"I don't know. And the people most likely to have the truth tricked out of them are now dead."

"I knew she was trouble."

"Yes. And now we have to worry about Vera. She is more and more vulnerable."

"But what does Muriel want from her?"

"I'd say everything she has, wouldn't you, Kev?"

OKAY, SO MY intuition told me the dead father and son were the same people implicated with my attack and connected with Muriel. I had an idea how to confirm that.

I did realize that the red wig wouldn't work, but it wasn't the only arrow in my disguise quiver. I put on my black turtleneck and jeans. I found a short black bobbed wig and some fake heavy-framed glasses. Poof, I was a beatnik and a good one too. A quick trip down the back alley to the Kelly car storage area yielded a battered Ford Focus with Alabama plates. *We dare defend our rights.* Well, I hoped it wouldn't come to that.

I had to leave the dogs behind as too many people would recognize them and put two and two together. Ditto my deep orange purse.

It wasn't long before I pulled into the parking lot at Sullivan's. It was late afternoon and I was surprised by the number of cars in the lot.

I stepped inside the seedy bar and looked around. I thought I had my answer. People were talking in low voices, looking somber. At one table, a couple of dark-haired women were crying.

I stopped the waitress on her way to the bar. I recognized her from our earlier visit. She hadn't smiled then and she didn't now. She hadn't been too impressed with Cherie, but she'd never noticed me. Good. I fished out my best southern accent courtesy of my years of friendship with Tiff. "Sorry, but Ah'm from out of town and Ah'm looking for the Hudson Café. Ah think it's on Bridge Street?"

"Nowhere near here," she said. "You gonna order anything?"

"Ah should be going."

"Fine. Step outside and I'll point the way." As we stepped through the door she said, "You don't have a GPS?"

"Giving me real strange instructions. I almost found mahself in the river."

"Yeah, that happens. Stay out of the river. It's—" She bit her lip.

"Something wrong, honey?" I said. "Inside everyone looked like someone died."

She nodded. "Someone did die. Two some-ones."

"Really? Two?"

"Father and son. Frank and Junior Riley. Their truck went into the river today. They drowned."

The Rileys were pretty vile, but that was a terrible way to go. "You must be so upset."

She shrugged. "A lot of customers are getting emotional."

"Were they your friends?"

"No, they were not my friends. They were a pair of useless jackasses with wandering hands, but I wouldn't wish that end on anyone."

"Ah'm sorry to hear this."

"Not your fault."

I smiled and pressed ten dollars into her hand. A nice tip and one that would get me her attention if I needed to come back again.

"Thank you kindly," she said. "And no offense, but I spent ten years in the south and you should work on that accent until you get it right. Your clothes are all wrong too."

"Point taken." I added another ten. "I was never here."

"I never laid eyes on you even if you were." She turned and strode back in.

So now I knew. The Rileys were dead. Muriel could not have killed them.

So who was her accomplice?

OKAY, WHAT HAPPENED next was wrong. I was desperate. The entire situation with Muriel and Vera was out of control. I needed to talk with Uncle Kev. As I was persona non grata, that meant I had to do something—maybe a bit underhanded.

I was still determined to be the only person in my family to go straight, um, ish. Of course, I'd be happy if any of my relatives decided to join me in the world of solid citizens. But I wasn't planning thievery. Just a little light break-and-enter. The law might not see it my way, but I believed it was necessary and for a good cause.

I located my lock picks. They'd been a Sweet Sixteen gift from Uncle Mick and Uncle Lucky. I keep them with me.

I already had on the all-black outfit, including black wig. The watch cap and even my old black hiking boots would be nicely invisible. The temperature had been dropping in that end-of-November way, so I decided on thermal underwear first. Mine were black, naturally, and I added alpaca socks that were also black but worth their weight in gold. It wasn't much good to be invisible if I got hypothermia. I wasn't sure if I should worry about my white Irish face, but I chose not to put any shoe polish on it. A balaclava would have been perfect. Of all the houses in the world, you'd think this one would have a closet full of balaclavas. But I couldn't find one.

A girl's got to think about her complexion. Instead, I dodged the cats and found a long black scarf in Uncle Lucky's closet. I stuck it in my backpack and would wrap it around my face when the time was right. I'd look like a demented ninja, when I got where I was going, but so what.

I felt uneasy, especially as the last time I staged a break-in, I'd come face to face with a police uniform. Not a happy moment for either of us.

However, I didn't think this outing would end that way. I called Uncle Kev to let him know to expect me and to keep an eye out. I left a note for Uncle Mick (wherever he was) to say that I was taking the Civic. The Civic was unremarkable and looked just like hundreds of other cars. I didn't want to take the Ford Focus or the Accord in case someone recognized them after all my snooping. Needless to say, the Civic's license plate was somewhat obscured by a selective layer of "dust."

I put on a brilliant yellow jacket with a hood to go to the garage and for my drive. I was extremely noticeable and that was the plan. A few miles out of town, I turned down a bumpy road on the property that bordered Vera's. The road led to an old farmhouse I knew was unoccupied. I angled the Civic into the bushes, ditched the bright yellow jacket in the passenger seat and began the trudge across the farmer's field. I was glad I'd worn the hiking boots as the furrows and ruts in the earth were frozen. My ankles thanked me, at least until I twisted my left one on a particularly vicious rut. I limped the rest of the way most inelegantly.

It was an eerie walk and the hulking presence of a thresher parked nearby didn't help much. I felt like I was being observed by a giant insect.

The moon was in its third phase, not as helpful as a full moon would have been, but enough to see by. Of course, seeing clearly is overrated. If you can see, you can be seen. Even so, I was grateful for the lack of cloud cover.

It took about twenty minutes to walk and I congratulated myself on choosing that long underwear and the alpaca socks. I approached Van Alst House from the rear, keeping to the shadows of the evergreen trees on the edge of the property.

Kev knew I was coming and once I reached the house, I did my excellent imitation of an owl hooting to let him know I'd arrived. I only hoped that he wasn't yakking and drowning out the sound.

The lights were on in the dining room. It was

eight o'clock, when everyone must be at the table. I felt a pang for the days of "We dine at eight, Miss Bingham." If Vera and Muriel were at the table and the signora was pivoting around with one of her platters, then no one was going to see what I did. Kev would be stuffing his face too. It would give him an alibi if one was needed.

The doors were locked, the alarm blinking. Vera might have changed the locks, but I had my picks and Kev had given me his code.

Sure enough, "HANDYMAN" worked like a charm. I let myself in, closed the door behind me and reset the alarm. I hugged the wall of the endless corridor, being careful not to dislodge any portraits of Vera's constipated ancestors.

It seemed like a year before I reached the library. It had a code too. Again, my luck held. This code had not been changed. I let myself in and locked the door, keying in the code again, in case someone came by and tried the door.

I sniffed the air. I loved everything about Vera's library, especially the aroma of the old volumes, leather covers and armchairs, real rosewood shelves and beeswax furniture polish. I loved the feel of the Aubusson carpet. I loved the wrought-iron banister of the circular staircase to the mezzanine. I paused to soak it all in, realizing this might be my last visit.

"I'll be back," I said out loud to the room. It would have been nice to curl up in the worn leather club chair and leaf through one of Vera's treasures. But I had a job to do.

A light was out of the question, but I had a flashlight that was barely enough to keep me from crashing into the furniture or tumbling off the circular staircase.

I crept up the stairs without a sound. We were a decent distance from the dining room, down two endless corridors. The attack cats were away, but you never know. On the mezzanine, I looked around, flashing the light. There were, as I feared, gaps in the books on the shelves. Were these the ones that Muriel had told Kev to sell? I scratched my head and stared at where the Nero Wolfe collection used to be. Not a single book remained.

That witch. It must have been pure spite.

Vera's father's battered Nero Wolfe books didn't reside in the library. Vera moved them between her bedroom and the study, reading and rereading the old paperbacks. But Vera's library collection was relatively recent and, except for the new *Fer-de-Lance*, consisted mostly of attractive mass-market paperbacks in excellent condition. This was the kind of collection that an obsessive collector like Vera might cherish, but it was in no way that valuable. There were many volumes in the library that would fetch thousands of dollars if Vera decided to sell them, but these were not among them. This collection had sentimental value to Vera because Rex Stout's Nero Wolfe books had been a hobby she'd shared with her father. We had worked to upgrade it, but it was far from first-rate.

What reason would anyone have for taking any of them? Even as I asked myself that, I had to admit that there could be reasons unrelated to the value of the book, as I had learned the hard way in a couple of tough spots since I came to work for Vera. I was chewing my lower lip and puzzling over the missing books when I heard a scraping at the door.

What was that? Someone was fumbling with the keypad, from the sound of it. Vera? But what was she doing here? This was the appointed dinner hour and nothing except illness on Vera's part interfered with that. On the other hand, who else but Vera would be using the library?

I extinguished the flashlight and felt my way to the end of the mezzanine. There's a leather club chair up there too, not that Vera could venture up the stairs. She had people to carry her precious collection up and down the circular staircase for her. I missed being one of those people.

So I wasn't really worried about Vera thumping up to the mezzanine and discovering me, but she might easily be able to spot me from the main level. I reached the chair, tucked myself behind it and hunkered down.

Voices wafted up to the second level. I was certain one of them was Muriel. Of course, she would have managed to get the security code, but who was the other person? Vera's gravelly voice was unmistakable. I'd spent months listening to her. That voice wasn't Vera's.

Muriel was speaking in low tones. I strained to hear what she was saying, but without moving from my hiding place, it wasn't possible. I caught the odd word and phrase. I couldn't catch what her companion was saying or even if it was a man or a woman. For sure it wasn't Uncle Kev, because low tones are not his best thing. Even more ridiculous to think it might be the signora. She'd never be able to resist shouting *demonio*!

What were they saying?

"Yes, she loves those stupid Wolfe books. I'm having fun taking them from her. One by one. Turning the knife. She hates it."

The malevolent glee in her voice when she mentioned taking the books from Vera made me feel sick. The black widow had turned into the Wolfe widow. Of course, that didn't make sense. I shook my head and listened.

"What? No, that's all taken care of . . ."

"Not long now . . ."

"Before she . . ."

"Interfering . . ."

"Nosy bitch . . ."

"Yes, we'll get rid of them next."

Well. Something told me that I was the nosy bitch. The rest of it sounded ominous. Who would they get rid of next?

Me? Kev? The signora?

Who was Muriel talking to?

A thunderous knock on the door caused me to gasp. Luckily the thundering was from Kev, so my gasp was drowned out.

Kev said, "The lawyer's here."

"He's early," Muriel barked.

Kev said, "You want me to tell him to come back at the right time?"

Muriel said, "Don't be stupid. Tell him I'll be right there. We don't need to be tripping over you, Kelly. Go to the kitchen with old Mrs. What's-her-name and keep out of our way. Do you understand me?"

"Sure thing, ma'am," Kev said in an unusually servile tone. If I were Muriel, I wouldn't have fallen for that.

I heard the door close, presumably behind Kev.

Muriel said, "He's another snoopy type, that guy, but he's got his tail between his legs. He'll hide out in the kitchen as he was told, so he won't see you or your people on your way out once we're done with the lawyer. We won't have to worry about Kelly or the old lady for much longer. You slip out the back. It's too bad I couldn't show you this room. It's really fancy. I'm going to enjoy it when . . ."

The response was a low murmur. The door squeaked open and then closed again. Silence descended. After a while, I did too.

I waited five minutes to give the mystery guest time to get along the endless corridor before I headed that way myself. Muriel was still around and that was bad, even though I figured she was probably with the lawyer.

As I tiptoed along approaching the back exit, the kitchen door opened and I found myself caught by strong arms. I yelped and a hand clapped across my mouth. I managed to stifle a scream as I was pulled through the door.

I didn't stifle my furious whisper. I swatted at my uncle. "Kev, are you nuts? Do you want Muriel to hear?"

"We need to speak to you!" Kev was white and shaking. The signora danced a little dance of distress.

From the hallway, we heard Muriel bellow, "What is going on there?"

The signora's eyes bugged out. Kev swayed. The signora shrieked, "Eees big rat! In kitchen! Aieeee!"

As I dived under the large kitchen table, Kev took up the challenge. "I'll kill it, Fiammetta! Muriel, do you want to help?"

"No, I certainly *don't* want to help. Get the exterminators in here tomorrow. I'm not having rats on my property. And stop shrieking. I have a business meeting and I don't want people to think this is an insane asylum."

Kev stuck his head out the door. The signora let

out one more whoop. Kev said, "Don't you worry, Ms. Delgado. We'll get rid of the rats."

Starting with you, Muriel, I thought.

"See to it. Or you'll be out of a job."

Once the door closed, I crawled out from under the table. "Did you know she was seeing a lawyer, Kev?"

"Just found out when he arrived."

"Do you know what that's about?"

He shook his head. "No idea."

"It has to be the property, some scam to get it from Vera. Did you notice Muriel said 'my property'?"

"We have to stop her."

"For sure, but there's more to this. She's not working alone."

Kev goggled. The signora made the sign of the cross.

I said, "I heard her talking to someone in the library. She took him or her there to show off the room. That person's visit has to do with the lawyer. You interrupted, Kev, when you came along to tell her that the lawyer had arrived. Otherwise, I'm pretty sure they would have gone to the mezzanine and I would have been discovered."

"That was close, Jordie."

"No kidding. Did you see Muriel's visitors?"

Kev shook his head. "But what were you doing there, Jordie?"

"You knew I was coming. I figured everyone

would be in the dining room. You're always at dinner at eight o'clock. I wanted to look around in the library and the office to see if I could gain some insights into whatever Muriel is up to. I wanted to check the caller ID on the phones."

Kev said. "You took a chance. Our routines have changed. Muriel doesn't like to eat that late. So now we eat at six thirty. Or whenever she gets hungry."

I did think that Kev might have mentioned this when I told him I was coming over. "Vera must be furious."

Kev shook his head. "She's not really. She just seems . . . defeated."

"*E un demonio!*" the signora added.

"Well, we have just begun to fight." I felt very Archie Goodwin as I said it. Archie and I love overwhelming odds. "Before we can outwit Muriel, we need to know who she's working with. There's probably no way to find out who it was."

"Man or woman?" Kev asked.

"All I could hear was a low murmur of voices. The books must have muffled the sound and I'm pretty sure Muriel and her guest didn't want to be spotted."

"Why not? She walks around here like she owns the place. What would she care if we saw her visitor?"

"It must be Muriel's accomplice. That's probably

the person behind the Rileys' deaths. Muriel mentioned getting rid of the nosy bitch."

"Who's the nosy bitch?"

"I think it must be me, as I am asking a lot of questions. Unless, of course, it's Vera."

"Vera? No. She's just slumped in her room, all the time. She's not nosy. It sounds more like you."

"Thanks, Kev."

"We need to figure out who it is."

"I am sure going to try to find out. In the meantime, we should find a way to learn what the lawyer is here for. Do you know his name, Kev?"

"No. Yes! He said his name was Dwight Jenkins. Does that sound like a lawyer's name to you?"

"I've heard of him. We need to know for sure what he is doing here."

"How?"

"I have an idea. I'm going to head out now. You need to keep a real close eye on Vera. You too, Signora. I'll be in touch. Cover me in case Muriel shows up. I'm cutting across the farmer's field. My car's parked on the next road. I'll follow the lawyer. Call me when he leaves. What? No, Signora. I really can't carry any food with me. It's going to be—"

I managed not to spill the thermos of hot soup or the pasta or the cookies I was carrying on my furtive trip through the furrowed fields to my car.

I crawled into the car, started it up and positioned it by the side of the road. I couldn't resist eating some of the hot soup. It was a delicious reminder of the life I had left behind. It probably also kept me from freezing to death.

My phone buzzed and Kev whispered, "He's leaving now."

As the lawyer's Buick purred past me on the road, I swung the Civic into position a safe distance behind him.

Part of my driver training from Uncle Lucky was learning how to follow someone without being observed. I don't think any of my friends or class-mates received the same training from their relatives. Never mind. It hasn't been necessary all that often, but the instructions stuck with me. On that lonely country road, I kept my lights off.

I followed him right to his imposing brick home (I was betting nineteen twenties) on St. Lawrence Crescent, a lovely tree-lined street within sight of the river and within easy walking distance of the downtown area. I slowed down and pulled in as he turned into the driveway. He parked the car and then lumbered to the front door with a briefcase. Yes! Shortly afterward, the lights went on inside. I inched forward without lights and parked right in front. I sat in the dark and watched. I figured the light was in the front hall and the house had the traditional central floor layout. Then a light went on from a window on the right side of the house. Two minutes later the lights went on toward the back. Kitchen maybe?

The lights were quickly switched off. Minutes later the upstairs lights shone out and the hall light was shut off. I could see the lawyer silhouetted against the curtains in the front window. Early to bed, early to rise? Or a den on the second floor? No way to tell.

I headed home for a rest. I had a busy night ahead of me.

I DO REALIZE that breaking into people's homes is not strictly speaking "going straight," a key point in my life plan. I'd convinced myself it was for the greater good. I wasn't out to steal anything. I needed to know what the lawyer had in his briefcase. I was certain it held legal papers that were very relevant to Vera's situation. I had to see them. After that . . . well, time would tell.

First I had to gain access. And to do that, I needed to check how well the home was secured. It was close enough to walk. It couldn't have been more than half a mile from Uncle Mick's, but people on foot at two a.m. are always suspicious-looking unless they're walking a dog. I didn't really want to involve the dogs in this caper. Walter had helped me with my reconnaissance in the past. But tonight was, as I believe I've mentioned, very cold and very windy. Walter does not do cold well. He was more likely to trip me up trying to jump into my arms to get warm than to provide an unobtrusive cover. And Walter was capable of raising a racket if I left him tied up.

Cobain, on the other hand, didn't give a hoot about the weather. But he was Officer Tyler "Missing Somewhere in Action" Dekker's dog. There was a good chance one of the officers on patrol would recognize the shaggy black creature at a glance. And because people knew that Tyler Dekker and I were in a romantic relationship of sorts, recognizing his dog would then make a connection. I didn't want anything about my illegal outing to lead back to me.

So, there I was, on my own. Too bad, because the dog thing usually worked so well. I was already in my black gear and I had my lock picks. I added a glass cutter, some clear Mactac, and safety gloves to avoid being cut. I put on a red fleece under my black gear and packed a silly red-and-yellow hat with braided ties. A small hammer, a pair of glasses with black frames, a lightweight folding black nylon bag and the black scarf completed the kit. My kingdom for a balaclava. Walter hid under the covers in case I got any ideas, but Cobain thumped his tail, full of hope at getting a W-A-L-K at this unaccustomed time of night.

"You're too identifiable, I'm afraid."

"So fix that," Cobain said.

All right, he didn't say anything. But I got an excellent idea. Shortly after, I set out with a black-and-white shaggy dog. A very happy dog, despite the fact I'd used my nontoxic Wolf brand wax-based face paint to give him two white ears and a number of large white markings and a spectacular white tail. The face paint was left over from Halloween. I figured Wolf was a fitting sign. I loved this big lumbering dog even if he wasn't mine. We walked the few blocks to the lawyer's place on St. Lawrence without seeing a soul. Of course, it was now two thirty in the morning so no big surprise there.

"You are a very good dog and when I tell you to stay by the tree you are going to. Right?"

Cobain seemed to agree. Of course, "tree" and "treat" sound a lot alike.

I headed toward the house. This lawyer broke every scrap of advice offered to anyone who'd ever inquired about security.

He had lots of large busy mature shrubs around his foundation. They were really quite perfect for sidling behind to get access to the house. I did a quick test and was pleased that no lights turned on. No motion detectors. A troop of burglars could hold a dance competition in his yard and he'd never know about it.

The bushy shrubs around the house were more than matched by the unruly cedar hedges that divided his property from his neighbors' on either side. Nice. And cedars are thoughtful enough to keep their form all year long. Again, a good shield. There was a slight chance that someone across the street might get up in the middle of the night and notice a woman and a dog prowling, so I kept to the side and the back of the house. Sure enough, by the back door was a security camera. It was focused on the backyard. On the back door was the decal for a security company. If the back door was alarmed, I knew the front would be covered too.

No point in using the lock picks. I knew I could get in and out of the building before the cops got there in their usual four to five minutes' response time that was fairly standard. But I didn't know how much time I needed. And I didn't know how the lawyer would react to a burglar alarm. I didn't want to find out. He might have a gun or he might have a heart attack. I was aiming for an outcome where no one ended up dead or with extra perforations. I'd just have to find a window that wasn't alarmed. Given the lousy security, I felt confident. The basement windows had the type of bars you buy in the hardware store. I knew ways of getting past them, but because of events in the not-too-distant past, there was no way I would be going into this or any other barred basement. No matter what was at stake.

Hugging the foundation, I explored, trying to figure out which windows belonged to which rooms. The living room seemed fairly obvious—I used the bay window as a clue—but sometimes professionals with these large older homes will convert the front area to offices. I knew nothing of this man, except that he was "the lawyer," Dwight Jenkins.

I ruled out the kitchen. From what I knew about houses of this era, the dining room was across the hall from the living room and had a door to the kitchen. That left what I hoped was a smaller room at the end of the dining room, a den or study. I had no way of knowing if it would be. I spotted the piano window. Homeowners never think to alarm transoms or piano windows, according to some people I know well.

Despite my association with Signora Panetone and the Hudson Café, I am slim and agile. There was a good chance I could pass through it. Lucky me, some outdoor furniture remained. I dragged over a wooden chair that really should have been put away for the season. I took my roll of Mactac and my glass cutter. I stood on the chair and was not only able to reach the window, but to attach the Mactac and to use the glass cutter around the edges. The glass came out nicely.

Then I tucked myself behind a bush and waited for the sound of an alarm. None came. To be on the safe side, I took five minutes and hung around to be sure that the cops weren't on their way. If they showed up, I'd melt into the neighborhood and home. Once I felt confident they weren't, it was back on the chair. I put on the safety gloves to avoid getting cut and pulled myself up to the window. Inside, things started off well. There was an upright piano and so I was able to slide onto it and then hop to the floor instead of dropping from the window. I groped my way into the next room. Direct hit: It was an office. A briefcase lay on the desk. It was closed and locked. Damn.

I had a couple of choices at this point. I fiddled with the briefcase lock and soon realized it was complicated. I picked it up and headed across the hall to the dining room. I snatched up a bit of silver and dropped it into the black nylon bag to reinforce the idea of a burglary. I paused. Was that a creak from upstairs?

It was.

And then another one on the stairs. I wouldn't have been surprised if the person descending on the stairs heard my heart thumping.

I legged it from the dining room into the kitchen, wrestled the door open and fled, dragging the black bag and briefcase. My panic increased because lately so many doors I'd opened had nasty surprises—like fires and police officers—behind them.

The alarm sounded instantly as the door opened. The sound propelled me in my escape. A light from the house illuminated the yard somewhat. Without thinking, I turned back and saw what I took to be the lawyer backlit in the door, scratching his head.

I ran, only stopping to collect Cobain. I dumped the black nylon bag behind the bush and used my little hammer to smash the lock on the briefcase. In the morning, I'd have to make restitution to the lawyer, who was probably an innocent bystander. I took all the papers out, except a few that seemed unimportant, and stuffed the rest into my backpack. The rest I left to blow around in the wind. Once I was through the adjoining yard, I took off the scarf and stuffed it down my shirt. I removed my black jacket, revealing the bright red zippered fleece. I added the silly red-and-yellow knit hat with the braided ties and finally donned the black-framed glasses. At least I wouldn't match any description given by the lawyer.

A police car whipped along the street. I stopped and stared at it in surprise as innocent people tend to do.

The car stopped and the cop rolled down his window. He was a heavyset guy pushing fifty. He had a slightly receding hairline. Maybe it had just migrated to his upper lip, where the mustache was doing well. I was pretty sure I'd seen him at the station. I walked over to see how I could help.

"You see anyone suspicious around here, miss?"

He didn't really look closely at my face. I think my silly hat was a distraction. Now there was a training gap, I thought.

"I did." I pointed to the yard with the bush where I'd left my stash. "Skinny white guy. He went that way. I think he dropped something. He looked kind of scary-looking. I was glad I had my dog."

Cobain wagged his new white tail and smiled at the officer. No doubt they'd met before.

The officer stared at me for a second. I think it was hard for him to take me seriously while I was wearing that hat.

I stroked Cobain to show my thanks. My hand came back covered in white and I hastily tucked it behind my back. Fortunately the officer was busy on the police radio. I hoped no innocent skinny white guy was about to become collateral damage because of my description.

I left the officer to find the "evidence" and hustled home before he came back to ask me for a statement.

At home, I got out of my highly identifiable gear and cleaned off Cobain. He licked my hand. Walter scampered around jealously.

I dug the papers out of my backpack. My heart rate was still high as I began to read.

I couldn't believe my eyes.

Vera had made a will leaving everything to her natural sister.

Muriel Delgado.

And in a separate set of documents, she had given power of attorney for health and financial matters to the same Muriel Delgado.

There were two witnesses to all the documents. I'd never seen their names before.

This was a disaster.

Vera had literally signed her life away. Now she was a sitting duck.

CHAPTER FOURTEEN

COBAIN WENT STRAIGHT to bed once I wiped off his disguise. I gave him a few treats to reward his actions as an accomplice. Really, he could have turned pro any time.

Walter woke up at the possibility of a T-R-E-A-T and now decided he needed to go out. I took a ring of keys from Mick's favorite hiding place. I gathered up my disguise and the legal papers. Then I slipped on my old plaid coat and my poor boy cap and stood shivering outside with Walter. Once the important stuff was taken care of, I crossed the street. I checked carefully to see that I wasn't spotted. Then I hustled down the alley in back of the vacant dress shop that Uncle Mick had recently purchased, not that I knew that officially.

This skulking around investigating was a pain in the rump. I'm not sure how Archie Goodwin remained so cheerful through all those books.

The fifth key on the ring opened the door. I headed up the rickety stairs to the vacant space over the shop. The place was full of shrouded machinery, from the look of it. I didn't want to snoop on my uncle, although it all looked suspiciously like high-end copying equipment. I realized I had made a mistake in choosing this location. It might be part of Mick's current project and therefore off limits, but it was too late for the moment. I found a loose floorboard, made it a bit looser, and deposited the will, the red fleece, the silly hat and the tools. It wouldn't fool a search team, but I didn't figure one would be showing up. Anyway, it was only temporary.

Just as I reached the other side again, a police car came slowly rolling along the street and stopped. I recognized the officer as the same one who'd stopped me before.

What if he recognized me?

"I know you," he said.

I gave him my widest smile. "Yes, I think we've met at the station. I have a friend who works there . . . sometimes."

"Oh yeah. You're Dekker's girl. Did you see a woman and a dog come by?"

I laughed and pointed at Walter. "Well, we are a woman and a dog."

"Different one. The woman was a bit thinner than you, maybe your height, stupid hat, glasses. Did you see them?"

Thank you, stupid hat, for total anonymity.

I shook my head. "I was asleep until the bossy pooch decided he couldn't put off a trip outside. Didn't see anyone."

Too much info, I told myself. *Don't pile it on, you'll trip up. A simple "no" would have done.*

He said, "A black-and-white dog. Weird looking."

I shook my head and pointed to Walter. "This is the only dog I've seen. Walter's kind of weird. Did it look like this?"

"Not even a little bit."

I was hoping that Cobain wouldn't wake up and show his face in an upstairs window and make an obvious liar out of me.

He said, "What about a skinny white guy running?"

I glanced around nervously and pulled my coat around me tightly. "Should I be worried, Officer?"

"Nah. Go back to bed," he said.

"I won't be able to sleep now."

"Lock your doors," he said, and drove away.

Gee, thanks. Fat lot of good the cops were. Locking his doors and putting on his security system hadn't saved the lawyer from me. If someone really wants to get in, they'll get in.

I turned toward the house and the cop car rolled on. Inside, I fished out my phone and called Kev.

"Mmmmph?"

"Wake up, Kev. Cruella's named in the will."

"What?"

"You have to find the will and hide it."

"But Bo Peep, what good would that do? The lawyer has the other copy."

"Not anymore, he doesn't."

Kev gasped. "She'll know that was us. She'll call the cops."

"So? Why would we take it? We're not going to inherit. Hard to imagine we'd be in any of Vera's wills. But as long as Muriel is the beneficiary in this will, Vera's life is in danger."

"Muriel will just insist on getting another will made. Vera's eating out of her hand."

"Just do it, Kev. Go fast. I am sure the lawyer will call Van Alst House to let them know as soon as he realizes that the will is gone. If the one at Van Alst House is gone too, I'm guessing they'll do up another tomorrow. But it buys us some time to help Vera."

"They'll probably figure it was you, Jordie."

"They won't be able to prove it."

"They might search your place."

"And if they do, they'll find me and two dogs. They won't find any will."

"Good."

"Kev. Make it look like a burglary. Break a window."

"Righty!"

I knew he'd love that.

"It's starting to snow again. Don't leave foot-prints outside. Or if you do, wear someone else's boots."

"Outside?"

"You do know that a window broken from within the house is a sign of an inside job."

"Of course, everyone knows that. You caught me sleepin', Jordie. I'm not thinking a hundred percent yet. Footprints, yeah, that's right."

I hoped that hundred percent thing kicked in soon. "When will you do it?"

"On it now."

"I'll dial 911 to give myself an alibi."

I told the dogs to stay put and headed for the back. I knocked over a few garbage cans. I smudged up the snow so that no sign of my footprints would remain, not that I was expecting a full-fledged police investigation into a possible intruder in my alley. Still, you can't be too careful. Luckily, we have no neighbors on either side. That's a benefit of my uncles' having bought up most of the property on the block.

Two minutes after I got in, I practiced my hyperventilating and called 911. I whispered breathlessly, "I think someone's trying to break in. Please come right away."

After a few sorting-out questions, the dispatcher said that help would be there shortly. She advised me to remain calm. I said I'd try.

The same officer rolled back up to Michael Kelly's Fine Antiques and grinned when he saw me open the door.

I blurted, "I think that guy might have been here."

Walter greeted him with great enthusiasm.

"What happened exactly?"

"Something or someone knocked over the aluminum garbage cans in the back. I had just gotten back to bed and it woke me up."

"You see anything?"

"No. I don't think he got in. The dog started to bark and I think maybe he changed his mind."

"Anyone with you?"

I shook my head. "My family's away. Anyway, it's back here." I gestured to the lane that separated our building from the next. "Aren't you going to call for backup?"

He laughed. "I'll be able to handle it."

"It really couldn't hurt to call for backup, could it?"

He was still laughing when he headed down the lane. He wasn't when he returned. "Cans are all messed up. Can't get any tracks, but it looks like someone was trying something. Has anything been disturbed inside?"

I shook my head. I silently asked my uncles to forgive me as I brought the forces of law and order inside and showed him the various doors.

He was frowning. "Looks like you scared him off. Sure you're all right?"

I smiled, wanly. "Spooked the heck out of me."

"Yes, he's probably looking for an easier target. Might even have been a raccoon. Even so, you got someone to stay with you? You're shaking."

"Thanks. I'm okay." My teeth were chattering and I wasn't even faking it.

"Give it some thought. Call a friend. I'd want my kids to do that."

Ah yes, my "friends." Of course, they'd vanished off the face of the earth. I didn't want to mention that to him. I really hate people feeling sorry for me, even nice fatherly cops. Especially nice fatherly cops.

If Mick arrived home to find me being consoled by another cop in the shop, well, we might have to call a hearse.

"I'm in the area and I'll patrol as often as I can tonight. How about I park down the street when I do my paperwork? Call 911 if you need to. I'll get the call."

"I appreciate that." That at least was true at this point.

He said, "And if I'm not on duty and you need help or for some reason they don't reach me, here's my cell." He passed me a generic Harrison Falls Police Services card with his own number written on it by hand.

Well, that was kind but weird.

As soon as he left, I texted Uncle Mick and Uncle Lucky to let them know it wasn't a good night for any, shall we say, unusual activity. I made myself comfortable and waited for Kev to call.

When he did, it wasn't good news. Not at all.

"We've got a problem here, Bo . . . Jordie!"

"What?"

"There was a break-in. Muriel's saying I did it."

Assuming that Kev was on speakerphone, I played it straight.

"A break-in? That's awful, Kev. What did they take? Not Vera's silver?"

"Not the silver. Well, I don't think they took the silver. No one mentioned it. Did they take the silver, Vera?"

I could hear Muriel raging and Vera's gravelly tone in the background.

"I can't hear Vera, Muriel," Kev said peevishly. "And I didn't have anything to do with breaking that window. I am offended you would suggest that."

"*Il demonio!*"

"I don't know what was taken, Jordie, but the cops are on their way. Muriel is saying that you were in on it."

"In on *what?*"

"I don't know 'in on what.' But she says you'd better have an alibi."

"An alibi? Why?"

"Because of whatever happened here, maybe twenty minutes ago."

"*Oh dio!*"

"Please, Signora, try to calm down. You're not helping anyone."

"Muriel is saying the police will want to talk to you about where you were when this was going on."

"As a matter of fact, I was right here with the

dogs, and I have a very good alibi for twenty minutes ago."

"Well, that's good, Jordie, because I'm wondering what kind of alibi Muriel has. Although she seems to have the cops in her pocket."

I heard Muriel's deep voice say, "Watch it, Kelly."

Kev kept going. "There's a window broken. From the outside, and guess what?"

I sighed, "What, Kev?"

"Muriel's boots are dripping from the snow, even though she claims she hasn't been outside all night. There's some kind of legal documents missing apparently. Who else but Muriel would care about that? Vera can't get outside and the rest of us have nothing to do with any legal documents. Do we, Signora?"

"*Povera Vera!*"

"You know what, Jordie? I think Muriel broke that window to fake a break-in for her own nefarious purposes."

"Nefarious. Kev?"

"Yes. Because—"

"Kev, I can't hear you."

All hell appeared to have broken loose at Van Alst House. I did hear a bit of the signora's high wail. The rest was just shouting and then the phone went dead.

"WE BEEN FIRED!"

"What?"

"Muriel found out that I got Eddie's phone number from the signora. She told Vera and I've been fired. I guess the break-in didn't help either. The signora's fired too. We're already off the property."

I barely stopped myself from saying "what" again. "The signora too? Off the property? It's the middle of the night."

Of course, Uncle Kev didn't actually have a vehicle at the moment. That's another story that would take too long to explain. "You mean you're standing on the road?"

"With everything I own in the world."

"I'm coming. Just wait for me and try to keep warm."

"I kind of miss the kitties, so that will be nice. But, you know, I'm worried about the signora. How is she going to cope?"

"She'll stay with us too. We'll find a way to deal with it in the morning. I'm on my way."

My heart was thumping. Kev might be a walking disaster, but he cared about Vera and he understood the way the household worked. This was bad news, especially with Muriel working so hard to get Vera's new will. As for the signora, that was just plain heartbreaking. I hustled out and the dogs hustled with me.

Ten minutes later, in the Saab, we picked up Kev and the signora, shivering on the side of the road. With the two dogs in the car, at least there was plenty of body heat to keep them warm.

My phone vibrated in my pocket. By the time I got it out, it was too late.

"Shoot. I've missed a call from Eddie. I'll call him back from home."

Beside me, Uncle Kev was shivering pathetically. I couldn't give him a rough ride about not wearing his warm clothes. He'd been through enough. I stepped on the gas and we rocketed the rest of the way to Uncle Mick's. The signora wailed. The dogs loved it all.

IT TOOK A few minutes to get everyone warm, dry and calm. While I tried unsuccessfully to return Eddie's call, the signora helped her own mood by whipping up a bit of pasta for Kev.

"Eat," she said. "Eat to help Vera."

I wasn't sure what you call a meal at four in the morning or how that meal would help Vera, but Kev enjoyed it. And the cats who had been yowling from behind Uncle Lucky's door may have scored a morsel or six. I decided I would check with the vet the next day to see what they should be eating, but for the moment I let it go. My head was buzzing with fatigue. I headed to bed and left them in the kitchen.

I was changing into my pajamas when I heard a thundering at the front door, which is actually the front entrance to the shop, of course. Did I hear a shout of "Police"?

Archie Goodwin would never have opened up for Inspector Cramer or Stebbins at that time of night, no matter how much they bullied. At the best of times, he gave them plenty of attitude. But for some reason Kev and the signora rushed to open the door and the rest, as they say, was history.

Of course, it was the police and it seemed that they had a warrant.

"What for?" I said, looking my most surprised as I arrived late to the party. "Kev, I think you should both go to bed now. We're all exhausted. No, don't argue. We are not letting them in any farther. Kev, the signora will be fine at Lucky's. Help her to settle in. The cats will be happy."

I felt something like joy when they actually disappeared back into the house, yawning and dragging their feet.

Detective Jack Jones was standing inside the front door of the shop, which is technically our place.

"It's a search warrant. Therefore it's to search."

"Go right ahead and search whatever you want," I said. "But first shouldn't you be telling me why?"

"You're kidding, right?" he said. "And don't get too comfortable because we're going to take you downtown to talk about a couple of break-ins tonight."

"Break-ins?" I thought I did a great version of outraged virtue. But my heart was thumping. Being dragged into the police station and grilled did not bode well for the future of my relationship with Smiley—if I had one, that is, considering his absence and silence.

"Don't act all innocent. I know for a fact that you broke into the office of Dwight Jenkins and the home of Muriel Delgado tonight."

"You certainly do not know that." I held my chin high.

"Where were you tonight?"

"Here, except when I walked the dogs. I walked them separately, if you must know. I did leave to pick up my uncle Kevin and Signora Panetone at the home of Miss Vera Van Alst tonight. That's Vera Van Alst's home and not Muriel Delgado's. Important distinction. They were fired after this alleged burglary."

"Uh-huh. And can anyone verify your where-abouts before that?"

He was being tricky. Of course, an innocent person wouldn't know what time the break-ins took place. Archie had also taught me that police give away how they want to trip you up. He liked to call it telegraphing. I said, "It depends on the time that you are talking about."

I looked past Jones's shoulder to see my own personal patrol officer loom into view. "What's going on here?" he said with a glower at Jones.

"We're arresting Jordan Bingham on suspicion of burglary." To me he said, "You're coming to the station."

"I'm in my pajamas," I bleated. "I have bare feet."

"Should have thought of that when you broke into Van Alst House an hour ago."

"I didn't." I managed to inject a half sob into my voice. Very effective, I thought.

"You ask me, she didn't," said the patrol officer. I was wishing I knew his name.

"What do you mean?"

"I mean that someone tried to break in here and she called 911. That was before we got the call about the Van Alst place. I came by here after the 911 and checked things out. I kept an eye on her because she's alone and there's some crazy guy in the area."

I sniffed. "I told you I was here."

Jones wasn't done. "There's still the robbery at the lawyer's house. And I think we've got you on that."

"I don't see how."

I actually felt bad by now, lying in front of my alibi, who seemed like a really decent person.

"We'll find those papers." Jones attempted to shoulder past me.

"Can I see that warrant?" I said. It had belatedly occurred to me that they'd never have been able to get a warrant that quickly for something as mundane as a couple of break-ins in the middle of the night. Thank you, Archie, for that inspiration.

"Why?" he said.

"Because it's the law."

My own personal patrol officer was frowning. Maybe he wasn't impressed watching Jones play fast and loose with a citizen's rights. Of course, he was seriously outranked by the detective, but still he was a witness to bad behavior.

Jones curled his lip, not a good look for him. "It won't take long." He turned to the officer. "And you, keep an eye on her and make sure she doesn't leave or make an attempt to hide the stolen papers."

"What papers are you talking about?" I said as he stormed out.

Jones squealed his tires taking off.

The patrol officer said, almost apologetically, "You really shouldn't try to leave."

I said, "I'm not planning to leave. I'd just like to get some sleep. And I don't even know your name, but thank you again."

"Gus Melski. Glad to help. I've got three girls of my own and I want to believe that people are out there keeping an eye on them."

I felt a pang of guilt. That's the thing about lying to decent people, but, honestly (as most of us say when we're producing whoppers), I couldn't think of another way to deal with this situation.

"Go to bed. I'll be in the car, outside your door so I can assure Jones you didn't hide anything."

THAT ONE HOUR of sleep really made a difference. Unfortunately, that was all I got. Then all of a sudden, the dogs appeared to be barking, and Walter was circling in a panic and nosing me. It took a while to come to the surface. The cats were yowling next door, so maybe that contributed to the general confusion.

Voices were raised in what sounded like hysteria. I pulled on my slippers and staggered downstairs.

My phone rang at the same time, but I'd left it upstairs.

Uncle Kev was leaping like a deranged leprechaun in the kitchen. The signora was wailing. Officer Melski was scratching his head.

"Something wrong, Officer?" I said.

"You tell me. I heard dogs barking and someone shrieking in a foreign language. Thought I better check to see if you were all right. This gentleman let me in."

At that, Kev managed to look extraordinarily guilty, even though all he'd done was answer the door.

"Thank you, Uncle Kev," I said.

Melski glanced at Kev and then at the signora. "So, let me get this straight. These people say they live here. That right?"

For a brief moment, I almost succumbed to the temptation to say I'd never seen them before. But of course, I couldn't do that as I'd already acknowledged Kev. Before I could add a thing, Kev sputtered, "Yes, we live here. We were fired by Vera Van Alst because of a woman who is trying to kill her. The police are no help at all!"

"*Il demonio!*"

"One at a time and in English," I said, collapsing into a chair. "Yes, I'm afraid they do live here now, temporarily. We all used to work for Vera Van Alst. I'm hoping this is just a bad dream, but in case it isn't, would you mind closing the door, Officer Melski? It's getting cold in here."

Everyone spoke (and "spoke" doesn't quite capture it) at once. I raised my hand to silence them.

Uncle Kev was trying to get Officer Melski to understand how awful it all had been. ". . . and we were tossed out in the snow to wait for our ride because someone broke into the house. We were already inside. Why would we break in? What do you think of that?"

"*O dio!* Vera!"

I said, "Zip it, Kev. And Signora, please calm down."

Officer Melski turned to me. "Are you sure they belong here?"

"Yes, they do, Officer. We've all been affected by whatever criminal takeover is happening at Van Alst House."

"Sure," he said. "I knew that."

"Oh. Did you? Well, this so-called burglary at Van Alst House may have been staged to give a certain person unfettered access to the assets of

Miss Van Alst, without the protection of her trusted staff."

Gus Melski stared at Kev and then at the signora. "Trusted staff."

"We all care about her." I felt my lips twitching. "And we're not just any employees, we're like family. That says a lot, considering Vera—"

"—is not the easiest person to get along with," Kev said, his baby blues glittering in a slightly deranged fashion.

"*Povera Vera!*"

"Right," I said. "Poor Vera. It's a bad situation."

"It's worse than bad," said Kev. "In fact, it's even worse than the worst."

No point in my arguing there's no such thing as worse than the worst.

I felt exhaustion settling on my shoulders. "Maybe we can talk about it in the morning. Let's get a bit more sleep."

Kev said, "What if that's too late?"

Speaking of too late, I ran upstairs to check my phone. During the hubbub, I had missed a return call from Eddie. At least this time he'd left a message.

But I could hardly believe my ears.

"Eddie's on his way," I said, coming back downstairs.

"From Florida?" Uncle Kev said. "I thought he was on a cruise."

"Apparently the cruise is over. The minute he

330

got our message, he seems to have raced to the airport. His flight got into Syracuse just after midnight. He's driving from there."

"Whoa. Must have cost him a bomb."

"He says he's going straight to Vera's."

"Oh boy. You don't want that, Jordie, but maybe he could make sure that nothing happens to her."

Kev and I stared at each other. The signora crossed herself. Eddie had always floated like a ghost through the kitchen and back rooms of Van Alst House, buoyed by his devotion to Vera. I hadn't wanted Eddie for his muscle. I was hoping he'd explain Muriel's hold over Vera. If there were secrets, maybe Eddie would know them.

My message to him was high-pitched. "Eddie. Wait for us. We'll come with you or get the police. For Vera's sake, remember it's dangerous."

Officer Melski gazed at us, bemused and possibly befuddled.

I figured Eddie would put Vera's safety way above his. I turned to Kev. "We need to make sure he doesn't get into that house. He's probably rented a car and it's a good three hours from Syracuse. Even so, he could arrive any minute now if he's not already there. You take my car and make sure he doesn't get down the driveway until we speak to him. I have to wait here for Detective Jones, unless Officer Melski will authorize me to leave."

Officer Melski shook his head. "Nothing personal, but no way in hell."

The phone rang.

I snatched it up. Eddie again.

"Eddie! You're where? Taxi? From Syracuse? Really? Oh. Well, since you're there, you have to listen to me. Vera's in real danger."

Kev blathered. The signora wailed. Officer Melski cleared his throat.

I said, "Hold on, Eddie, I have to find someplace quiet so I can hear you." I shot a sheepish grin at Officer Melski and headed up the stairs before resuming my conversation. I didn't want Melski to hear that I knew the contents of the will. Talk about an admission of guilt. I said, "Eddie, Muriel and her minions have weaseled their way into Vera's will. Muriel will get everything. I know, it's a shocker. Yeah, I went to the cops, but they couldn't care less about Vera. You know how some people still hold a grudge. I'm pretty sure Muriel got Frank and Junior Riley to run me over with a truck. Oh yes, I was hit by a truck. Well, there's been a lot going on here. Muriel has a solid alibi for the time it happened. I'm sure the Rileys did her dirty work. Now Frank and Junior are dead.

"Like I said, there's a *lot* going on. This woman is dangerous, Eddie, and I'm counting on you to help me figure out what she has on Vera." I returned to the kitchen still talking to Eddie. "The cops have been worse than useless. I need you to be on Muriel twenty-four-seven. Muriel's sneaky. Thank you. Don't even go to sleep. Please try to convince Vera to let Kev back in, and the signora. No. Of course, they didn't rob her. Did Vera say that? Of course, it's not true. It's all part of Muriel's shakedown."

After Eddie hung up, Melski crossed his arms and said, "Worse than useless?"

I glanced at Melski. I didn't want to accuse Melski of being useless. He was, after all, my alibi. I didn't feel secure enough to tell him that I thought Detective Jones was part of the whole conspiracy. "Not you, of course, but I brought some very credible concerns to Detective Jones and he dismissed them. I don't see how two hit-and-runs involving the same people couldn't even warrant some follow-up. Then I saw him buddying up to the two guys who most likely ran me over and next thing I know Jones is breathing down my neck over the B&Es at Vera's and what's-his-face the lawyer."

"Dwight Jenkins," Melski said.

"Whatever. Do you see where I'm coming from?"

"The Rileys are dead."

I sank onto the kitchen chair, feeling exhaustion and hopelessness wash over me. "Yes, I know."

"You know? Their names haven't been released to the media yet."

I didn't want to mention Sullivan's. "It's a small town. People start talking right away. I think I was at the gas station when I heard it first."

"And you believed it?"

"The guy at the pumps has never steered me wrong before. I believe the Rileys tried to kill me." I added, "The woman who witnessed it is terrified. She won't talk. Here's why I think Muriel Delgado's connected. Her own stepfather was killed in a hit-and-run nearly forty years ago and her mother inherited from him. When the mother died shortly after, Muriel inherited from her. There was a million-dollar insurance policy in the pot too."

Melski looked stunned. "You think she murdered her mother?"

"No, her mom was in very poor health. Muriel didn't get along with her stepfather. If her mom died first, Muriel would have been out in the cold. Conveniently, Pete Delaney wound up dead before that could be a problem for Muriel."

"And you know all this how?"

I was unwilling to throw Audra and the Snows to the wolves, although I didn't really think that Melski was a wolf.

"You understand that I am not trusting everyone from the police, present company excepted."

Melski stared at me for a long minute. Then he said, "What about this blond woman?"

"What?"

"We have a BOLO for a blond woman who was seen with the Rileys not long before they died. Detective Jones believes she's involved."

Cherie.

Cherie had made quite a splash at Sullivan's. And Detective Jones had been there too, fraternizing with the two murderous landscapers. Naturally, I couldn't let anything slip about me being there spying on them. Somehow I knew that admission would blow up in my face and I might lose this new possible ally.

I shook my head. "No blondes at Van Alst House. Or here."

I was thinking fast. Could Cherie really have been involved? Or was Detective Jones just pointing the finger to get attention away from Muriel and possibly himself?

Tricky situation.

I said, "It's hard to believe all this stuff is happening in Harrison Falls."

"And that's not all," he said.

"What?"

He leaned in, conspiratorially. "I hear there's a big bust going on too."

I stared at him, exhausted and slack-jawed. "I don't understand."

"There's been a sweep and it looks like the feds have broken up a counterfeiting ring."

Uh-oh. "You think that has something to do with the Rileys?"

"Like you said, there's all this stuff happening in our little town."

"Here? Counterfeiting seems a little sophisticated for Harrison Falls." My Spidey Senses were doing backflips. *Please, not my uncles.*

"Apparently here and Grandville and downstate."

"Albany?"

"New York City."

Counterfeit ring. Of course, my uncles would be all over that. Kellys love a crime with zero violence and a lot of sleight of hand. This must be why they'd been so elusive lately. I'd been thinking more along the line of a jewelry heist. But then there was all that equipment in the building across the way. Were Uncle Mick and Lucky caught up in this sweep?

My eye began to twitch. I wasn't sure I could hide my anxiety, so I tried a diversion.

"You don't think this has anything to do with Muriel and Vera, do you?"

"Oh no, just making conversation."

At the sound of heavy footsteps from the shop, I whirled to face Uncle Mick. Safe and sound. Wild Irish hair standing on end. Yawning and stretching, he whipped off his jacket. As usual his shirt was unbuttoned just enough to show off the gold chain nestled in the ginger thatch on his chest. "What a night. Long drive back from Baltimore. Can't wait to hit the hay. What are you doing up so early?" He glanced around, staring at Melski. Then turned to Kev and the signora. He frowned at the door to Lucky's, where a cat protest could be heard. Finally back to Melski. "Perhaps I'm already asleep and this is a nightmare. Wake me when it's over."

I barely managed not to collapse with relief. "Officer Melski, this is my uncle, Michael Kelly. This is Officer Melski, Uncle Mick. Officer Melski's been a huge help. He kept me out of jail tonight."

"Huh. You are the last person in the world who would ever get arrested, my girl."

"That's changed, apparently."

Melski ruined the mood. "I suppose you can account for your whereabouts from two to three this morning, sir?"

Uncle Mick chuckled. "Sure can. Got pulled over in a roadblock on 81. Some FBI thing as far as I could tell. You guys keep records of that kind of thing, don't you?"

Perhaps the stars were in alignment for the Kellys tonight.

Kev said, "We heard they were looking for a bunch of paperhangers."

Mick chuckled. "Counterfeit—paperhangers? In Williams County? That's shocking. What's the world coming to?"

He was light and breezy, so I figured whatever he'd been up to, it wasn't counterfeiting.

I had to ask, "And Uncle Lucky?"

"Still a happy honeymooner in the big smoke. Home again tomorrow, I think. Well, I'm off to bed."

Only an innocent man could saunter up the stairs leaving us in the kitchen. Surely.

I stood up but felt my knees buckle. All that adrenaline.

Officer Melski said, "Maybe you should get some rest too. I have a feeling you won't get much today. I'll be outside if you need me."

I barely made it up the stairs. Cobain and Walter came with me. Although I hoped Melski didn't recognize Cobain, I was too tired to question why a patrol officer was free to spend his night keeping an eye on us.

Kevin checked that the signora had everything she needed in Lucky's place and he crashed on the sofa there, giving Bad Cat an opportunity for a bit of fun, I figured.

Just before I went to sleep, I texted Cherie asking a very special favor. I needed a wireless webcam set up in Vera's room, one at each entrance and one in the study if I was to keep an eye on whatever was going to happen in Van Alst House. I probably needed a spare too and a laptop. If anyone could make that happen, Cherie could. That is, if she got my text and if she really was one of the good guys.

At this point, I had very little to lose.

CHAPTER FIFTEEN

I F THINGS HAD been bad up until that point, at nine the next morning they got much worse. For the first time in my life, I was arrested.

This set up a wave of opposition from Uncle Mick and Uncle Kev, Signora Panetone, Walter and Cobain and, unless I was wrong—given how shocked I was—a cat or two in the distance. Everyone had been caught flatfooted competing to make breakfast in the small kitchen.

Everyone except me. I was caught flatfooted enjoying the results of competition between Uncle Mick and the signora. The only flatfoot in our group seemed to have gone home when his shift was over.

"I'll get you a lawyer," Uncle Mick said.

"Make sure it's not Dwight Jenkins," I muttered.

Uncle Mick shrugged. "Don't worry. He's useless."

Detective Jones scowled at Uncle Mick. His expression radiated menace.

If I had an expression it would have radiated stunned, just plain stunned. The fact of the pot calling the kettle black just added to my stunnedness.

I was ushered from the house by Detective Jones after being given time to get dressed. What does one wear to the interrogation room? Something that would survive a spell in a cell? I wore black tights, black boots and a gray dress. I decided against jewelry and a scarf. They'd just take those from me.

I had no role models for this. Although some of my uncles were no strangers to jail, Mick and Lucky had never spent a minute behind bars, giving new meaning to "the luck of the Irish." Kev was a different story, but who would ever use Kev as a role model for anything?

As Detective Jones put his hand on my head and I slumped into the back of a Harrison Falls Police Services patrol car, Uncle Mick called out, "Don't say a word until the lawyer gets there. Not a word, my girl."

After being fingerprinted, having my mug shot taken and being left to twitch in an interrogation room for at least an hour, I decided my model would be Archie. An innocent person might be puzzled, angry or panicked, but, of course, I was not an innocent person. Still, I did not intend to become a convicted person.

The interrogation room wouldn't win any prizes for décor. It was Vera-sweater-beige with a single table and four hard plastic chairs. The lights were unpleasantly bright and humming, the worst that fluorescence has to offer. Naturally, the door was locked.

I sat there and tried to remember the details of Archie's interrogations. I assumed a languid and relaxed position, not to give anyone on the other side a moment's satisfaction. Of course, I was guilty of the burglary of Dwight Jenkins's house and of orchestrating the theft of the will at Van Alst House. I doubted that they could prove it. Still, I worked on remembering my uncles' many tips on convincing lies.

I did not trust this guy Jones. I wouldn't put it past him to manufacture evidence to frame me. He had bad taste in drinking buddies and I bet his integrity was subpar.

After an eternity, he showed up, well groomed as always, with a young officer and a tape recorder. I looked bored. I declined his offer of a soft drink or some bottled water. Coffee too. Did he think I was a fool happy to hand over my DNA?

"Thanks. Still enjoying memories of breakfast."

"It could be a long day."

I shrugged. "Bring it."

"Your choice."

He made himself comfortable in the plastic chair next to the younger officer. The tape was already running.

"You know why you're here?"

"I've been advised not to say anything without my lawyer."

"Why would that be? An innocent person doesn't need a lawyer."

I resisted an urge to blow him a kiss. I think that was Archie's influence. I managed a smile.

And so it went. Questions about where I was, who I was with, who I had contacted, what time this, what time that. All the answers were the same: not until my lawyer gets here.

"You sure you have a lawyer?" he said with a sneer after a lot of wasted questions. "Why would you need one?"

"I didn't before this morning actually, but my uncle will contact a family friend."

"Name?"

I figured the most innocuous question could blow up in my face. I could become rattled, and once rattled I would be a sitting duck for whatever shots Detective Jack Jones wanted to fire. "You'd have to call my uncle for that information."

Uncle Mick was more than equal to anything Jones could dish out.

Archie would have dished back, never answering the question as asked, pushing and even taunting the cops as he went. There were plenty of entertaining examples of that. Inspector Cramer's face always turned bright red. Of course, Archie was brave about being beaten up and I was pretty sure that I wouldn't be, even if it led to a successful litigation. I kept it to smiling and hoped that Jones would be only manageably enraged. Unlike Cramer, his face never got the slightest bit red.

I thought the younger cop got a bit wide-eyed

from time to time, but we all have to grow up sometime. After what felt like weeks but was probably only hours, an officer came to the door with my lawyer, a guy named Sammy Vincovic from Syracuse. I had heard my uncle speak of him in respectful tones. Unlike the dapper Detective Jack Jones, Vincovic looked like he'd slept in his suit. Regularly.

Jones would underestimate him.

I was allowed to consult privately with my lawyer. I hadn't been sure if that was just on television. "When they question you, say nothing," he advised.

"I haven't been answering anything without you."

"No comment. That's what you say, if they pick you up again or question you about anything."

"I have an alibi." I filled him in on Officer Melski.

Vincovic shook his head. "Say nothing."

"But—"

He shook his head sadly. "You want this to go well or badly?"

"Well, I am the one in the family who's gone straight."

"Then you want it to go well. There's no way they can get a conviction and most likely no way that it will even come to trial. If it does, we can look forward to a case for malicious prosecution. Those are good."

"They are?"

"Sure. Moneywise. Of course, you'd need to go to trial and to be acquitted and we'd need to prove that the cops deliberately messed up."

"You could probably make that stick. Something bad is going on with my former employer, Vera Van Alst. Detective Jones is mixed up in it." It took a while to explain. At the end, I think Vincovic got it. He smiled, maybe imagining the fun of a suit for malicious prosecution. I just wanted it all to end.

By the time I got bail, I was starting to unravel.

As I was on my way out of the station, Detective Jack Jones narrowed his eyes. "You're not off the hook yet."

"No comment," I said.

Vincovic smiled like a proud daddy.

AT HOME EVERYONE fussed over me, including two excited dogs. Somehow in the homecoming, I managed to get scratched by Bad Cat. I almost had to admire his initiative. Speaking of initiative, Vincovic was described in admiring terms as a "piranha." When I voiced my worries about the cost of a piranha, Uncle Mick said, "A treat on me, my girl."

The signora had won the battle for kitchen supremacy and was serving giant bowls of fresh pasta with a simple tomato sauce. I knew that meal was out of this world. My uncles were in for a treat of a different kind.

On the off chance someone had planted a listening device on us, I couldn't reveal what I'd done or ask Uncle Mick about the equipment across the street and if he'd had a close call in the sweep on 81 last night.

"I ran into your old friend, Cheryl," Kev said. "She said she has everything you need for your sound system if you're still interested. All the components."

As I didn't have a friend called Cheryl and I wasn't looking for a sound system, I assumed this was code for Cherie and the webcams and laptop being set up in Van Alst House. "Oh yeah. I'll be glad to get that old turntable hooked up. That way I can play some of those vinyl classics in the shop, Uncle Mick."

"You're looking tired, Jordie," Kev said. "Maybe you should have a rest."

"I lost a night's sleep and today was really rough. Detective Jones has a vendetta against me."

"Vincovic will make mincemeat out of Jones, my girl. He's obviously making it up as he goes along. Just another dirty cop trying to protect a murderer. Now why don't you head on up and get some rest."

Mick headed up the stairs, treading as girlishly, but audibly, as he could, while I sneaked out the back door with Kev to the second garage, the one the police almost certainly didn't know about, to have a private chat.

"We made contact with Eddie," Kev said.

"How?"

"Cherie got to him when she installed the surveillance equipment."

"Great. By the way, how did she get access to the house?"

"Did something to mess up the cable connection, and then knocked on the door and told them it had happened while she was working in the area and she needed to make repairs."

"They fell for it?"

He shrugged. "Told you Muriel's a cable addict. She was flipping because she couldn't watch her morning programs."

"And they let her in?"

"Apparently the lawyer's been back and a new will is all signed."

"Oh no."

"It's okay. Cherie was asked to witness it. Don't worry. She didn't use her real name. I don't think that will would be legal, do you?"

"That will be a cold comfort if something happens to Vera."

Kev's eyes widened.

"Things are really serious," I said.

"But there's good news too."

"What is it?"

"Eddie's been booted out."

"That's not good news. He was supposed to protect Vera."

"He got agitated about the will and blew it. But he wants to talk to you. So Cherie brought him here. Wait until you hear this."

"But the police are actively looking for this blond woman. They might figure out it's her."

"Give her some credit. She's no dummy, Jordie."

No dummy, but was she a good guy or a bad guy?

A soft knock on the door caused me to whirl. Eddie entered. If he was pale and insubstantial at the best of times, tonight he looked like a puff of smoke, ready to dissipate.

"You have to help her."

"That's the idea, Eddie," I said. "Did Vera talk to you?"

"She wouldn't. You're right. She's under Muriel's thumb. This will says Muriel's her sister and she gets everything."

"Muriel *is* her sister, illegitimate, but a half sister anyway. Did you know about Muriel being Leonard Van Alst's child?"

"You hear things."

"And do you remember about Vera and Muriel's relationship in high school?"

He slumped in a chair. "What's to remember? They hated each other. Vera was embarrassed by her father's affairs. She wasn't really popular to begin with. Then when the factory closed, everyone hated the Van Alsts with a passion."

They still do, I thought. Jack Jones was one of them. Probably the Rileys too.

Eddie said, "Muriel was really nasty and she was big too. Vera had never even gone to public school. She had her head in her books and she kept to herself. She was different from everyone. Exotic."

I didn't add, *and a total snob.* From his expression and tone of voice, I figured this was the point where Eddie began his lifetime of unrequited love for Vera.

I patted his arm. "And?"

"She needed protection. I made sure I was between them all the time. Everyone knew that Muriel was a Van Alst b—well, you know." He blushed.

"Did Vera know?"

"Aside from the gossip, Muriel made it clear to her."

"That doesn't explain the hold that Muriel has on her then. If Vera was aware of it and she knew everyone else was too, what else could it be?"

"Something big. I don't know what. Muriel was really horrible, nasty. The kind of person who would need psychological work before she could become a decent person. I think Mr. Murphy took her aside and gave her grief for the way she was treating Vera. Not long after that, Muriel started to cozy up to Vera. She apologized and said she was wrong. She wanted to make amends and be a friend and she didn't want anything from Vera. She knew she wasn't a real Van Alst."

"You heard all this?"

"I was right there."

"Did Vera accept it?"

"After a while she came around. It would be easier to have Muriel as a friend than an enemy."

"No doubt."

"They started to spend time together and I got kind of left out. It was the end of the school year and I'd been hoping to take Vera to . . ."

Oh boy, that was heartbreaking. But we couldn't go there. "And what happened between them?"

"I don't know. They went to movies and walks and even to an art gallery somewhere in Syracuse one day. Muriel couldn't go to Van Alst House because Vera's mother was still alive. They went to restaurants. They were best friends."

"For how long?" The time must have been right around when Pete Delaney was killed. Then school would have ended. Vera went off to college. Muriel's mother died six months later and then Muriel left town. Until one week ago.

"Not long. Muriel's stepfather was killed. That's when things changed. After that Muriel didn't have anything to do with anyone."

"Really? That was when they fell out?"

He nodded. "I know Vera tried to see her, but Muriel refused. Maybe because old man Van Alst still wouldn't acknowledge her. Vera was crushed when Muriel ended the friendship. That was her only girlfriend. She was more sensitive back then. I think the rejection damaged her."

"I'm sure." I was beginning to feel the power Muriel had over Vera. But only two people knew that story.

Poor Eddie was the picture of grief. "That's all I can tell you. What can we do for her?"

"I have an idea. You'll work with Kev. You will distract Muriel and get her out of the house. I'll get in and speak with Vera. I think I can make her listen to reason. But even if we can't, um, a friend of Kev's has rigged up some video and audio recording equipment in Vera's room. We'll have eyes on her."

"But she values her privacy. She's so . . . well, that seems wrong."

"Well, she'll have all the privacy she needs if she's dead, Eddie. To prevent that, I'll be watching from my old rooms again. It will just be me and you know I'll do the right thing. I'm Vera's friend too. I don't want to do this, but we have to."

Eddie was clearly conflicted. "I suppose it's necessary. And what do I do?"

"Kev will tell you. I'll be in touch. And if there's any danger to Vera, we'll let you know and you go get help."

"I'll call the police."

"I was thinking the fire department might be a better bet. Everyone will show up then. Fake some smoke or whatever. And please, please don't use any of Kev's ideas."

Kev looked wounded.

I said, "No offense, Kev. And Eddie, if you get the signal from me, you have to call Officer Melski and tell him that Vera and I are in danger. I think we trust him. Here's his number. Can you handle all that?"

"Of course. Why wouldn't I be able to?"

Not everyone was like Uncle Kev. I could trust Eddie not to burn down Van Alst House while faking a fire. Pretty sure.

"Okay, I'll get ready and then we'll head out in separate vehicles. My Saab is still parked in front of the shop, so that will look like I'm still here. At least it usually works."

"As long as the cops don't check here in the middle of the night, Jordie. If you're at Vera's place, your bail will be revoked and Mick will be out a bundle."

"Positive thoughts, Kev," I said, trying not to think of how much Mick would be out. I crept back to Uncle Mick's place and upstairs to get my burglar clothes, warmest boots, tools, backpack and a good book to read for the long night ahead. I picked up the copy of *Some Buried Caesar*. It also involved unfamiliar surroundings and a lot of bull.

HALF AN HOUR later, we were parked in the same place as my last furtive visit and we checked that our phones had a signal. Everything was a go. Kev handed me packages of food for me and Vera, including Uncle Mick's best thermos. The signora doesn't miss a chance.

I stuck the food and thermos in my backpack and picked my way across the fields and toward the Van Alst place. Kev and Eddie got in place at the end of the Van Alst driveway.

We had agreed on an SOS on the horn to warn me when Muriel was coming back.

As I reached the house, I texted *GO!*

I waited. Eddie and Mick drove forward to the house and began to blow the horn loudly. After ten minutes, the front door opened and Muriel appeared. I used that time to sprint across to the back door and pick the lock. Of course, Muriel had turned off the alarm when she stormed down the driveway. I dashed in. I hurried along the endless corridors to the grand foyer and then up the broad stairs to the second floor. I reached Vera's door. To knock or not to knock? I decided that picking the lock would get our unscheduled powwow off to a bad start. My heart was thundering, a feeling I should have been getting used to.

I knocked.

"What is going on?" Vera said.

I muttered.

I could hear her complaining as she wheeled toward the door. As she opened it, her face contorted and she did her best to close the door in my face.

"Sorry, Vera, but we need to talk," I said, foot firmly blocking that possibility. "You are going to listen to me. Muriel is outside. She doesn't know I'm here. Let's keep it that way. I can't believe you let her get rid of Eddie."

"He shouldn't have been here."

"I know she has something over you and that's why you have pushed away every friend, every supporter, everyone who could save you."

She tried to bluster. "I don't need saving. And definitely not by you, Miss Bingham."

"Is that so? You are alone here with Muriel and whoever her accomplices are."

"What accomplices?" Vera barked out the words, but I could tell that was unsettling to her.

"Don't know yet, but will find out. Now I need you to tell me what she's got on you."

"Miss Bingham. You will be arrested if you don't leave."

"Do you want to end up dead just to keep a secret? Is that the best you can do?"

She blinked.

"What are you thinking, leaving everything to her?"

"That's none of your affair."

"But—"

"But nothing. She is my sister and I owe her."

"You don't love her, though."

"My emotions are hardly your concern."

"They *are* my concern. I care about you, Vera, no matter how you act. I love being part of your world and I have learned so much from you. You are not going to get rid of me, when you need my help. Muriel is dangerous and you know it, so stop pretending. Whatever you might have said or done when you were just a teenager doesn't matter. You can trust your friends, no matter what."

"There's nothing you could do."

"How awful could it possibly be?"

The bleakness in Vera's eyes was hard to bear.

"It can't be that bad," I said, before swallowing. "Even for *crimes* there's the statute of limitations."

"Not for everything."

"Well, it's not like you committed a murder, Vera."

She met my eyes and I felt my blood chill.

"I don't believe that for a second."

"How would you know?"

I told myself to be calm. Muriel had outdone herself if she'd convinced Vera that she'd committed murder. "There's no way, Vera."

"I will tell you because I know you won't tell anyone. That's one positive trait from your criminal relatives."

I blinked. I hadn't realized that Vera knew that about my relatives.

She said softly, no sign of her usual gravelly voice. "I was driving a car."

I let her speak.

"I hit a man. He died. I kept going."

"Anyone could have an accident, but you're not the type to run from one."

"I was drunk."

"Oh."

"And there were drugs in my system."

"Drugs?" A picture of Vera in bell-bottoms smoking a bong flashed through my brain.

"I'm not proud of what happened, Miss Bingham." I didn't believe this had happened, but, clearly, Vera did.

"Was the man Pete Delaney?"

She nodded. "I knew him. He was a very nice man, very important to his wife, very good to Muriel, although she loathed him. I killed him. I ruined Muriel's life. That will is the least I could do."

"That's ridiculous, Vera."

She stared at me, her face haggard. "Miss Bingham, which of us was there?"

"Start at the beginning. What do you remember about the accident?"

"Nothing. I have blocked it out. But it happened."

"Do you remember driving the car?"

"No. Apparently, I was quite drunk and I had tried some recreational pharmaceuticals."

It was laughable to imagine Vera soliciting a drug dealer for "recreational pharmaceuticals." But the situation wasn't funny. "What kind of drugs?"

"I don't remember. I didn't even know."

"Was it Muriel's idea? Was it peer pressure?" Something didn't smell right.

"Does it matter? I did it."

"Do you remember drinking?"

"We decided to have some wine. I brought it from home and we shared a couple of glasses."

"And you passed out and you don't remember taking anything."

"That's right."

"A couple of glasses of wine wouldn't have that effect, Vera. Muriel must have drugged you. Let me guess, she said she was with you the entire time."

"She could have hated me, but she chose to protect me. She told the police we were together and I didn't have to worry about it. She was my alibi. Of course, it was the end of our rather strange friendship."

"Listen to me, Vera. She was your alibi, but, more important, you were *hers*."

"More nonsense, Miss Bingham."

"You went off to college at the end of the summer and three months later, Carmen Delgado died. When Pete Delaney was killed in June, his wife had less than a year to live. He left everything to her, including a million-dollar life insurance policy. Then when Carmen died, Muriel inherited the house and what was left of the insurance money. That was enough to get her out of Harrison Falls and off to a new life in the big city where no one knew her. Muriel had a powerful motive to kill Pete."

"She left because she was heartbroken. I am responsible for that."

"She left because she had enough money to. You didn't kill Pete Delaney, and Muriel didn't either. She arranged for Frank Riley to do it."

Something changed in Vera's eyes. A spark of hope? "Frank Riley?"

"Yes."

"I remember him. He was a rough boy from over on Lilac Lane and not too bright, but he had quite a crush on Muriel."

Lilac Lane? Well, that explained a few things. The old couple were probably still in touch with Frank and Junior. Maybe they were even relatives. They probably knew about Frank's connection with Muriel. That would account for the woman's instant hostility at my questions.

I turned my focus back to Vera. Time was an issue. "He tried to run me over. The same way that he ran over Pete Delaney all those years ago. I know it's because I was asking questions about Muriel. And no one will get him to admit that because he's dead, as is his brute of a son. Muriel, of course, has an alibi for both incidents."

"You can't prove she was involved."

"And no one could prove you hit Pete Delaney. Vera, let us help you. We need to get you out of the house."

I heard the car horn beeping our SOS signal.

"No," Vera said.

"Staying is too risky."

"You think I'm in danger?"

"Yes. That original inheritance must be used up, but Muriel gets another big payoff if something happens to you."

"There's not much you can do to protect me from these so-called unknown accomplices."

"Vera, please. Come with me."

"You'd better get going, Miss Bingham, if she's as dangerous as you say. What could she do to me?"

"She could push your wheelchair down the stairs. She could smother you in your sleep. She could tamper with your food. So don't leave the room with her. Keep your door locked. Don't eat or drink anything she gives you."

I hightailed it down the hall and up the steep and dark back stairs to the third floor and my beloved little apartment. It looked so forlorn without my stuff, but I was glad to see the curling cabbage rose wallpaper and the iron bedstead with the flowered quilt.

Somehow Cherie had managed to install the web cam in Vera's room, and the interior of the room was visible on the small screen of the laptop she'd left for me. I also had a good view of Vera. One good thing, there was no sign of the signora's package.

I gasped at a knock on Vera's door.

Vera stiffened. She raised her chin.

"Come in," she said.

CHAPTER SIXTEEN

I AM CHECKING to see how you are." Muriel strode into the room, looming over Vera in her wheelchair. She was as large and coarse and scary-looking as ever. Her loose and flowy black clothes still swirled around her like a dark specter. For some reason she was carrying a small tray.

One floor up, I hunched over the screen and held my breath.

Vera said, "How kind, Muriel. I am fine. What was all that fuss outside?"

"That idiot Eddie and that other idiot, Kevin Kelly. They're drunk."

"Drunk?"

"They were acting crazy. I could smell alcohol on Eddie's breath."

"Could you?"

"Sure could. You are lucky to have gotten rid of them. If they come back, I'll call the police."

"The police would be a good idea."

Oh, Vera. You caught that, didn't you. I sat up straight. Of course, Eddie was allergic to alcohol. We all knew he never touched it because it made him instantly ill. Muriel wasn't very good at lying on the fly. Rule One: *Keep It Simple*. Guess she didn't have an Uncle Mick to guide her. Vera was staring at Muriel. I could almost see the wheels turning. Was this finally enough to convince her that Muriel was determined to do her some harm?

"Oh, I almost forgot," Muriel said, "I brought you a snack. I'll put it on the table here. Those two fools have me distracted."

"We wouldn't want that," Vera said.

Yes! At last, a peek at the old Vera.

"They're double-chocolate mocha brownies with truffle icing and some ginger tea. Very nice." Muriel put the tray on the small table near Vera's wheelchair. I recognized the Royal Derby china. And I recognized something else.

"Thank you."

"Aren't you going to try one?"

"I certainly am," Vera said, "But I have a little acid reflux, so I'll take a tablet for that first. I'd like to savor them, Muriel." She extracted a pill container from her bedside table and popped a pill into her mouth.

"Of course, well, eat up. I'm feeling rather unwell myself." She picked up Vera's copy of *Over My Dead Body* and fondled it. Even from my position, I could feel Vera seething. It was one of her favorite Wolfe stories. Muriel dropped the book carelessly into her bag and said, "I can't reach my doctor, so I'm going to the emergency room at Grandville General. They say you should follow up immediately if you have pain in the jaw and tingling down your arms."

Even on the small screen, it seemed to me that Vera's eyes glittered. "Would you like me to go with you?"

"And why would I want that?"

"It would be ill-advised to drive yourself."

"I'm not stupid. I've called a cab."

"Good thinking," Vera said.

I snorted and said out loud, "Right, because you need that alibi, Muriel."

Vera obviously had figured that out too. "Well, there will be lots of people to keep an eye on you at the Emergency room."

"Yes. Are you nervous alone?"

"Ridiculous. What could I have to fear in my own home?"

Muriel's thin mouth squirmed into a smile. Every hair on the back of my neck stood up.

The door closed behind Muriel, and Vera rolled toward the bathroom. I heard the toilet flush in a minute. When Vera rolled back into view, the plate was empty and I assumed the cup was too.

There went the evidence.

I gasped when there was another knock. Muriel was back. This time she'd added another layer of swirling black outerwear. "My cab has arrived," she said in a doom-laden voice. "Oh, I see you've finished the brownies and ginger tea. Let me take the plate and cup out of your way."

I bit my lip. That would get rid of any traces of drugs.

Vera said, "You have outdone yourself."

Muriel turned and said, "I imagine I'll be back by midnight."

I raced to the top front window in the attic—to be sure that Muriel actually got into the cab—before I dashed down the steep stairs to Vera's room. I called Kev. "Muriel's gone. I think she's sending her accomplice to finish Vera."

"Roger, Bo Peep."

I caught my breath at Vera's door. It was open. She was holding the poker to her fireplace set.

"You were right, Miss Bingham."

"Whoa. You didn't eat those brownies, did you?"

"Do you take me for a fool?" Ah, the old Vera was back.

"What did you do with them? I should have mentioned they'd be useful evidence."

"Of course, they'd be evidence. I hid them in the bathroom cupboard. I poured the tea in my toothbrush glass. I wanted Muriel to believe she'd succeeded. I didn't realize you were still in the house, Miss Bingham."

"I've been watching what happened on the webcam that shows your room. I didn't want you to worry about giving anything away."

Vera's eyebrow arched. It told me what she thought of that.

"Well, Miss Bingham. What now?"

"Now we get out of here. And Kev and Eddie will wait to see who shows up. We don't know who's helping Muriel and whether there's one accomplice or more."

But even as I said it, I had an inkling.

"My car's on the other side of the field, but we'll take your Cadillac from the garage. Are the keys still in the kitchen? Wait for me by the back door. We need to get out of here as soon as possible."

Vera said, "I am not leaving."

"We've got to get out of here before Muriel's collaborator shows up. Part of keeping yourself safe means making a new will tonight. Name any beneficiary except Muriel, even the cats if you want. As long as this last will is valid, you're in danger."

While we were talking, I rearranged the pillows on the bed to make it look like Vera was sleeping, then dimmed the light. Perhaps in the rush of the moment Muriel's sidekick wouldn't notice the wheelchair was missing. Any attack on Vera's sleeping form would be captured through my webcam.

"I will not be driven from my home."

"Don't think of it as being driven. Think of it as choosing not to be murdered in your home. We have webcams in place in your room and at the front and back doors. We'll capture images of the other scumbag on the computer. And if we get them on tape in your room, we'll have something concrete to bring to the police and then you can come right back home. Really, we're just going to visit my Uncle Mick and have some untainted tea."

"I'm not going anywhere. I shouldn't have let her manipulate me. I am ashamed of myself. This is what comes of pride, Miss Bingham. She found my weakness. I was afraid of exposure, scandal and a trial. At the time, I thought it would be even more disgrace for my family name. I see now how I was used."

"Fine. But you'll have to lie low until we get a few things under control. Let's go to the library. I'll make it seem like you're in bed here, and you'll be safer in the library with the security system activated. In the meantime, we'll be working to spring a trap. Why don't you take along *Where There's a Will* and enjoy that at least?"

"One of my favorites and it does seem apropos, Miss Bingham. I won't fight you on relocating to the library. And the trap?"

"I was thinking a gathering of witnesses and suspects, Nero Wolfe style. If all goes well, you'll be vindicated, Muriel will be stopped and the accomplice will be exposed."

"If all doesn't go well?"

"How long has it been since you've seen some theater?"

Vera tilted her head. I was glad to spot a slight upward curl at the corners of her lips.

As we waited for the elevator, I pulled out my

phone and called Mick. "Drop everything. I need you to pick up Dwight Jenkins, the lawyer, and bring him to Van Alst House now. He needs to draw up a new will for Vera. She'll be in the library. Come around to the back, bring Jenkins right to the library and stay with him and Vera. You and I can be witnesses." I held the phone away from my ear as Mick gave me his opinion of this plan. "It's Code Red, Uncle Mick."

In our family, Code Red trumps everything.

My phone vibrated as soon as I hung up. I'd missed a call from Kev and apparently I had also missed one from the Poocherie earlier in the day. I checked to discover that I had a message from Jasmine. I almost let it go. Cat food and dog treats seemed very unimportant with everything that was going on. Even if she'd remembered something else about the Rileys, that wouldn't help much at this stage. After all, they were dead.

I got Vera settled in the library with the door locked. Her job was to phone the security company and change the code to the library door. I didn't want anyone but the good guys joining her there. I headed back upstairs to keep an eye on the webcam. I settled on the bed with the laptop and played Jasmine's message.

Her voice was apologetic. "Very sorry it took so long to get back to you. I've been *so* busy. I forgot that you'd asked me about those guys. Call me if it's important. My number is—"

I called her.

Lucky for me, she answered right away.

"Once I got away from the chaos, my head cleared and I remembered them."

"Where did you see them?"

"I had to come back to the Poocherie late one night because I forgot my wallet. I saw these guys coming out of the Hudson Café around midnight, long after it closed. They caught my eye because they didn't seem like the usual clientele, if you know what I mean. They were pretty grungy with muddy boots and all. I thought maybe they'd broken in."

"The Hudson Café? Really?"

"It is kind of weird and it's probably nothing."

I swallowed. Visions of the double-chocolate mocha brownies with truffle icing swam in my head. "Was anyone with them? Maybe they were friends with some of the staff."

"I may be wrong here but it seemed like they were tight with Lainie, the owner, and another person that I didn't know. They all acted like old friends. Like they went way back."

Lainie Hetherington had only been in Harrison Falls since the summer. She and the Rileys couldn't have gone that far back unless there was another connection. And she'd never mentioned that she knew them personally. I could feel pieces falling into place.

"Did you see the other person, Jasmine?"

"Yes. But I didn't know her."

"Would you recognize her if you saw her?"

"I think so."

"This is really important. Thanks so much. Don't mention it to anyone at all. And I will need you to do a huge, lifesaving favor for me."

Jasmine said. "I love it when you're mysterious."

"Just sit tight and be available."

I called Kev. "You and Eddie better get in here. Hide your car somewhere. Vera is refusing to leave so we're bringing the lawyer to her to update the will."

"We're a mile or two away, Jordie."

"A mile or two? Why, Kev?" Of course, because he was Kev, it was physically painful for him to follow instructions.

"Just thought it might be a good idea to get the kitties."

"What?" Like bringing a stick of dynamite to a bonfire is a good idea.

"But the signora wouldn't let them go. I took the dogs instead."

"Aw, tell me you didn't."

"I thought they might cheer up Vera. But don't worry. Eddie's gone back to get the kitties and the signora."

Funny, I didn't remember taking a handful of crazy pills. I spoke slowly so as not to startle my already stunned uncle. "Kev, the pets will not cheer Vera up if she's dead. Do you understand what I'm saying? I need you here."

"Ooooh, okay. I get it, Jordie. Should I pick up coffee or snacks?"

I massaged my sweaty temples. "No, Kev. No doughnuts. I just need you. Here. Now."

I was pretty sure I knew what would happen next. Vera had been intended to consume one or two drugs that interacted badly in the brownies and the tea. I imagined sleeping pills and muscle relaxants. Enough to kill her and yet still look like an accidental overdose by a fragile woman with health and sleeping issues. Then someone would show up to make sure she was dead. And if she was still breathing, I imagined they'd hold a pillow over her face until she stopped. It would all be hard to prove and it would happen while Muriel was being her highly visible self at the hospital.

I figured I knew who the someone was. The source of the brownies. One of the people I'd talked to about Muriel. The same one with whom I'd shared my concerns about the Rileys. I'd trusted the new owner of the Hudson Café completely. I'd been sucked in by her lovely compassionate manner and her sweet desserts. I felt foolish and naïve.

I used my iPhone to check some facts, starting by Googling Lainie Hetherington. I found several articles about her and her cognitive therapy practice.

Why had I never thought to do that before? It didn't take long before I found a nugget. Lainie Hetherington had been charged with fraud last year following a complaint by a former patient. Further investigation showed that charges had been dropped, but her license had been suspended, meaning she couldn't practice in the state. So not retired, but unable to practice.

What was the connection between her and Muriel? Muriel had also lived in New York City. She'd left Vera alone for nearly forty years. What had caused her to return? Had she been a patient of Lainie's? Whatever you could say about Muriel, she was still a damaged person. Was she bitter and angry? Had she been desperate to be acknowl-edged as a Van Alst? Had she confided that to a warm and sympathetic therapist? Did Muriel's hatred of Vera and the so-called secret spark an opportunity for Lainie after she lost her license and livelihood?

I figured the answer was yes.

Muriel would have been a sitting duck. Just like Vera.

But now I just had to prove it.

The time was now ten o'clock. Uncle Mick had arrived with Dwight Jenkins. They were no sooner through the door when Eddie showed up with the signora and the cats. The cats vanished instantly. I rushed down the stairs to get everyone settled. Uncle Mick and Dwight Jenkins were ushered into the library. Jenkins was sputtering at the inconvenience. He was ill-advisedly using the word "kidnap" in that sputtering.

I said, "You can stop that talk now. You've been used as part of a murder plot and you'll cooperate with Miss Van Alst and hope you don't have the full weight of the law and the licensing body on your head. Uncle Mick, as soon as the will's witnessed you need to put your car out of sight. Try behind the garage." I headed off a bout of outrage. "Not for long and incredibly important. You too, Eddie. No one must know we're here."

Uncle Mick's mouth snapped shut. It didn't take long for Vera to sign the new will leaving everything to the cats. Uncle Mick wasn't keen on that, but he did witness. Eddie did too.

"I hope this will be the last time," Jenkins complained.

Vera said, "You're not being paid to whine and you're not the only game in town."

Kev popped his head around the corner and said, "Where do you want the dogs?"

I rolled my eyes. "I don't. Take them to the library and hope they'll just go to sleep during our big moment. Mick will stay with Vera and you can help me by setting up the study. Eddie, I need you to get Mr. Murphy, your old English teacher, and bring him here."

"Does he know he's coming?"

"He doesn't and he won't like it, but he knows something about Muriel and Vera and this is the time to make him see how important it is."

"But how can I—?"

"We are going to stop two people who wanted Vera dead. If we want to bring them to justice we need to hear from him. Talk him into it. I don't care how."

"I don't even know where he lives."

"I've looked that up for you."

I called Cherie and Jasmine next and set up the next arrivals. Lucky for us Harrison Falls is small and compact. It didn't take long for everyone to return.

I felt very Archie Goodwin as I met them in groups of two and ushered them into the study. This room, as I may have mentioned, is every bit as noteworthy as Wolfe's study. There's no globe, but the room was grand and elegant with its ten-foot ceilings and faded silk draperies. The furniture was exceptional, if past its prime.

Kev brought in extra chairs from the nearby sitting room without doing any damage. I was sorry there wasn't a red chair, like Archie's, but you can't have everything.

Twelve chairs were arranged in a semicircle facing the desk. Cherie, who was no longer blond, as fallout from that BOLO, set up a laptop on the desk and adjusted the angle of the spare webcam to capture everything.

Kev had done an excellent job of setting up an antique bar cart complete with almost every liquor bottle in Van Alst House and a selection of Waterford crystal highball glasses and wineglasses. I surmised that he'd logged a few hours as a barman somewhere. Best not to know details.

I made a call to the police and sure enough in a matter of minutes, Detective Jack Jones was ushered into the study. I said, "You'll find this instructive."

Jones stared around, glaring at Cherie, Jasmine, Uncle Kev and me. He'd just started to rant when Eddie arrived with Mr. Murphy. I guess Mr. Murphy's authority was still in effect after all those years, because Jones snapped his mouth closed and took a seat.

"This better be good," he said. Cramer couldn't have said it better.

Eddie scurried back to the library to spend a bit of time with Vera and wait for the magic moment. Two minutes later, Dwight Jenkins entered the study guided by Uncle Mick. Uncle Mick made the universal symbol for "not a word" and Jenkins slumped into the seat closest to the door.

All we had to do was sit and wait. I glanced at my watch. I'd been hoping that Melski would show up.

The signora threw herself into a whirlwind of preparation and somehow managed to swing through with a tray of cheeses, sliced bread, prosciutto, Genoa salami and olives.

"Eat!" she said. I could tell from her jubilance that she knew Muriel was not likely to win.

Kev took the tray from her hands and offered it around along with napkins. No one but Kev was hungry.

He followed that with offers of drinks. Jenkins went for Lagavulin. Uncle Mick is not one to say no to a drop of Jameson. Cherie accepted a Bacardi and Coke, Jasmine a Cosmo. Mr. Murphy agreed to a glass of merlot; Jones shook his head. Needed his wits about him, I supposed.

I did too.

So did Kev. I shook my head as his hand reached out to get himself a glass.

Every now and then, someone's eyes would glance at the four empty chairs.

Cherie said, "We've got company." She pointed to the screen.

Lainie had already entered the foyer. I hightailed it to the front of the house and caught her as she was starting up the stairs.

"Lainie? What are you doing here?" I feigned surprise.

She was more surprised; hers wasn't feigned. She frowned. "Well, what are you doing here?"

"Something terrible has happened." I was shaking. And I wasn't entirely faking that. I had a pretty good idea who I was dealing with. She was looking as good as ever. The silver bob neatly pulled back in a classic ponytail, the red lipstick fresh, her clothing chic and becoming. The well-dressed and elegant murderer. Nero Wolfe and Archie had unmasked many of those.

"What is it, Jordan?"

"But why are you here? I don't understand, Lainie. Do you know Vera?"

"Muriel Delgado called me from the hospital. She's been coming by the café and she seems so lonely and out of place here, I thought she needed a friend."

"Oh." How stupid did she think I was?

"She thinks she's having symptoms of a heart attack. She asked me to meet her there to help. I'm pretty sure it's just nerves. She was completely overwrought."

"Really? Why?"

Lainie blinked. "She was worried that Miss Van Alst might mix up her medications and she insisted that I come over and check. Vera's been doing that lately. It's so dangerous."

I sniffed, then shuddered. "You're too late. I think Vera's dead."

"What?"

"She's not breathing. She's in her bed. She's just lying there and—"

"Are you sure?"

"Pretty sure. I was afraid to touch her." I

simulated a bit of hyperventilating, nicely done if I did say so myself.

Lainie put her arms around me and I managed not to flinch.

I pushed back and clutched her hands. "Do you have Muriel's cell number? We need to let her know. Muriel needs to come right back. Now!"

"Shhh. You have to be calm, Jordan. I'll call her. But if she's having a heart attack . . ."

"You said you thought it was just nerves."

Lainie tossed her silver ponytail. "Yes. And this terrible thing won't help those nerves."

I wailed, "You have to."

"Yes, yes, I agree. I'm calling now. Muriel? It's Lainie Hetherington. Yes. I am there. No, I'm afraid that she's not all right. Well, I don't want to say over the phone. Have you seen a doctor yet? No, don't take a chance, please. No. I didn't find her. Jordan Bingham did. Well, I don't know why she's here. I will ask her, but you should— hello?" She turned to me. "Oh dear. She's pretty upset."

"Let me tell you about upset."

"What were you doing here, Jordan? Why did you go to Vera's bedroom?"

"I wanted to try to reason with her about firing me and the others. I waited until Muriel left and let myself in. When I went to her bedroom, I found . . ."

Lainie's eyes glittered. "You can see how this won't look good for you, can't you?"

"No one needs to know that I'm here, Lainie. Please check on her. Maybe she's not dead. I . . . I'm not sure."

I followed her up the stairs and turned away while she went into the room. The light was dim enough for my purposes. "I can't bear to go back in there."

Outside, I texted the signal to Cherie, who was set up in the study. I hoped she'd see on the screen what we needed.

The text came back. *She has picked up the pillow. Got her.*

Kev began to holler downstairs. I opened the door. Lainie was leaning over the supposed sleeping form of Vera, with the pillow in her hands. That would have been recorded.

Lainie dropped the pillow. "What's he yelling about? Why is he here? What is wrong with you people?"

"Fire!" Kev shouted, convincingly. "Get out of there now! This place will go up like a Roman candle."

Our fire idea was going to come in handy after all.

Lainie hesitated. I said, "The place is on fire. It's too late for Vera. Save yourself, Lainie."

We raced for the stairs and down. At the foot, we were met by Uncle Mick. He has more natural authority than Kev. "Sorry, false alarm," he said, raising his crystal glass of Jameson in a salute. "But there's something you both should see. Matter of life or death."

With his free hand, he shepherded the puzzled Lainie down the hall and into the study. She glanced around at Jasmine and Cherie and Jenkins. She frowned at Mr. Murphy, couldn't quite place him. Her eyes widened when she spotted Jones.

"What's going on here?"

"Drink?" Kev said.

Lainie shook her head and stared at Jones before moving toward the door. But Mick was standing there and he was more than enough Irish uncle to keep everyone in the room.

"You can't keep me here," she said. "I'd like to leave now."

"That would be a very big mistake," I said. "Don't you want to hear what Muriel has to say when she comes back? She may try to suggest that you enticed her to do things."

"She's a very disturbed person," Lainie snapped. "You can't listen to anything she says."

"But we'll hear what you both have to say. She should be here any minute."

Lainie went on the offensive. "At least the police are here. If you played a role in Vera's death, they'll find out."

I glanced at my watch and smiled.

The tension in the room was nicely ratcheted up

by the time Muriel made her grand, black and swirling entrance. Kev went to meet her. We could hear her bellowing. "What are you doing here, Kelly? Get the hell out! And is that a Siamese?"

Uncle Mick opened the door to the study as Muriel pursued Kev down the endless hallway. I peeked out. "Do come in, Ms. Delgado. We have some bad news for you about Vera."

Muriel boomed from the corridor, "It was just a matter of time before she mixed up her medications. I need to see her body."

Lainie slumped into the nearest empty chair and put her hands over her eyes. *Oh, Muriel, bad when your confederate decides to act like an ostrich.*

Mick stepped aside and so did I. Muriel stomped into the room, glaring.

"What are all these people doing in my house? Get out, all of you!"

From behind her came a gravelly voice. "It's not your house yet, Muriel."

It was hard to know who was most thunderstruck, Muriel or Lainie. Both jaws dropped as Vera rolled into the room. A Siamese shot through the door too.

Vera made her way to the desk and with Eddie's help moved from the wheelchair to the desk chair. I knew she could do that herself, but I think it made Eddie happy.

She smiled. "In the words of the great Mark

Twain, 'The report of my death is greatly exaggerated.'"

I couldn't remember when I'd last seen her looking so cheerful.

"What's this about?" Muriel blustered. "Everybody else but Vera out!"

"It's about you putting drugs in my brownies and my tea."

"That's ridiculous."

"Not ridiculous in the least. I did hang on to the evidence."

Muriel blurted, "But the plate was empty."

This was confirming what I'd suspected. Muriel wasn't bright enough to have conjured up all this. Lainie, on the other hand, stood up to leave. "This has nothing to do with me."

"But it does. And so in fact do the Rileys. You and Muriel also employed them."

"I don't know any Rileys."

Now the spotlight was on Cherie. She looked good as a brunette too. She whipped the laptop around, fiddled a bit and clicked play.

The room was silent as we watched Lainie standing over Vera's bed. We had a clear view of her picking up a pillow and leaning in.

Jasmine inhaled sharply, then gulped her Cosmo.

Jones looked like he was about to have a stroke. His hand shot to his head. His expression as he stared at Lainie told me he hadn't been involved in the plot. It also told me he had been taken in by her and perhaps romantically involved.

I said, "So you were willing to kill Vera, Lainie. Did you also do in the Rileys because I was getting close to them?"

"I didn't know any Rileys. I'm not sure what you're trying to pull off here, but it won't work."

Jasmine piped up. "That's not true. You did know them. I saw you together outside your restaurant. You were all really chummy."

Muriel turned to Lainie and roared, "You killed Frankie and Junior? Why, you—"

"Forget the hokey movie lines, Muriel," I said. "Nobody's falling for it. This is all on your head, including Frankie and Junior."

"That is definitely the woman who was there with Lainie and those landscapers," Jasmine added. "She'd be hard to mix up with anyone else."

Vera at this point was leaning back in her chair, enjoying the show.

I said, "Of course, the brownies came from your café. That will be easy to establish. Using your signature dish to murder someone? Not so bright. You both conspired to do that. Of course, now we realize that you took Muriel under your wing as a patient before you lost your license."

Lainie fell for the bluff. Her eyes widened.

"Did you think we wouldn't find out, Lainie? Muriel was just what you needed: a damaged and vindictive woman who could have access to a big estate, if only she could get rid of her half sister. Did it take long to coach Muriel to take over Vera's life, to undermine her and get rid of her friends and support system?"

"This is foolishness. I want a lawyer."

"It won't be me," Jenkins said, picking up his glass of Lagavulin again. "I'm glad Miss Van Alst changed her beneficiaries from Muriel to her cats."

Muriel shrieked and her black garments swirled. Her eyes bulged.

Lovely.

I continued, "You agreed to Muriel's need for an alibi and came here to make sure Vera was dead while Muriel was still in plain view at the hospital."

Jenkins put down his single malt with a thump. "I'm having trouble following."

"Let me bring you up to speed," Vera said, leaning forward again. "Many years ago, Muriel tricked me into believing I killed someone."

Muriel's eyes glittered. "You did! You ruined my life."

"Not at all. Because I was foolish enough to believe you, I provided you with an alibi for the death of your stepfather. I had no reason to harm him."

I interjected, "But you had a million reasons, Muriel. And you had your friend Frankie, even then."

She paled and swayed. "You can't prove it. I never said anything like that to you, Vera. I never did."

Mr. Murphy got to his feet. "I imagine this is why I am here."

"It is," I said. "We need to hear what you know about this."

"It was so many years ago. I did overhear Muriel bullying Vera outside the schoolyard, insisting she'd been drunk and stoned and something horrible had happened. I didn't hear what the horrible thing was. It never occurred to me it was something so serious. Vera kept denying it. She said she never did drugs. But eventually she broke down and agreed that it must have happened the way Muriel said. I didn't know what it meant at the time. It was a very disturbing scene, but it wasn't in the school. I had no authority. I didn't know what to make of it or what to do about it. There was never a word about either girl in the media. Shortly after, Vera left for college and Muriel departed right after her mother died. That conversation has troubled me ever since and, in my mind, it's as clear as the day it happened. I truly regret not speaking to Vera about it. Perhaps I could have helped."

Vera shrugged. "I wouldn't have told you. She had me believing it in the end. It's always weighed heavily on me. I won't forgive her for that."

"You? You won't forgive me? You stole everything from me! My father, my life. This house should have been mine, and everything in it. You should have been living in poverty alone."

"Ah, yes, the poverty that only a million dollars and the price of a house can alleviate. I am the true Van Alst, Muriel. You are a fraud, a criminal and an interloper."

No one expected it. In a swirl of black clothing, Muriel lunged and grabbed Vera by the throat.

Chairs were knocked over. The bar cart went flying. The smell of alcohol filled the room. I raced to Vera's side and caught someone's elbow in the head. Kev landed on his backside. Cherie grabbed the laptop. I believe Jenkins hid under his chair while Mr. Murphy and Jasmine pressed themselves again the wall. A cat launched through the air, followed by a human scream. Uncle Mick would need to make a twenty-dollar deposit in the swear jar. Eddie wailed and pulled at Muriel's fingers. Vera's eyes bugged out of her head. Was she turning blue?

Somewhere a dog howled.

Detective Jones drew his weapon and pointed it at Muriel. "You've just bought me a world of trouble and I'll shoot you if you don't let go." I believed him and Muriel must have too, although he had to repeat it. Her fingers loosened. Vera slumped into her chair. Eddie wept. No one saw Lainie making for the door in the fracas.

But once again, Officer Melski was in the right time at the right place.

"Sorry I'm late," he said, as he snapped handcuffs on Lainie a minute later on Jones's instructions. A passing Siamese took a swipe at her legs.

"You missed the best part," I said to Melski.

"Glad I got here," he said with a tired grin. "I did promise Dekker I'd keep an eye on you. Wouldn't want to tell him I failed in that."

Uncle Mick said, "Shame about that bottle of Jameson."

THE DOOR OF my garret creaked open; the air inside was cold and a little stale, but I didn't care. I was back in my own little cabbage-rose-wallpapered heaven. Muriel and Lainie were locked up. Jones was in hot water. The witnesses to the first will had turned out to be two innocent servers from Lainie's café, just doing a favor for a customer. The poor kids would be out of a job now that the Hudson Café would be shuttered.

The signora, the cats, Uncle Kev and I were officially reinstalled in Van Alst House. Vera was home from the hospital. Her throat was badly bruised and she had broken blood vessels in her eyes, but she was alive and relieved to get her life back. Eddie was a happy man.

I let my bags slide off my shoulders to the floor. Kev had already brought my boxes up; they were stacked neatly in a corner and the Lucite coffee table was back in its place. Good Cat and Bad

Cat wove in and out of my legs before making themselves at home on the bed. The signora had made it up for me with crisp linens and a puffy duvet. We were home. I was so lucky, but why did I still feel so sad?

My iPhone buzzed in my pocket. A text from Lance:

> Poke.
> Poke??? I haven't seen you or heard from you in a week, you missed me getting fired, run over and solving a 40 year old murder and now all you have to say is POKE!???

The phone buzzed again. This time it was Tiff. Poke poke

I'll poke you, lady, with a sharp stick, I thought. Then I heard footsteps on the stairs. The cats tilted their heads in curiosity. Bad Cat extended his claws in anticipation.

Tiff and Lance and a humongous bouquet of stargazer lilies filled my doorway. I had meant to give them some attitude, but instead, my stiff upper lip turned into a trembling lower one.

"Where have you been? I got run over." I stiffened my spine before a wave of tears washed over me. I was still, after all, a Kelly. We know how to pull ourselves together even when we don't feel like it.

Lance and Tiff rushed forward. I think Lance may have been welling up; Tiff had streaks of tears on her cheeks. I was soon smiling from being wrapped in love, hugs and the delicious smell of my favorite flowers.

"Where were you?" My squeak trailed off. I was herded to the sitting area.

Lance's eyes definitely had tears in them. His handsome face was twisted in guilt. "I'm a horrible liar."

This was true. Tiff patted him on the back. Not a romantic gesture by any means. "He was afraid he wouldn't be able to lie to you. And that's my fault." She sat beside me. "Please, don't freak out with what we're going to tell you."

"I'm making no such promise."

Tiff said, "I've been really tired lately. Not merely tired, but exhausted."

"Tell me about it. Try getting smacked by a truck."

"But I also had a bit of a swollen gland in my neck. My doctors . . ." She continued but I heard nothing after that. My mind raced like WebMD as I ran possible causes through my database of human afflictions. I knew what she must have been afraid of: the same kind of cancer that killed her mother when we were in school. My hands started shaking.

"The same day, you said you'd lost your job. I heard that just as I got a cancellation to get in early. I knew that Lance would never be able to lie to you and I didn't want you to be worried. I asked him to come with me. I made him leave his phone when we went to Syracuse for the tests." My chest tightened. Panic spread goose bumps across my skin. I was so wrapped up in my reaction to her illness, I hadn't even heard the rest of what she was saying.

"Jordan, it's fine! I'm fine, really. They think it was anemia and maybe a mild case of hypothyroidism." In order to avoid a waterfall, I grabbed Lance and Tiff in a hug/double nelson.

Tiff said, "So you understand why I didn't want to tell you by text or by phone until we knew what was going on?"

"I do, of course. You must have been sick about it. I'm sorry I wasn't there for you. I feel bad you had to worry about me and worry about my reaction. I shouldn't have been such a delicate flower."

Obviously, I wouldn't have been a very strong support during this time for Tiff. All that over-thinking had led me to believe Tiff and Lance had ditched me for some magically splendid love affair in rainbow land or, at least, inconsiderately browsing in the outlet mall. But they were actually drinking stale coffee in a waiting room in Syracuse. "I thought you went off to ride unicorns without me." I knew I had a goofy grin. "Now it all makes sense."

Tiff and Lance exchanged glances. "Okay, Jordan, maybe you need a lie-down?" Tiff angled me toward the pillows. Lance said, "Is hallucinating unicorns a sign of a head injury?"

Tiff said, "Something must explain it." Lance arranged my flowers in the vase he'd brought along. I saw him wiping his eyes.

After a lot of catching up, they left. I never once mentioned during our emotional gathering that I had pretty much learned to stand on my own feet without them. It seemed wrong to bring it up, and after all I'd had Kev and Cherie.

I climbed into bed still filled with relief. Good Cat took up residence on my belly. And I finally let myself fall into a deep sleep and joined them on the unicorn ride. Or maybe I dreamed that.

Except for Smiley, all was right with my world.

CHAPTER SEVENTEEN

THE FOOD DROP was practically unrecognizable. Festive paper turkeys decorated the place. Who doesn't love turkeys and pumpkins and pilgrim hats? Phyllis managed to look rather rakish in hers. Not sure what the original pilgrims would have thought.

The pumpkin spice candles gave the place a warm glow. Phyllis's team of retired teachers were kept busy setting tables, seating families and serving. I saw Mr. Murphy from a distance. He didn't acknowledge me. I suppose I wasn't his favorite person. Jasmine did dance by, bringing little bone-shaped packages for people to take home to their dogs.

The long tables were done up with yellow tablecloths and orange napkins. It was all the best the Dollar Daze had to offer. Lance had put his considerable decorating talents to work, with Tiff as the able assistant.

The aroma of turkey and stuffing was intoxicating. Even more intoxicating was the sight of my nearest and dearest, all working hard to get back in good grace.

It was hard to believe how many families and

individuals were here for this special dinner. I was glad to be able to help them and sorry that they needed the help.

Vera Van Alst, generally the most hated woman in Harrison Falls, got some strange looks as she worked her wheelchair in between the long tables, offering hot rolls.

"You've never had anything like these," she said with authority. I knew that was true because the signora had made a gazillion of them and they were simply the best. Their fragrance was wonderful, even with all the competing aromas.

"And you may never again, so hurry up," Vera added to anyone who was slow on the uptake.

The signora danced behind her bearing an enormous soup tureen filled with ravioli simmering in homemade broth. Eddie followed reverently with a dish with freshly grated Parmesan. All right, so this wasn't a Thanksgiving tradition in Harrison Falls, but who knew what the future held.

To my surprise, Dwight Jenkins was also volunteering. I spotted him with Tom and Mindy and they all waved. They were restocking the dessert table with plated pumpkin pies, cakes and other goodies. I guessed that Tom and Mindy's kids had canceled again, but I hoped this event brought them some joy.

In the kitchen, Uncle Mick was inspecting the turkeys. I had left strict instructions that he wasn't in charge of turkey doneness. The Kellys favor birds cooked to the texture of jerky. Luckily, Karen was there and able to exercise a bit of influence over Lucky, who in turn could get Mick to step away before complete desiccation set in.

Officer Melski had brought his family's traditional sweet potato dish, complete with nicely toasted marshmallows. More surprising was a cameo appearance by Detective Jack Jones, in casual clothing, although I was pretty sure that charcoal pullover was cashmere. He made a donation under Phyllis's eye and sauntered over to me. He nodded, reached out and shook my hand. "No hard feelings?"

"None. You made it right in the end." I didn't mention that it must have been a blow to him to learn that the lovely Lainie was a murderer. I never got details, but I figured she'd put certain ideas into his head about Muriel and Vera and me. At least he was man enough to admit he'd been had.

Tiff, bearing Brussels sprouts, created an impact. She would touch a shoulder, an arm, or pat a hand. She radiated happiness.

Lance was serving potatoes. Most of the women in the room fixed their hair as soon as they spotted him approaching. He is even more magnetic than Uncle Kev and far less catastrophic.

That reminded me, where was Uncle Kev? He'd said something vague about adding some pizzazz to the party. Cherie was blond again and also showing lots of pizzazz and cleavage. She was the sexiest pilgrim I'd ever seen. Would he dress as a pilgrim too?

I thought the dinner had already had plenty of pizzazz.

My phone buzzed and I put down my platter and checked. Everyone was there, after all.

Smiley.

Home tomorrow. Love U . . .

Love U? Love *me?*

What just happened?

And wait, tomorrow?

Maybe I'd get my unicorns and rainbows after all. Although they'd better come with a good explanation. I had a feeling that explanation would be coming too. After all, Smiley had made sure that Officer Melski kept an eye on me.

Even I had to admit that things were just about perfect. Of course, that was before Uncle Kev arrived and most ceremoniously opened a crate releasing a gang of angry and confused wild turkeys. Pizzazz? Not so much.

Eventually, the screaming subsided and there was general rejoicing.

Everyone gave thanks.

RECIPES

PUBLISHER'S NOTE: The recipes contained in this book are to be followed exactly as written. The publisher is not responsible for your specific health or allergy needs that may require medical supervision. The publisher is not responsible for any adverse reactions to the recipes contained in this book.

The Signora's Rustic Roast Chicken

With a salad and a glass or two of Tuscan wine, the signora's version of roast chicken is like a mini-vacation in Italy!

Half a loaf of rustic Italian bread, cut in 1-inch thick slices, enough to make a bed for the chicken
4–6 tablespoons olive oil, divided
Salt and pepper, to taste
1 chicken, about 4–5 lbs
½ to one whole garlic head (rub off outside papery skin and slice in half horizontally through all the cloves)

Half a lemon
Half a lime
Sprigs of fresh rosemary or two tsp of dried
½ bunch fresh thyme, coarsely chopped or two
tsp dried

Preheat oven to 400 degrees F.

Place bread slices in center of a metal roasting pan.

Drizzle 2 to 3 tbsp of olive oil over bread and sprinkle with salt and pepper.

Season cavity with salt and pepper. Stuff with prepared garlic head, lemon, lime and herbs.

Rub outside of chicken with remaining olive oil and season with salt and pepper.

Place chicken, breast side up, on bread slices.

Roast chicken for about 1½ hours, until it is very brown and crispy and pan juices run clear when you cut between the leg and thigh. Internal temperature should be 165 degrees F.

Remove from oven, cover with foil and let chicken rest for 10 to 15 minutes before carving.

Serve with slices of the fabulous bread from the pan.

Smokey Roast Peppers in Olio

The signora grows amazing peppers in her kitchen garden at Van Alst House. In the late summer and early fall, you can smell them roasting. Uncle Kev has been commandeered to roast them on the charcoal grill which gives them an amazing smoky taste.

6 red, yellow or orange peppers
6 cloves of garlic, peeled and slivered
¾ cup very good quality extra virgin olive oil
Squirt of lemon juice
Sprinkle of sea salt

Place peppers on the charcoal grill or over a medium gas flame. Let them roast for 15 to 30 minutes, using tongs to give them a quarter turn every few minutes, till the peppers are charred, soft and collapsing. Once they're blistered, remove and place them in a brown paper bag. Close the bag and leave for 30 minutes to an hour. This will steam off the skin.

When the peppers are cool, remove from the bag, and peel off skin. This will be easy but a bit messy.

Once they're peeled, remove the stem, cut in four and remove the seeds and the white membrane.

This is messy too and there's no way around that. Never mind. It's worth it.

Slice peppers about ¼-inch thick. Place in a shallow serving bowl. Sprinkle with lemon juice.

Cover with your best olive oil.

Add the garlic slivers and sprinkle a bit of sea salt.

This is a wonderful side dish for meat or chicken. It keeps very well in the fridge.

Pan di Spagna

Pan di Spagna is a traditional sponge cake. Signora Panetone has at least three different Pan di Spagna recipes as far as we can tell. This one has a bit more sugar and flour than the other two, but it is Jordan's favorite. The signora might serve it with whipped cream and fresh fruit, or she might slice it into layers and put jam and custard in between each. Or she might drizzle it with a lemon icing sugar glaze. Jordan likes it all by itself with a light dusting of icing sugar.

6 eggs at room temperature, separated
½ cup water
2 cups white sugar
2 cups white flour
2 tsp baking powder
1 tsp good quality vanilla
Icing sugar (optional)

Preheat oven to 325 degrees F. Butter and flour an angel food pan.

In a bowl add water to yolks. Beat until thick and fluffy.

Add sugar gradually, beating until very thick and glossy.

Combine flour and baking powder. Gradually add to yolk/sugar mixture, beating until well blended.

In a separate bowl, beat the egg whites until stiff peaks form.

Gently fold egg whites into yolk mixture gradually, being careful not to overbeat. You should still see streaks of white.

Bake for about one hour until a tester comes out clean.

Cool on a wire rack and carefully remove from pan. Serve plain or with whipped cream, lemon glaze or any other tasty addition.

Center Point Large Print
600 Brooks Road / PO Box 1
Thorndike, ME 04986-0001 USA

(207) 568-3717

US & Canada:
1 800 929-9108
www.centerpointlargeprint.com